FIERCE

CLARISSA WILD

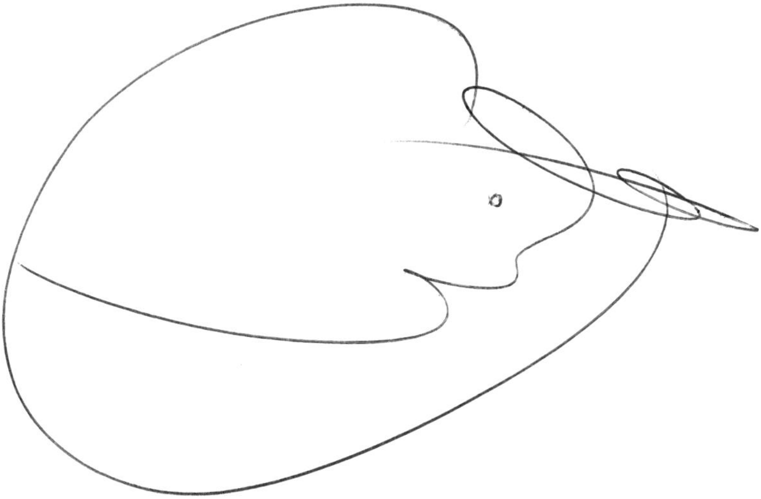

ISBN: 1494957612
ISBN-13: 978-1494957612

CONTENTS

FIERCE Playlist

This is a list of songs special to me, because they really brought life to FIERCE. You might enjoy listening to them. Especially the ones by Muse, which have their own special place in this book.

"Iris" by Goo Goo Dolls

"Skyscraper" by Demi Lovato

"Wonderwall" by Oasis

"The Reason" by Hoobastank

"The Fighter" by Gym Class Heroes ft. Ryan Tedder

"Uprising" by Muse

"Supermassive Black Hole" by Muse

"Radioactive" by Imagine Dragons

"Demons" by Imagine Dragons

"Holding on and letting go" by Ross Copperman

"Hold Me Now" by Red

"All I Ever Wanted" by John Tyree

"Wherever You Will Go" by The Calling

CHAPTER 1
EMBARRASSING MOMENTS

Geeks at new schools are like boats trying to sail on dry, uncharted land. They never fare well.

I draw in a huge breath and blow it out before stepping out of the bus. The driver behind me chortles at my reluctance to leave the comfort and safety of the bus. Of course, he isn't used to people actually preferring his bus over the outside world. I'm sort of an exception to the usual people he deals with, and that's not a good thing.

On the contrary; I'm chicken-shit, and it's even worse that I know I am.

Seeing this gigantic campus and college in front of me is terrifying. My legs are shaking, my heart is pounding, and I wish I could just step back into that bus and get as far away from here as possible.

But that would be sad. So sad, I think I might cry from laughing at my own cowardice.

It's really pathetic that these new things scare me so much. Most girls would love new schools, getting to know new people, experiencing the boys.

Just the thought of it makes my heart race.

Nope, that's not for me.

But I have no choice, either. I want to do this. I always wanted to study. I need it. My family needs it.

I just have to stop whining, stop thinking about it, and just go for it. Just do it!

Shaking my shoulders a little, I take a deep sniff to smell the trees surrounding me, and march forward.

Suddenly, a cold jet of air surges toward me from the left and catches me by surprise. I shriek as the waft of air tangles my hair in front of my face and blows up my skirt. There's a loud noise coming from the thing blasting air at me. Holding down my skirt so my panties aren't exposed, I use my other hand to keep my glasses straight and try to see what's happening.

"Sorry," someone yells, and the turbulence is turned off.

I'm left gasping while catching my breath. A leaf blower had been pointed straight at me.

"Sorry about that," he repeats as I pat down my skirt.

"Thanks," I mutter.

Great. What an awesome start to the first day at college.

"You all right?" he says, directing his leaf blower somewhere else.

"Fine," I say.

"Uh … You might want to take a look at your hair," the guy says, clearing his throat.

"What?" I say, grasping for my head. Crunchy leaves are coiled up in my hair.

My eyes widen as I start plucking all the leaves out. I work to unravel the knots, trying to get it to go down again, but my frizzy hair never gives in.

Oh, why does this always have to happen to me?

Looking around I can see people staring at me, hiding

laughs behind their hands. I feel like I'm in the center of attention, the focal point of the show. This is making me sweat like crazy.

My eyes narrow as they catch the gaze of one person in particular. A long, lean guy wearing a black leather jacket, who's standing a few feet away from me with a couple of other guys. His flaring gray eyes narrow as I catch myself staring right back at him. I blush when his plump lips slowly curl up into a cheeky smile.

I smash my lips together to prevent a squeal from escaping. He's hot, but I look like a mess. No, correction, I am a mess.

I'm like a fully decorated Christmas tree in the middle of fall.

Embarrassing. I can't believe this is his first impression of me.

Well, it's not like I have a chance with guys like him. They don't go after nerdy types like me.

Straightening my glasses, I try to ignore everyone looking at me. I put up a horrible smile as I walk toward the dorm halls, trying to pry the last pieces of leaf from my hair that just won't come off. It's like they're glued to my head or something. I couldn't have imagined a worse time for my hair to turn into its usual giant magnet, attracting and attaching to all kinds of strange things, because it's as sticky as spider legs.

Sometimes I think I'd better just cut it off and be rid of it. Maybe I could donate it to science, so it can become the new-and-improved Velcro.

I smirk from my own jokes, which are terrible, I know. Still, they make this day a little better after that scene.

My dorm's at the end of the campus, a ten-minute walk from the bus stop. I'm glad my parents helped me move in my stuff last night so I wouldn't have to do it alone today. As I enter the door, a deafening squeal makes me plug my ears.

"Autumn!" Evie yells.

She throws herself against me and wraps her arms so tightly around me that I can't breathe. Wheezing, I wriggle myself free from her hug so my lungs can expand again.

"I can't believe we're going to be roomies," she says, squeezing my arms.

She bites her lip and looks at me with big eyes, like she's about to explode into her usual happy dance. "Isn't it awesome?"

"Yeah, I can't wait to make myself at home here," I say, nodding, trying to make it sound genuine.

"Wow, you sound excited," she says with a sarcastic undertone.

"Sorry, I do like that you're my roommate. Honestly, I do." I sit down on my bed and she sits down next to me. "But I think I just made the worst and most laughable entrance ever."

"What happened?" she asks.

"Oh … you know … a leaf blower … my hair … the usual crap."

She snorts. "Well, that's just you being yourself."

I shake my head and smile. Evie nudges me with her shoulder and winks. "Oh, c'mon. It's not like they'll remember you for it. Who'd remember girls like us anyway? We're the nobodies. The 'invisible.' Nobody's going to blink at us." She makes quotation marks with her fingers.

I laugh. "You got a point there. 'Not being anyone' makes life a lot easier."

Evie lets her head rest on my shoulder and I sigh.

"Dork for life and proud of it," she muses.

And then we both burst out into laughter. We fall flat down on the bed and Evie puts her arm around me like she usually does when it's just the two of us. I don't remember her any other way. We've always been this close. Ever since I met her in high school she's been my best friend. Both teased, we sought comfort in each other's presence. Dorks have to stick up for each other. That's the only way to make it through that thing called puberty.

I'm so glad we're both past that now. I expect college life to be different. A lot better, maybe.

Someone clears his throat, and I immediately push myself up on my elbows.

"Am I interrupting you guys? I can come back later, no problem."

"Brody!" I scream, and jump up from the bed. He's standing in the doorway. I run to him and wrap my arms around him.

"I get that you're happy to see me, but no need to crush my ribs," he says, almost choking on a laugh.

"Sorry," I say, releasing him from my grip.

"So, had a look around campus yet?" he asks.

"Yeah, I did the tour yesterday. I can't believe how huge it is!"

"I know, right?"

We look at each other, and I can't help but squash him between my arms again. I haven't seen him in such a long time. It feels like it's been forever since we were at the same school together. I never liked that he was three years older than me, but when he left to go to college, I was even more distraught. Suddenly, my best friend was gone, and I had to fend for myself.

Luckily, I met Evie not long after. She's been my only friend since. I think I can safely say I have two best friends. Although I don't really know if it'll be the same now that I'm here. Brody looks so different now, I can hardly tell it's him. I hope things will be the same like always, though.

"Hmm …" he mutters. "Seems ages ago since I was last a newbie. Wasn't the greatest experience."

When he sees my scaredy-cat face, he chuckles a little. "Relax. You've got me to back you up. I didn't have anyone to show me around, to help me out when I needed it. But you two have me now."

Evie rolls her eyes when he looks at her. "Don't go thinking you're a mogul now." She walks up to him and pinches his cheeks. "Still little Bro-bro to me."

He scowls at her, and she laughs.

"And now for the formal introduction: Autumn Blakewood and Evie Carder, I hereby welcome you to campus."

"Why thank you, generous lord." Evie makes a bow, and I muffle a laugh behind my hand.

"It's tradition. Well, it's not like you understand any of that," he says, snorting. "Evie Peeved."

She frowns and nudges him forward. "Okay, that's it. Out."

"What? Can't take a joke?"

"I hate that name."

"Exactly. That's why it suits you perfectly."

"Well, if you'll excuse me, I have other stuff to do besides talking to an annoying dork." She storms out the door and walks through the hallway.

"You're a dork yourself, too!" Brody yells, laughing out loud.

"I know. That's why it's even more pathetic!" she yells back, laughing too. Then she disappears through a door with a 'ladies' sign above it.

"That's what you get when you push her buttons," I say when Brody directs his attention back to me.

"No, *you* push her buttons."

"What's that supposed to mean?" I say, and I put my hands on my waist.

"You know what I mean … cuddling up on the bed and all

that."

I blush. "We're just friends. It's no big deal."

"To her it is."

I sigh. "I'm not into that kind of thing, and you know that."

"I know, but she won't give up, and I can already tell this is headed toward disaster. Someone's going to get hurt, and I know it won't be you."

"Stop making such a huge deal out of a hug. She's not … we're not. It's nothing. Forget about it."

Brody holds his hands in the air and closes his eyes. "Don't come crying to me later when your friendship is on the line, because I'll only say 'I told you so.' Don't mess with chicks, that's all I'm saying, and I know plenty about that."

I grimace. "Yeah … What do you know about relationships? Last time I saw you trying to hook up with a girl you got a milkshake in your face instead."

"Hey, I'm not that guy anymore. It's been three years since then, Autumn; I've changed."

I purse my lips. "We'll see about that."

Brody squints, a devilish smile creeping onto his face. "I guess so. See you around!"

He walks through the hallway, and I hear him go downstairs before I turn around again and go back into my room. Staring at the clock, I pull up my sleeve so I can fiddle with the bracelet I got from Evie before summer. The only problem is, it's not there.

What? I stare at my wrist, but my bracelet is clearly missing. What happened to it? Did I take it off? I remember twiddling with it in the bus, so it can't be at my parents' place.

I grab my suitcase and rummage inside, but it's nowhere to be found. Oh God, I hope I didn't lose it. What if that leaf blower blasted it away into the grass? What if someone else picked it up? I'd never find it again.

Frantically I search my room, but can't seem to find it anywhere.

"Looking for this?" someone says.

I turn around only to stare into those piercing gray eyes again. It's him: the guy who was staring at me when I left the bus. The one who turned my cheeks redder than a beet. *That* guy.

He leans against my doorpost, casually holding up his hand. Pinched between his index finger and thumb is my bracelet.

My bracelet. He's holding it. Him. The guy who caught my eye the moment I saw him.

And he's talking to me.

Oh God, I can't breathe.

I swallow away the lump in my throat as I walk toward him, holding my breath.

"This is yours, right?" he says. His voice is deep and husky, and I don't think I've ever heard anything sexier.

I nod, still staring at him. I'm only just close enough to be able to reach for the bracelet, but not nearly far enough away for my liking.

My heart is beating like crazy as his eyes scan my face, while I try not to breathe. I feel like if I do, I might start panting.

He looks so goddamn ridiculously handsome up close. I don't think I've ever seen a guy this gorgeous before.

His spiky hair all gelled up, the tan skin of his hands peeking out from underneath his leather jacket, his broad pectorals visible through his tight white tee. All of it is making my head explode.

A hot guy is standing in my doorway, talking to me, giving me back my stuff. Stupid as it sounds, it feels like a dream.

Things like this never happen to me. Hot guys don't come

so close to me.

I never anticipated something like this happening. I don't even know how to behave. I didn't expect this at all.

I catch myself staring at his amazing features so I raise my head to look up at him. His eyes follow mine, and then I know he knows exactly what I was looking at.

Oh God. This is embarrassing.

A cute smile curls up his lips. "You can't talk?"

My mouth feels like it's stitched together, as if I'm unable to pull it open and say anything. I must look ridiculous.

I push my glasses farther up my nose so they're not askew anymore. Flushing, I force my lips to part. "Yeah," I say. "I was so scared I lost it. Where'd you find it?"

He cocks his head, and it shows me his muscular neck, making me blush even more. "Outside. Thought it was yours. It looked expensive."

I hold out my hand, but he doesn't give it to me.

"I think it's important to be careful with stuff you think is valuable. Money doesn't grow on trees. Besides, not everything can be replaced."

"I agree, but I lost it by accident. Can I have it back now?" I say. I'm not in the mood for a lecture. I try to snatch it from his hand, but he grasps my bracelet and pulls back his hand.

"What kind of a 'thank you' is that?" he says, squinting, taunting me.

Suddenly, he looks a lot less attractive. I cross my arms and say, "Thank you."

He smiles and tilts his head, dangling the bracelet in front of me. "That all?"

"Yes. What else do you want from me?" I snap.

"Your name." He mimics my stance and crosses his arms, burying the bracelet deep within the socket of his elbow. His biceps bulge against his leather jacket, and I have trouble not gaping at them.

"Autumn Blakewood. Yours?"

"Autumn? What kind of name is that for a girl?"

With furrowed brows, I say, "Well I like it."

He starts twirling my bracelet like it's some kind of toy. I risk a chance and reach for it, but he pulls back again. Goddammit.

"I don't have time for games …" I say, sighing.

"Oh … I'm not playing games, Leafy."

"Leafy?" I say, scowling.

He points at my hair and immediately reminds me of the embarrassing scene outside. Now I have to fight off the heat rushing to my cheeks.

"Here," he says, and he tosses me the bracelet. "Name's Hunter Bane," he says.

I barely manage to catch the bracelet before he saunters off again. Frowning, I watch him walk off.

"See ya, Leafy."

"My name isn't Leafy, it's Autumn!" I yell after him, but he only waves as he walks into his room.

Which is only five feet away from mine.

CHAPTER 2
THE FIRST DAY

Glaring at myself in the mirror, I brush my fingers through the frizzy mess that is my hair. My brown curls don't bend to my will, nor that of my brush. It's like a bomb exploded on my head. I swear, sometimes I think I'd rather not sleep at all than wake up with this hair.

I get dressed and wake up Evie, because we'll be late if she doesn't get up soon. She swings her hands in the air, trying to shoo me away, thinking I'm her mother. It makes me laugh when she starts growling at me. As she snores, I open the window and pull the blanket off her. She squirms from the cold rush of wind on her bare legs.

After she's dressed, we get a quick breakfast at the cafeteria. Evie and I make our way to our first classes of the first trimester. We have completely different schedules. I'm studying English lit and she's studying linguistics. We both have a love for language, but I like my books close to home and she prefers to learn more about other cultures. I'm glad she found what she likes to do, but it's unfortunate that we have only a few classes we both follow.

I'm going to miss having her close by. I'm not used to being on my own and not having my friend around to support me. Walking through these massive halls makes me feel like an ant. A tiny, miserable little ant that could be squashed underneath big feet at any moment.

I'm never comfortable around a lot of people. It's something that stuck with me after that hellhole they call high school.

Right now, I don't have my best friend to back me up, and Brody's already in his political science class, so I have no choice but to venture through the campus alone. Still, it surprises me I've not yet bumped into someone. That nobody has called me any names yet.

As I find my way to the classroom I'm supposed to be in, I sit down on the nearest empty bench seat I can find. I don't want to have to walk all the way down the steps, knowing people are going to look at me. I don't like being watched. Maybe I'm too insecure, but when the focus lies on me, I get the creeps.

I unpack my books, pens, and paper and put my bag under my seat, while someone sits down next to me.

As I look up to see who it is, I almost jump up from my seat.

Just seeing his big gray eyes makes me want to run.

"What are you doing here?" I say, perplexed.

"Following this class," Hunter retorts. "What else?"

Pursing my lips, I gather my pencils and line them up neatly like I always do when I'm nervous as hell. "I uh …"

"And what are you doing here?" he asks playfully, putting up a curious face like it's the most serious question in the world.

"Do you really want me to answer that?"

"Well, do you want to be here?"

I arch one eyebrow and he does, too, mimicking my

expression, as if he's making fun of me. "Of course I do," I say.

He chuckles. "Figured. You seem like the nerdy type."

I gasp. "I am *not* a nerd."

"No?" Hunter reaches over to my books and opens the first one he can find. "Looks like it to me." He points at all the notes I've made. "I don't know anybody who writes this much before class has even started."

I snatch the book from his hand and shut it. "I just like to be prepared."

"For what? The apocalypse? It's just college."

I sigh. "Whatever."

"Or are you just afraid you might have to deal with stuff you're not prepared for?" He inches a little closer. When his leg briefly touches mine, I squeeze my thighs together and shudder. He's too close for comfort. I've never had a guy come this near.

"You're scared, aren't you, Leafy?" he says. His low voice is soft, and I can feel his breath near my ear. Shocks course through my body, and it's unlike anything I've ever experienced. I feel completely naked.

"Can I borrow this?" he suddenly says, and grabs one of my pens from my neatly lined stash. I look at him in astonishment, and he stiffens for a second. "I promise I'll give it back," he says with a cutesy voice, and then he flashes me a smile. "Thanks."

He scoots back in place and glares at me from a distance. I don't need to see his eyes to know that he's watching me; I can feel his eyes piercing my side.

I close my eyes for a second to regain my composure. Since I sat down in class I haven't caught anything of what the teacher is saying. I don't even remember the man starting his class. All I know is that Hunter is toying with me, and I don't know why. Am I funny or something?

"Autumn?"

My head shoots up from dreamland and I look around. The teacher and almost every student in class is looking at me.

"Autumn Blakewood?"

"Yes?" I stammer, ducking between my own shoulders, because I feel scrutinized.

"I asked a question."

"Sorry, I didn't hear it."

A few muffled laughs are audible throughout the auditorium, and I can feel the heat rush to my cheeks. Shit, I'm totally making a fool out of myself.

"Can you name the primary source for Shakespeare's famous plays?" the teacher says.

"I … uh …" Crap, I don't know the answer. I haven't been listening at all.

"Holinshed's Chronicles," Hunter whispers as he leans forward.

"The Holinshed's Chronicles!" I shout.

The teacher squints and waits a second. "All right."

Then he continues his lesson, and I let out a huge breath, falling back into my chair. God, I can't believe Hunter helped me. Him, out of all people.

Turning my head, I see Hunter smiling cheekily at me. I'm dumbstruck with his sudden helpful answer.

"What?" he says, as I gape at him.

"Nothing. I just didn't expect that."

"There's a lot more you can't expect from people."

I chortle and shake my head. "Well, thanks anyway."

"Yeah, I pretty much saved your ass there."

My eyebrows draw closer together. "Hey, don't get cocky."

Hunter wriggles his eyebrows, and it makes me laugh. "Comes with the jacket."

His eyes drift off to the teacher, and he starts penning down notes. I'm surprised by the mere fact that he even seems remotely interested in learning something today.

As I start some pre-work on today's assignment, I notice his face turning my way every couple of seconds. I glance sideways and see him studying my notes.

"Hey!" I exclaim.

He's seriously peeking at my notes? First he helps me find the right answer to the teacher's question, and now he's cheating? I don't get this at all.

"Shhh," he whispers, shushing me.

"You're cheating."

"Who cares?"

"I do," I say, slamming my notebook shut.

He frowns and gazes at me. "Aren't you uptight."

I smile pretentiously. "Comes with the skirt."

He laughs. It's a deep sound, a manly laugh, one that makes my heart flip over in my chest. Then he licks his lips in a way that makes my toes curl. Watching his tongue come out and flick along those thick lips makes me zoom in on them. It's the first time I notice how sexy those lips look. It's also the first time I feel like I want to lick them, too.

"Good one," he says and winks, making my heart stop.

The teacher clears his throat, and I notice he's doing it because he wants us to shut up. I crawl back into my shell, drawing back, and hide my reddened cheeks by leaning on my hands. I focus on my textbook just to avoid seeing the class stare at me. Just to avoid seeing *his* narrow eyes watching me.

As the class comes to an end, Hunter says "See ya, Leafy," and he throws me my pen.

"It's Autumn."

He shrugs and gets up. My gaze follows him as he walks out of the classroom, and then I spot Evie standing behind the huge windowpane. Her eyes are widened, and it looks as though her face is glued to the glass. Just as Hunter leaves the room her eyes zoom in and follow him, as if she's tracking him.

Then she gazes at me and tips her head, nodding, beckoning me to come.

I hurry to grab my stuff and run down the steps toward her.

"What the hell was that all about?"

"What are you talking about," I say, as we start walking through the halls.

"You. And that guy sitting next to you. I saw you guys talking, you know."

"He just asked me for my pen. No biggie."

She laughs. "Yeah right! You guys were talking. A lot. I could see everything," she scolds.

"Were you watching us or something?" I say, laughing with my mouth open.

"No. I was waiting for you. Then I noticed who was sitting next to you. Hunter Bane. Jesus."

"You know him?"

"Brody told me about him," she says as we head toward our joint class. "Supposedly he's got a reputation here, and I don't mean the good kind."

"Hmm …" I start mulling over what that means. I don't really know the guy at all, but he doesn't seem that bad. Besides, having a bad rep could mean loads of things. Actually, now that I think about it, only loads of bad things.

"I wonder why he sat down next to you," Evie continues. "I mean, he could've picked any pretty girl in the room and buttered her up, but he chose to sit next to you instead. What does he want with you?"

"I don't know," I say. Now I'm also wondering why the hell he sat down next to me. The more I think about it, the more it creeps me out.

"To peek at my notes is the most likely answer," I say

eventually.

"Well I sure hope so. I also hope that's the only thing he wants from you."

Frowning, I bump my shoulder against hers. "Evie! Are you jealous or something?"

"No, I just don't like it when you hang with bad boys."

"Hey, don't worry." I hook my arm around hers. "I'm not hanging with anyone, and I have no interest in him."

She smiles, and I smile back, but my stomach churns. What I just said doesn't ring true. I know it should be, but somehow his presence has two totally different effects on me. One part is freaked out and wants to run, and the other part is curious as hell.

We walk to one of the few classes we share and find two spots in the middle, but before the class can start a loud scream draws my attention. I turn around in my seat and see Hunter.

He's yelling words into his phone, but I don't know what. He's outside, pacing up and down the hallway. I can't hear anything he's saying, since there's a glass wall in between us, but his face predicts thunder.

I wonder what's going on. He looks pissed, and just seeing him like this scares me.

When the conversation is over, he smashes the phone on the floor.

I spring up from my seat, and a bunch of other students who see it also gasp and point at him. Hunter kicks the wall, and with each thump my body jolts up and down. Then he straightens his jacket and stares at his fists.

Suddenly he turns around and gazes at me.

I freeze in place. With his piercing gray eyes on me I feel like a brick wall. Unmoving, but breakable just from his glare.

His eyes scan my face, and I can see the anger and pain. It's flowing out of him like a seething, bubbling volcano. He continues to stare at me, and I feel like I'm the only one in this classroom. This moment in time feels like an eternity.

Then he turns around and storms out of the building.

CHAPTER 3
BITTER CHANGES

It's been days since I last saw Hunter. He hasn't been to class, and I haven't seen him walking around the dorm either. Something tells me he hasn't even slept in his own room. I wonder what's going on with him. I wonder what that phone call was all about. What made him so angry?

I don't even know why I care so much.

Why do I care?

I barely know him, and yet I can't stop thinking about what's wrong. That scene of him kicking the wall, furious as hell, keeps replaying in my mind over and over again. His flaring eyes follow me wherever I go, even when he's not around.

I've never had this before, but it's almost as if I'm desperate to find out what happened to him that made him so upset. He seemed so aloof and carefree in class before. I didn't expect him to explode like that. At least, not because of a phone call.

I really wonder what's going on ...

Sighing, I read the same sentence I've been reading for the last couple of seconds. I'm trying to study, but it's really going nowhere like this.

"Hey, Autumn."

I look up and see Brody enter our room. There's a girl with wavy blonde hair standing behind him with her hands on her hips, and she's gazing at us with a smirk on her face. She's shaped like an hourglass, and her brown skin looks like she tans at least once a week. In her short pink dress she reminds me of the Barbie dolls I used to play with when I was little.

"What's up?" Evie says. When she sees the girl she scowls. "Who's that?"

Brody clears his throat. "This," he grabs the girl's hand, "is Scarlet."

"Hi!" the girl says with a perky voice. "I'm Scarlet Fox."

"Pleasure," Evie says, and she stares at the girl's feet as she steps into our room. I can see from the grim look on her face she doesn't like it. Sometimes she gets a little territorial. It's weird, but I like weird.

"I'm Autumn Blakewood," I say. "And this is Evie Carder."

Scarlet smiles gently, but seems confused when she sees Evie's unwelcome, snarly face.

"I'm going out with some friends. Catch up a bit. Wanna join me?" Brody says.

"No thanks," I say, and I shut my book.

"Why not?"

"Because I need to study and get all my homework done."

Brody chuckles. "It's only been a few days since the first trimester started. There can't be that much work. Besides, you have the rest of the year to study. C'mon."

"No, I really need to get this done," I say, frowning.

"We'd love it if you'd come," Scarlet suddenly says, as if she has a say in the matter.

"Brody …" Evie says, glaring at him.

I know she means she wants him to put a leash on her, and it makes me chuckle a bit. I know Evie hates dolls. Especially when they wear dresses. They're her pet peeve.

"Don't you want to enjoy college life?" Brody says.

"We do. In our own way. Without make-up, and dresses, and parties," Evie says.

Brody squints at her. "By locking yourselves up in your room?"

"I just want to keep up so I don't fall behind later. Nothing wrong with that," I say.

"You did that in high school, too, and look what happened to you then."

"Hey, don't put that on her. It was not her fault she got teased!" Evie says. Teased is the understatement of the year. Bullied is more like it.

"No, neither was it my fault; I tried to protect her."

"Guys … don't fight, please," I say, sighing.

"Well, why won't you try something new? I don't want you to have to live through that again. If you can socialize with the crowd this time, maybe you can enjoy college life a little more."

"I'm already enjoying it," I say with a smile, hoping he'll stop asking me to do things I don't want to do.

"What's it to you anyway? Why are you so intent on getting her to go with you?" Evie says, frowning.

"Look, I just want to help out, all right? But whatever. Scarlet and I will just go together then. We've got plenty of other friends to hang with."

"Yeah, you go have fun with the popular crowd," Evie scoffs.

"Evie," I say with furrowed brows, and she rolls her eyes.

"Thanks, Brody. I appreciate the offer, but Evie and I really want to study."

"Okay … Well, see ya then."

"Bye!" Scarlet says, chirpy, and I smile at her because I don't know what else to do in an uncomfortable situation such as this.

We wave at each other, and Brody wraps his arm around Scarlet. My eyes widen. As they leave, I notice his hand is on her ass.

Evie throws her pillow across the room and lets out an annoyed moan.

"Oh. My. God. Was that his girlfriend?" I stammer.

"Seems like it. I can't believe he wants someone like that." Evie closes her eyes and lets out another groan.

"Hmm … maybe she isn't that bad. I mean, we don't know her, really."

"True …" Evie mumbles. "Still, I don't get why you still hang out with that guy."

"Brody? Why not?"

"He's turned into a total ass."

"No, he hasn't."

Evie points at the door. "Well, what do you call that then?" She rolls onto her back and stares at me from her bed. "He thinks he's all that now that he's part of the popular group. And he's trying to pull you with him."

"It's not that bad. He just wants to help."

"By making you remember your shitty time at high school?"

"He's just trying to convince me, that's all."

"Don't make excuses for him," she says, sitting up. "I'm trying to help you, too, and I'm telling you that he's changed."

"Maybe …" I say, opening my textbook again.

"I don't like those people he's hanging with. Ever since we've been here, he's done nothing but 'socialize,'" she says, making quotation marks with her fingers. "I don't think he's studied at all."

"Well, that's his problem."

She sighs. "I know."

It's quiet for some time, and I go back to reading the same page as last time, just to make sure I read it well enough to remember.

"Look, I'm sorry. I know he's your friend, and that you've known each other for God knows how long … I just don't want to see you get hurt."

She looks up at me and smiles.

"Don't worry. I know Brody and he knows me. He wouldn't do that."

"I hope you're right," Evie says, and she props up her pillow. Then she starts to laugh. "Did you see the look on her face when she saw me? Priceless."

I chuckle. "You looked like a hibernating bear who got disturbed in her cave. Not a pretty sight."

"Awesome!" she says, smiling widely.

"You really like scaring people off, don't you?"

"Hell yeah …"

Shaking my head while laughing, I turn the page of my textbook and try to read the next sentence, but I can't get Brody and that girl out of my head. I want to believe my own words and think everything will be all right, but some part of me also believes Evie. I know he's changed. And it'll probably only get worse. Can I deal with it?

♥♥♥

Evie and I have been studying at the library all day. After Brody came by, I told her I really couldn't concentrate and that I needed to be somewhere where we couldn't be disturbed. Or be distracted by weird thoughts. I have been having those a lot, lately. Especially about Hunter.

She went to our room earlier, because she was tired, but I stayed so I could do some homework ahead of time. I like being prepared.

After I jot down the last notes about Hamlet, I pack my stuff and make my way through the halls. It's already late at night, and it's dark outside. I hurry to my dorm and try not to make a noise as I walk up the stairs. Shuffling through the hall, I freeze when I turn a corner.

There's a guy in the shadows. He's leaning with his head against a door only a few feet away from my room.

I straighten my glasses to make sure I'm not imagining things, but it's real. Swallowing, I stay put and stare at the guy, who's just slumped forward, barely moving. Who is he? What's he doing here? Should I leave?

My heart races in my chest, and my muscles are tense. I know my body is preparing for flight or fight. My instincts tell me to make a run for it, but I know that's absurd. He could just as well be a student, someone who's drunk or had a rough night. Maybe I'm exaggerating.

Besides, I want to go to bed, and my room is just up ahead. It can't be too difficult to pass him, can it?

Shuffling, I press my body against the wall and start to walk. I slowly step forward, trying not to make too much noise. I don't want him to turn around. Actually, I'm hoping he won't notice me at all.

But it's too late now.

"Leave me alone." The voice is gruff and croaky, full of unspoken emotion. It sounds familiar.

Inching closer, my eyebrows tighten together as I try to see who it is. If I can reach my room safely. If he's dangerous or not.

It surprises me when I hear him sniff and take in short

breaths. Is he crying?

"Stay away," the voice repeats, and the more I hear it, the more I recognize it.

My jaw drops open, and I stare in confusion. "Hunter?"

His head lifts up from the wall and one look at his shiny gray eyes tells me it's him.

"Leafy?" he says, his lips parted in a way that make me focus on them.

His hand drops to his side, and he turns around to face me, still hiding in the shadows of the light. But I don't need any light to see the redness that clouds his eye. The patch of skin underneath is swollen, and the rest of his face is white. Too white.

"What's wrong?" I say, gazing at him. He looks sick, and I'm immediately worried about him. Even though I know he's been an annoying jerk to me in the past, I want to help him.

"Please just go," he groans, and he points at my door.

"Are you okay?" I say, and I bend my head so I can look into his eyes, but he turns his head away so I can't see. Is he trying to hide something?

"Don't come closer." His voice is getting thicker by the second, as if it's hard for him to talk.

When I look into his beautiful eyes, all I see is hurt. He looks broken. Beaten. As if he's been to a funeral or something. His face is dark and dreary, full of grief. But not the type of grief that comes with death. I just can't place it.

I wonder if anyone's ever seen him like this. It's like he's been crying all day and has been trying to hide it from the world. Like he's been hiding himself.

"Wait here," I say, and I walk past him and sneak into my room. Tiptoeing across the floor, I try not to wake Evie from her snoring sleep. We have a little fridge standing in the corner, and I grab a bottle of water from it. I hurry back to Hunter and open the cap.

"Here. Drink some."

I hold up the bottle, and he just stares at me with a bewildered look on his face.

"You look like you could use some help," I say.

He turns around and faces me. Then he starts walking toward me with slow, heavy steps.

I inch away until my back is against the wall, but he keeps coming closer. He towers above me, and only now do I realize how much larger he is. How much bigger, stronger, more muscular. His black tee can barely hide the straining muscles underneath.

He places both hands on the wall beside me and lowers his head to meet my eyes. I cower underneath him, shuddering from being so near to him.

"I don't need anyone," he growls, his lips barely parting.

I can feel his breath on my skin, and it makes me gasp. He's so close now, I could touch him if I reached for him. If he stepped forward a little more, he'd be on top of me.

It scares me to death.

My heart is thumping in my throat, and I can barely breathe. Lifting my head, I gaze into his glaring eyes. Those vivid gray irises that amaze me. There is something in there that sparks my interest, secrets and hidden emotions he keeps far away from the world. Things I want to know.

His chest heaves, and one of his hands drop. I swallow as he steps back again and stares at the ground. I wonder what is going on inside his head.

His hand reaches for mine, and for a second I'm almost convinced I'm going to pull back if he touches me.

But I don't. He grasps for the bottle, and our fingers briefly graze. I shudder from his touch as he takes the bottle from my hand and puts it to his lips. I watch him gulp it down with eagerness. Rivulets of water stream down his chin and end up on his shirt, making him look even rawer and more intense than before.

The way he drinks makes me swallow, too. As if there's some kind of lump in my throat. His lips suck the opening of the bottle, and it looks … My God … Too hot to handle.

For a brief moment I imagine jerking the bottle away and pressing my own lips on his.

It strikes me that I'm having these weird fantasies about him. I haven't seen him like this before. Somehow he looks sexy. And I like it.

As he lowers the bottle again, he gazes at me with a fierce look that makes me want to step back a little. He seems angry, but I know it's not because of me. I didn't do anything wrong.

"Thanks," he says in a gruff tone.

It doesn't sound thankful, but mostly because I know he's pissed at something else. The something that made him cry.

Hunter Bane, of all people, is standing outside his room, crying.

I didn't expect to witness something like this.

"No problem," I say, and I turn the cap back onto the bottle.

"Please don't tell anyone you saw me," he says, glancing sideways at his dorm room, avoiding my eyes.

My breath hitches. Why would he ask me that? Is he afraid or something?

"Good night," Hunter says, and he puts his hand on the door handle.

"Sure … good night," I say, and I turn around as well.

Biting my lip, I walk toward my room, every step feeling like a mile. Before entering my room, I turn my head to watch him walk into his room and close the door.

Sighing, I enter mine, too, and close the door behind me.

CHAPTER 4
OUT OF MY LEAGUE

I couldn't close my eyes last night. Not one second did I sleep. One moment I was thinking about Hunter so much I thought I was dreaming, but of course I wasn't. Sometimes I even wondered if he was awake, too.

Dragging myself out of bed this morning was no easy feat. Normally I wake Evie up, but this time it was the other way around, which is unusual, to say the least. With half-mast eyes I make my way to class and sit down somewhere comfortable.

Suddenly the door to the classroom opens, and someone comes stumbling in. Everyone turns around in their seats, but I don't really care today. I'm way too tired to check and see who it is.

"Well …" the teacher says, and puts down his book. "Mister Bane."

The moment I hear his name my eyes jerk open, and I turn my head like an owl peering around. Hunter walks down the steps, carefully watching where he puts his feet. His eyes look even more swollen than last night, which I thought wasn't possible until now.

"Be on time from now on. Next time you can wait outside," the teacher says, his eyes following Hunter all the way down.

Until he sits down right next to me.

I gulp the moment he slumps down in his seat, his arm grazing mine. I hesitate to look at him, because I'm afraid he might look even worse than before. No, I know he does. And I don't like seeing him that way.

The teacher glances sternly at him one more time before continuing with his lesson.

Hunter sighs and buckles. He drops his arms on the table in front of him and lets his head rest on them. With his head completely buried between his arms he looks like he's falling asleep.

When he starts snoring, I know he has.

I pick up a pencil from my stack and poke him with it, but he only groans. He moves around a little, but doesn't stop snoring. The more I try to wake him, the more he starts making noises, and I don't want the teacher to hear. What if he looks this way and sees him sleeping in the middle of class? I don't want Hunter to get in trouble. However strange it sounds, even to me.

I bend over and put my mouth close to Hunter's ear. I've never been this close before, and it makes me shiver. My lips are so near to his skin, I could kiss him and feel what it's like. If I could only do it. If I had the courage.

God, what am I thinking?

The smell of his aftershave is intoxicating, and my lips start to quiver the moment I try to speak. "Wake up," I whisper.

He takes in a huge breath, and suddenly his face is turned to me.

A squeal almost comes out of my mouth, but I stop it by jamming my lips shut. He's looking straight at me, eyes wide open. His lips are parted, his hair is messy, and I can feel his breath tingle on my lips.

Holding my breath, I just stare back.

"Well hello there," he says, a devilish smile appearing on his face.

"I … uh …" I stammer.

I scoot back to my place and draw back as far as I can. I suddenly feel very, very exposed. Like I just kissed him or something.

As if I would ever do something like that.

"You what?" he says, leaning on his hand.

"You were sleeping in class. I was waking you up," I say, staring ahead.

I don't dare look him in the eye, because I realize what those eyes are starting to do to me. Once I see them, I can't look away. They're pulling me into something that's really not good for me.

But damn, those eyes. I just can't look away anymore.

"Nah," he says, closing his eyes. "I wasn't sleeping."

He yawns, and it makes me chuckle a little. "Guess you didn't sleep either last night."

"Not really, no." He comes up from his sleeping position and stretches, making me gaze in awe at his well-built features.

I can't believe I'm doing this.

Why am I drooling like this? This is so unlike me. I never fall for the bad boy. I never like guys who act like him, aloof and cocky. Why is this so different?

Frowning, I sigh, and start twiddling with my pen.

"You always come so close to guys you barely know?" he suddenly says.

I open my mouth to say something, but I have no clue what he's talking about. Shaking my head, I say, "What?"

"You were only a few inches away from my face a couple

of seconds ago."

I blush hearing him say that. I know I was, but I'd rather not be reminded of something embarrassing.

"I'm just trying to help," I say.

"I don't need any help," he says, clearing his throat.

"You said the same thing last night."

"Yeah, and I meant it."

"Well, you sure looked like you could use some help," I say, pursing my lips.

He sighs. "As if it could do anything. As if it could solve my problems."

"Maybe it could, if you'd accept it."

He slams his hand on the table, and the sudden bang makes me jolt up in my seat. He stares at me, the look in his eyes violent.

"Nothing, *nothing*, can help me," he says, his nostrils flaring.

My eyes sting with tears, and my hands form fists just from anger. "Fine. Whatever. I'm just trying to help. You don't have to take it."

His hand slips from the table, and he turns his head toward the exit, probably thinking of a way to escape. He's still breathing heavily, and I feel terrible because of his sudden outburst.

But we barely know each other. This whole thing, the way he's acting, is not because of me. Something must've happened to him to make him act like this. I wonder what's bothering him so much that it makes him so explosive.

Was it the phone call?

"Look … I'm sorry," he says quietly.

I bite my lip as I almost see him think. He's staring at his table, probably mulling over his words, over what is happening in his life.

Sometimes I wish I could see inside.

"I just had a rough night, and I'm kind of pissed about it, okay?"

"I understand," I say.

He nods, still looking like he's thinking about a whole lot of things at the same time. "Okay."

I know I said I understand, but I don't. I'm only saying it so he won't be so angry anymore. It frightened me, but at the same time I'm still trying to figure out what the hell is going on in his mind.

♥♥♥

It's hot outside, and the sky is clear blue. There's not a speck in the sky, and I feel good just being here. I'm sitting on the grass together with Evie. We're studying and enjoying the nice weather. I like changing the location sometimes, keeps my brain from dozing off. Besides, the excitement of a new room quickly fades if you spend hours and hours locked up there.

Evie's eating an apple, and every time she takes a bite it sounds like a horse is chewing.

I wince at the sound.

I look up, and before I can say anything I see a girl in a tight black dress stumbling over the grass, coming toward us in her sky-high heels. Scarlet.

I poke Evie in the side, and she almost drops her apple. With one eyebrow raised, I say, "Look who's coming."

When she sees Scarlet, she stops chewing. "Oh. My. God. Is she coming to us? Oh, please, no."

I nod, sighing. I try to put up a smile for the girl, but I know everyone can see it's fake.

"Hey girls!" she says with her usual cheerful voice. "What are you doing?"

Evie holds up her book and dangles it in the air without

saying anything. Then she takes another bite of her apple to ensure she doesn't have to speak.

"Studying," I say.

"Oh … interesting," Scarlet says, and she puts up a pretentious smile. "Mind if I join you?"

Before either of us can protest, she sits down on our blanket with her legs crossed like a real princess.

"Well don't wait on us," Evie snaps, and she throws away the apple.

"Wait for what?" Scarlet says.

Evie frowns and shakes her head, then she whispers in my ear, "Brains of a sheep."

I muffle a laugh and hide it behind my hand. "Look, we really just want to study," I say.

"I know. I was planning to do the same, but when I saw you girls out here I thought I could join you." She smiles brightly, as if she thinks it'll help convince us to let her stay.

Well, it's not like she's been mean. We have.

It's just that she's so not Brody's type. He used to like the geeky girls. The strong girls. Not the Barbie-doll types. And from the looks of it, that's all she's got.

"Oh, and you know about English literature?" Evie scoffs.

"As a matter of fact, I do. I followed a class about poetry in high school."

Evie chortles and has trouble stopping herself from bursting out into laughter. "Okay. If you say so."

"Besides, you guys and Brody are friends, so I thought I should get to know you guys."

Evie rolls her eyes and glances at me.

"Actually … I'm here to ask you for a favor," Scarlet continues. "I'm doing research about discrepancies between the different social classes and common portrayals of stereotypes. I thought you girls could help me out with that, since you seem just like the type to discuss this. I study sociology," she says.

My jaw drops. I'm struck in awe by the fact that her words came out in a way that make her seem smart. Her clothing and the way she acts hides all that, but now I'm starting to think she's smarter than we thought. Maybe we misjudged her.

From the corner of my eye I see Brody approaching. He's frowning heavily and his lips are smashed together. He doesn't look happy.

"Scarlet!" he yells as he marches closer.

She turns her head, and when she sees him she starts waving. "Hey!"

"What are you doing?" he says with a high-pitched voice, as if he can't believe she's here.

"What's wrong?" I ask.

"You know you can't be in the sun," Brody says to her, ignoring my question. "Are you just going to ignore the doctor's advice?"

"No, I was just talking. I didn't plan on staying long," she says, pursing her lips. "It's just sun. Nothing scary about that."

"You know it's too hot for you!"

"Brody. It's the sun. What's your problem?" Evie snarls. "She have a heart disease or something?"

"Yes," he snaps.

"What does the sun have to do with heart problems?" I ask.

"It's none of your business," he says, furious.

I draw back and look at him in confusion, while he grabs Scarlet's arm and pulls her to her feet.

"Your heart is too fragile for this. You know better than to expose yourself to danger."

"As if the sun is going to make my heart explode," Scarlet says. "C'mon, Brody. A little warmth isn't going to kill me."

"You don't know that. If you heat up too much your heart

has to work way too hard to cool you down. There are risks. You know all this," he explains.

She sighs. "It's *my* heart, Brody. *I know*. I know the limits. Don't tell me what to do." She jerks her arm loose and turns her head away from him in defiance.

He lets out a huge breath. "I'm just worried about you."

"Thanks, but I can take care of myself."

He frowns. "I don't have time for your nonsense. Stay if you want. I just want you to be safe."

"Well, thanks, but see ya," she says, still ignoring him.

In the meantime, Evie and I look at each other with raised eyebrows, both thinking the same thing. I don't know what the hell is going on, but it has something to do with her heart. And Brody is acting like a total bitch because of it.

God, this is so not how I remember him from high school.

Has it been so long? Has he changed so much in the last couple of years?

He storms off again, and after a while Scarlet gazes at him with a sad look on her face. "I'm sorry, girls. I don't …"

"Yeah, we know," Evie says, nodding. "Don't apologize for him. Not your fault."

She smiles lightly. "Thanks. I'm sorry. I really have to go. But I'd really like to hang with you sometime."

"Yeah …" I say, and a pathetic laugh comes out of my mouth. "Maybe sometime later."

"Okay. Well, see ya!" She waves and then runs after Brody.

"Jesus. That girl's something else," Evie says after a while.

"Tell me about it."

"I did not expect that."

"No, I didn't know she had heart problems. Kind of puts things in perspective."

Evie hums in agreement. I'm staring at the grass, thinking about the whole scene. Brody really reacted over the top. I'm not sure it was necessary.

"Well, even if she has heart problems, it shouldn't give Brody permission to act like that," I say. "I think Brody's really turned into a jerk."

Evie chuckles. "Now you're saying."

"Yeah, well, I hate to admit it, but it's true. He's changed. A lot."

"I wonder why. I mean, you always said he was the nicest guy you ever met. Then when I met him I thought you were crazy or something. He never struck me as a cool guy."

"We used to be best friends. He always stuck up for me when I got bullied."

"Yeah, I know. Still, he doesn't strike me as the type to care right now."

I nod and hum in agreement.

It's true, what she says. I'm starting to see it more and more, but I don't actually want to admit it. It means we're really growing apart, and I don't want that to happen. Before I came here I'd hoped we could be a tight bunch together, just the three of us, having fun, but now it seems he's totally disconnecting from us. I barely see him anymore.

I don't really want to think about it anymore, so I look at the people around me instead and focus on what they're doing.

As I turn my head, my heart stops.

It's Hunter.

He's stretching his back and legs, alternating positions while staring up into the sky. His face is blank, concentrating on what he's doing. The cut muscles hiding behind a thin layer of cotton are mesmerizing to look at, and he reminds me of those sportsmen who prepare for their challenge by increasing their limits.

He gets up on two feet and shakes off some of his energy. Then he starts hitting a large ball that's hanging from a tree by a thick rope.

His strikes are hard and fast, and his face turns into the face of a fighter. Full of energy. Full of anger.

I don't know which one I find more frightening.

He's like a massive force of fury aiming for the knockout punch. On a freaking ball.

Sweat drips from his face and makes his skin shine. He's wearing only shorts and a loose tank top, which moves fluently with his shuffling. I can clearly see his six pack through his wet shirt, and his brown nipples peeking through.

I gulp at the sight.

He looks marvelous. The way he jumps around, hitting that ball like it's his arch enemy. He's lightning fast and not heavy on his feet at all, even though he looks like a hulk right now. A big, fierce, manly man with biceps the size of small melons.

And it's making me drool like a teenager.

I can't believe I'm thinking about him like that, let alone gawking at him.

Each time he hits the ball, he sends it flying into the air, and I'm amazed at his sheer strength. The aggressiveness in his stance, his power. It's like a magnet to my eyes.

"Looks like he's working out," Evie says, jerking me out of my daydream about Hunter.

The moment she opens her mouth Hunter looks our way and stares right at me. My eyes widen, and my breath falters. I suddenly feel caught in the act of admiration. Dammit, I didn't expect him to turn around, and I certainly didn't expect him to notice me sitting here. What an embarrassment.

My face starts to glow. His lips quirk up into a smile, and he waves a little, so I wave back.

"Autumn!" Evie says, and she pokes me in the side.

I turn my face toward her. "What?"

"Don't encourage him."

"He's not even into me," I say.

"Well it's sure a coincidence he keeps wanting to sit next to you," she says.

"Maybe he just doesn't have many friends."

"I don't think so," she replies, and she points at something behind us.

I turn around again and see Hunter sauntering away. My eyes follow the direction he's going, and I notice he's walking toward the fence. A bunch of guys wearing ragged clothes and unshaven beards stand behind the fence. They're clustered together, and it looks like they're talking, but I can barely see their mouths move. Their eyes skid from left to right, scanning the area, as if they're checking to see if the coast is clear.

With a quick glance, Hunter checks if anyone's looking, and I quickly turn my head in the hopes he didn't see me looking. When I think it's clear, I turn my head again and see him talking with the guys.

"What do you think they're doing?" Evie says, squinting.

"I don't know."

One of the guys behind the fence rummages in his pocket and takes out something I can't see. Suddenly they exchange something, and Hunter pushes something deep into the pocket of his jeans. Then he does the same, giving something back to them. They're lightning quick in the trade. I can't even see what it is, just that it's small and lightweight.

They all nod, and the look in their eyes is harsh, as if it's a warning of some sort.

It freaks me out.

Everything. Not just the look in their eyes. Not just the exchange. Everything about it has bad written all over it. Just like Hunter.

"Nothing good," I murmur.

"What?" Evie says, and she crawls closer to me, lying down

on the blanket.

"Nothing." It just doesn't look good, but I can't say what it is either. I didn't see anything, but I know it's not cool. But I don't want to worry anyone without proof.

We both peer at the boys as they part. The guys stroll away from the premises, and Hunter comes back to the college ground. I quickly turn around on my back, and Evie does the same, and we pretend we've been laughing all this time.

Hunter passes us, and I know he's been looking. I don't want him to know we saw everything. There's no need yet. I don't know what it is he was doing, but I'm sure it's something he doesn't want everyone to know. And I intend to keep it that way, as I'm far too scared to face the consequences if I did tell anyone.

Yep, I'm chicken-shit.

CHAPTER 5
CHICKEN-SHIT

My hand is hovering close to the door of Brody's dorm room, but I can't pull the trigger and actually knock. I've been meaning to talk to him for the past couple of days now, but I can't figure out for the life of me how to start this conversation. I don't like fighting with my friends, but at the same time I don't want it to continue the way it's going right now. He's important to me, and I can't lose him. I want to see if I can change this.

I'm shaking from top to bottom as I blow out a final breath before knocking.

The waiting seems like minutes, but I know it's only been a few seconds. Still, he doesn't open the door. He doesn't even respond.

I knock again, but still there's nothing.

"Brody?" I call.

Nothing.

"Hey, Autumn."

I turn around and Evie's walking up to me.

"Do you know where Brody is?"

"Yeah, I just saw him downstairs. He's hanging in the

lounge room with a couple of his weird friends. Not a good idea," she says.

"Well, I still want to talk to him."

"Why? Is it important? He seemed too busy laughing his ass off at fat girls passing by."

With furrowed brows, I say, "What? He would never do that. That's not like him. At. All."

"Tell that to the girl who ran past me, bawling her eyes out."

I bite my lip. "I think we just need a good talk."

"And you think that's going to help?" One of her eyebrows lifts.

"We've been friends forever, he'll listen to me."

She sighs. "Look, Autumn, I get that you were best friends and all, but Brody's really changed. And it's not for the good."

"Maybe if I can talk some sense into him he'll …"

"Don't count on it."

I look down at the floor, mulling over my idea to talk it over, get this cleared up and out of the way. But Evie's words ring true. She's not one to make this stuff up. I know for a fact Brody's changed, but I still think I can get through to him. I shouldn't give up until I've tried.

"If you really want to do it, I'll come with you," Evie says, and she hooks her arm around mine.

I smile. "Thanks."

"What would you do without me?" She winks, and it makes me laugh.

We go downstairs and into the student lounge. Brody's sitting there with his supposed 'friends,' who don't fit at all with what I had in mind for his friends. They're skinny, well-built, have smug faces, and some of them have girlfriends hanging on their laps. I don't remember Brody being like this, but now that I see him sitting there with Scarlet by his side, pretending he's all that, he seems different than before.

They're talking loud, and I can barely hear what they're saying, because they're all yapping through each other's conversations. They're also smoking, even though that's not allowed, but it doesn't smell like tobacco. It stinks, and I feel like I've just entered a private party.

Evie coughs, creating a distraction, and the group stops talking. "Hello?"

"Hmm … fresh meat," one of the group members says. "What do you want?"

"Yeah, fuck off," another one says, and they all chuckle.

"Shut up!" Evie yells. "I'm not talking to you."

Brody calms down his peers. "Autumn, Evie?" he says. "What are you doing here?"

"Uh, hello? This is the student lounge room. Everybody's allowed in here." Evie taps her foot on the floor.

The group Brody's with laughs at her, and her tapping speed increases.

"Obviously." Brody looks annoyed by her comment. "What can I do for you?"

"What can I do for you? Boy, you sound like a real gangsta, don't you?" Evie says.

"Don't call him that," one of the guys cautions.

"Or else?"

"Evie," I say, and I put my finger on my lips. "Let me handle it," I whisper.

She crosses her arms and puffs. "Fine."

Clearing my throat, I say, "Brody, can we talk?"

The group bursts out into laughter. "He doesn't have time for you," one of them says.

"We're busy, can't you see?" another one says, and they lean forward, looking bored and annoyed.

"Stop being such assholes!" Evie screams. "Or I'll …"

Now they all stand up. "Or what, bitch?"

The relaxed mood has suddenly changed to a darker, scarier mood, and I'm not sure if I still want to talk to him. Heck, I'm not even sure if I should stay here one second longer. I don't feel safe.

"Or nothing," Brody says. "Look, girls, I'm sorry, but I don't think this is the right time."

"Yeah, fuck off," one of the other guys says. "Like you're even welcome anywhere. Fat ass."

Now I have to hold Evie back before she charges in to start a wrestling match.

"What did you say?" she screams.

"Stop!" I yell.

"What, huh? What d'ya wanna do? Wanna fight?" one of the guys says to her, and he tilts his head in contempt.

"Fuck you! Fuck you all!" Evie screams, and she jerks herself loose from my grip. "And you too, Brody! Autumn's your friend, and you've been treating her like shit."

"What? What did I ever do?" Brody says, holding up his hands.

"C'mon, Evie, let's go," I say, and I usher her out of the room with trouble. "They're not worth it." I can't deal with this right now, so the best solution is to cut it off.

"Damn right they're not worth it!" she screams, but I hope they can't hear her.

I push her up the stairs and pull her into our room. I have trouble containing her, because when she gets started she's like a bull with horns, ready to charge.

I slam the door shut and watch her pace up and down. Kicking the door, she rages some more until she's out of breath. Then she slumps to her bed and flops down.

"God, I hate them. *And* I hate him."

I sit down across from her, and just stare ahead.

"Wow …" I say. "I seriously did not know it was that bad."

"Do you see now? Those guys are *not* good, Autumn. I tried to tell you, but you've been blind the whole time."

"Well thanks," I scoff.

She sighs. "Sorry, I didn't mean it like that. I just mean that you really need to open your eyes to the truth. He's not who you think he is. Not anymore."

"Damn it …" I say, and I let my back drop onto the bed so I can stare at the white ceiling. It makes things a little easier to process.

Neither of us say anything else until she's calmed down. When I can no longer hear her panting, I sit up straight, and so does she.

"It smelled like pot in there. Brody's really gone nuts." Evie twirls her finger around in the air, close to her temple.

"I guess …" I say.

I don't really know what else to say. I've seen it with my own eyes now. He's hanging with the wrong crowd, and now he's even smoking weed. Their behavior is violent and frightening, and I don't want to have any part in it.

"Friends are supposed to be there for each other. To support one another. They don't laugh at you or let their friends treat you like dirt," Evie chides in anger.

"I know …"

The more she says, the more I feel tears stinging my eyes. It hurts to have her talk like this. Not because it's wrong, but because I know it's the truth. I don't like seeing my friends this way.

"Oh … crap … I'm sorry," she says, and she scoots off the bed and sits down on mine, putting her arm around me. "Don't cry because of what I said."

"I'm not." I wipe away a few tears I didn't manage to hold

back. "I just hate the way this is turning out. I missed Brody. All this time I was waiting to finally go to college so I could hang out with him again, and now he's like this."

"I know … I'm sorry …"

"And the worst part is that I can't change it."

She sighs and leans her head down on my shoulder, rubbing her hand over my back. "Let's not talk about it anymore. He won't ruin our day anymore."

"Yeah …"

"Hey, what do you say we go swimming? Let's do something fun."

"I can't." I reach into my pocket and take out the money I have left for the week. I don't need to count to know it's not enough to do anything else but buy food with. "It's not enough. I'll have to wait until my next paycheck, and even then I probably won't have enough."

"Oh …" Evie swallows. "Well, we can always go back to the library and pick out random books to read instead. Just something to get your mind off Brody."

I nod, and she claps her hands.

"All right, let's go."

She pulls me up from my bed, and we go outside.

We bump into Scarlet in the hallway. "Hey, where are you going, girls?"

Brody comes up behind her, and I wince at the sight of him. He quickly walks around us and grabs Scarlet's hand. "C'mon."

"No, I want to talk to them." She jerks her hand loose. "Sorry about his friends. They're a cranky bunch."

Evie snorts. "That's a big understatement."

"So, what are you girls up to?" Scarlet asks.

I clear my throat to stop Evie from starting a fight. "We thought of going swimming, but—"

"Oh, can I come?" Scarlet interrupts me.

"We're not really—"

"I want to make it up to you. Let's go together, I'll pay."

"No, you know that's not good for your heart. Now let's go," Brody says, and he swiftly grabs her arm and drags her through the hallway.

"Sorry! Rain check, then?" she yells, digging her feet into the carpet as he pulls her around the corner and out of sight.

"Not a chance …" Evie mumbles.

"At least Scarlet is nice," I say. "I can't say the same about Brody."

"It's like the world is upside down," Evie says. "Tan-and-pink chicks aren't bitches, and they suddenly want to hang out with us, and the nerd has turned into a complete asshole."

"Let's not go there again," I say as we walk downstairs.

"Right," she says.

We make our way across campus toward the library, and I spot Hunter in the middle of the open ground. The moment his presence catches my eye I stop moving. He looks confident, but unsure of what he's doing at the same time, and it alerts all my senses to what's going on.

He's standing with a group of guys that seem familiar. And now I know why. It's the same guys as the ones behind the fence, the ones he made an exchange with.

One of them has brown Justin Bieber hair, what I'd call a flowerpot cut, but he looks quite handsome, and I swear I've seen him before. Maybe in class.

It doesn't really matter. What does matter is that Hunter's having a suspicious conversation with them, and this time I can actually hear them.

"Shit," I mutter, and I push Evie against the wall.

"What?" she says, but I put a finger in front of her mouth.

"Shh … It's Hunter!"

"So? Who cares?"

"I want to know what he's up to."

"Why do you care? He's just a guy …" Evie sighs.

"Look," I say, and I direct her attention toward the guys.

Her eyes widen when she sees what I mean.

"Shit, this looks serious."

"Yes, that's why I want to know what's going on. Hunter's been acting strange lately, and I want to find out why."

She nods, and I turn my head and watch the guys. I'm completely focused on the voices, all unfamiliar except one. His. The gruffness of it never ceases to grab my attention.

Hunter's standing close to the group of guys, and they're whispering some things, but when actual words come out I can finally hear it.

"That guy," one of them says, and he points at a guy standing near a fountain, talking to someone else.

"What do you want me to do?" Hunter says.

"You know …" the other one says, and Hunter freezes.

Their looks are stone-cold sober, so serious it chills me to my core. I don't know what they mean, but it creeps me out. And the grim look on Hunter's face doesn't predict anything good.

He nods, and I gulp. They shake hands and then disperse, as if they were never even there, discussing secrets.

"I don't like this at all," Evie whispers.

"Me neither," I say, and we make a run for it before any one of them notices we've been watching.

But before Evie and I turn the corner, Hunters eyes meet mine. His piercing gray eyes zoom in on me, and he starts to squint the moment he realizes it's me.

Shit. I've been caught.

With his gaze on me I can barely breathe. I know he knows I've been watching him, I can see it in his eyes. I don't need to talk to him to know that he wants me to keep it a secret. His intent glare is enough.

And then we turn and bolt away.

CHAPTER 6
TROUBLED HEARTS

"Yuck, don't they have some real food here?" Evie throws the spoon she's holding into the lettuce behind the counter. The lunchroom lady grimaces at her, but turns around shortly after.

"Fat and juicy burgers aren't exactly real food either," I say, carrying my plate to the checking counter.

She snorts. "Hell, I'd prefer Mickey D's anytime over this junk."

I laugh as I pay the cashier and watch Evie snarl at the lunchroom lady to make her something that includes at least an ounce of meat.

When she finally has her slab of meat, we find a free spot and sit down to eat.

"I swear, one day I'll just drag you into a real lunchroom. Some place they serve nice, tasty food."

I roll my eyes. "You know I can't afford that."

"I know, but that's why I've decided that from now on I'm just going to save up every cent I have so I can take you with me to one of those damn fine restaurants maybe once a month."

I smile, but feel embarrassed because of my lack of money.

Evie's hand is suddenly wrapped around mine right on the table. "Hey, don't you even think about feeling bad. It's supposed to be a good thing."

"I know … it's just that—"

"Stop it. I'm not taking no for an answer. You'll come with me, and I'll pay, and that's that. No buts. No ifs. Once a month, we'll gorge on delicious junk food or better."

I chuckle. "All right. Thanks."

She smiles and squeezes my hand a bit.

"I'm really glad I have you as a best friend," I say.

The twinkle in her eyes disappears, and she lets go of my hand.

"That's what friends are for," she says. Diverting her eyes to her food, she grabs her fork and knife and starts cutting up the meat like a butcher, making me wince.

There goes my appetite.

"Could you be a little less …" My eyebrows draw together as my mouth drops open. "Is that Brody?"

Evie turns her head like a hawk in the direction I'm looking, so I say, "Don't stare! God, do you want him to see or something?"

"Does it matter? It's just Brody."

I sigh. "That's not what I meant. Don't you see who he's standing next to?"

"Yeah? So?"

"It's that guy. The guy Hunter was talking to the other day. When we were going to the library, we saw them talking about some weird business."

"Oh, *that* guy!"

"Shhh!" I say. "I'd rather not get caught staring again."

I blink again, but nothing changes. It has to be the same guy. I'd recognize that flowerpot hairdo anywhere. It's the guy Hunter was talking to. The guy who told him to do 'something' to 'someone.'

I wonder what the hell he's doing with Brody.

So many questions pop up into my mind. What does he want with Brody? And what was he doing with Hunter? If they both know him, does that also mean Brody knows Hunter?

So many things I don't know the answer to, and it's making me insane.

Brody bumps fists with the flowerpot hairdo guy, and they both take off in different directions. I wonder what they just talked about. I wonder how the hell they know each other.

When that guy passes us, I pretend I'm eating some lettuce and stuff my mouth full of it. As he leaves, I almost choke on the huge amount of food in my mouth. I wash it down with a bottle of water, and Evie starts cutting up her steak again.

"I wonder …" My voice stops working.

I don't know what I want to say anymore.

As soon as my eyes catch a glimpse of that guy entering the cafeteria I'm flabbergasted.

My mouth drops open and I stare at him. *Him.* I know I call him 'him' all the time, but that's because he is the only guy my attention is ever drawn to. It's like there is no other guy around *but* him.

"What?" Evie says, but I ignore her.

I completely zone out, my eyes glued to his being. He's not just another guy, not one of the many flocking into the lunchroom. No. This is Hunter Bane, the guy whose mood changes with a snap of the fingers. The guy who goes from being a complete jerk to a witty, cute guy. The guy who looks like a sex god, but seems to have no interest in other girls whatsoever. Or at least, not that I can see.

There is so much I still don't know about him, and for some reason I'm intrigued as hell. I want to get to know him. Maybe it's because he taunted me that day with my bracelet, because I want to know why he is the way he is.

Whenever I see him, all I can think about is him.

He's the guy I'm swooning over.

And it's making me look like a gasping, drooling girl.

Closing my eyes, I take a deep breath and focus on the here and now. I can't go to him. I can't talk to him. I'm having lunch with Evie, and it's rude to leave her like that. I have to keep my eyes shut to prevent myself from failing in my resolve. I can't look at him, because I know I'll falter and go over there eventually.

Still, I can't help but open my eyes.

He's much closer now, and he's leaning against a vending machine. He coughs and then looks at his hand, wiping something on his dark, frayed jeans. He's wearing unusually thick clothes today, which isn't at all like him, and from the looks of it they're cheap, too.

Jamming one hand into his pocket, he runs the other through his spiky hair. He fishes a few coins from his pocket, gazes at them, and then crushes them in the palm of his hand. The look on his face darkens, and I can see his chest heave as he stares with anger at the vending machine.

I gulp at the sight of him and can't get a word out of my mouth. Hunter Bane, the guy who seems to have it all, doesn't have enough to buy some snack from a vending machine?

The idea alone makes me gasp. I can't believe Hunter, out of all people, doesn't have enough to go by. Is it just a coincidence? Or is this what he goes through on a daily basis?

Just like me?

I shake my head when he suddenly turns his head and looks at me. We stare at each other, and my eyes widen. His eyes are bloodshot, and his eyelids are swollen. There's a huge purple mark on his left cheek.

My fork drops onto the table.

"Autumn? Hello? Earth to Autumn?" Evie yells. She's been calling my name all this time, but I haven't paid any attention to it. And I don't want to right now.

I need to know what's wrong with Hunter.

"Be right back," I say.

"Huh? What? Where are you going?" I think she follows my gaze, because she immediately says, "Oh, God, you've got to be joking. Hunter?"

"Sorry," I say. "I really want to talk to him."

She stammers, but I ignore her, and I hurry over to him.

When he sees me coming, he pulls up his hoodie, turns his head, and starts walking in the opposite direction.

I run up to him and grab his arm, but he jerks loose.

"Leave me alone," he says as he walks through the cafeteria door.

"What happened to you?" I say.

I push myself past the doors and step in front of him. He looks miserable. His face has all the colors of a rainbow, like he's been hit with a baseball bat. His eyes scare me even more. They look dreary. They're red and big, as if he's been sick or crying.

Or something way, way, worse. Drugs.

I can't even think of it without wanting to puke.

The abrasive look on his face sends shivers down my spine. The only time I've seen him more upset was when he leaned against his door in the middle of the night, crying.

He closes his mouth, leaving a small gap in between his lips, as if he still wants to say something but doesn't know quite what.

I swallow. "I asked you a question."

It's not like me to be this upfront, bold, but I have to. He looks sick, and it seems to me like he doesn't even care. It's as if he's completely oblivious to the state he's in. Or there's something else going on that makes him ignore it.

"And I said: Leave me alone." His hands curl up into fists, and I get the sudden urge to bolt away, but I don't. I have to make a stand. I have to help him. I don't know why, I just have to.

"I want to know what happened," I say.

"Why?" His teeth grate, and his lips barely part as he speaks the words. It almost makes me feel like he's angry with me, but that can't be. I didn't do anything. Or did I?

"Because you seem hurt," I say with the calmest voice I can muster. I don't want to make him angrier.

"Why do you care so much?" His voice is hoarse, and it almost sounds as if he finds it strange that anyone could even care.

But I do.

I don't know why, I just feel like I need to care. Like I have to find out what's wrong with him, so I can fix him.

As if *I* could fix him. Me. Little, goofy, broke me.

As if he's been waiting for that. He just said he wants to be left alone.

He doesn't want to talk to me. He's been avoiding me since the moment he saw me. He doesn't want my help. Doesn't even need it.

But I can't leave him alone. For some reason I feel this unspoken, undeniable connection between us. I can't put my finger on it. It's not tangible. I just know it's there.

And I have to find out why.

"Because ... I just do," I say.

Maybe I'm selfish for wanting to talk, but I think it's worth it. If I can talk to him, I can find out why he's been acting so strange lately. Maybe I *can* actually help him, even if he thinks I can't. Maybe we could become friends. Maybe ...

I look up into his eyes, which he keeps hidden behind his

hoodie, and I can barely spot his glinting gray eyes. They're half-mast and not even pointed at me. It almost makes me think he's ashamed to look at me.

But why?

When I first saw him, he mocked me, but he was just playing around. He's a cocky, confident guy with a cute, boyish smile I can't ignore. His jokes make my skin crawl with anger, but that's him.

This is not him.

He looks broken, damaged, beaten. Literally.

Seeing him this way breaks my heart, even if I'd rather be taken to hell than admit that.

Without realizing it, my finger lifts to touch the bruise on his face.

Hunter cocks his head and backs away before my finger reaches his face. "Don't."

His lip contorts, his eyebrows draw together, and for a second I almost believe I see tears forming in his eyes.

Then he storms off.

CHAPTER 7
DEVILISH GAMES

"Did you hear?" Evie says, as we walk to our classes the next day. "Someone got beat up yesterday. Here on campus. During the day. In plain sight."

"Seriously?" I say, gasping.

My throat feels like it's being squeezed together. Images of Hunter and his bruised face and bloodshot eyes flash through my mind. All I can think about is if it was him. Or maybe he did it to someone else.

"You know what's even stranger? There were only a handful of people who saw it, and they said it looked like it came out of nowhere."

"What?" I didn't think my mouth could drop any farther, but it just had.

"Yeah, I reacted the same way. I can't believe someone would do that. It was in broad daylight."

"My God …" I say, still baffled.

"I'm wondering if it's some sort of calculated, premeditated fight. Like it was set up, or something like that. I know it sounds strange, but it took ages for word to reach our end of the campus, and fights like this usually take no more than five minutes for everyone to know. I mean, the guy was busted up pretty bad."

"Who was it? Were there more?" The words roll over my tongue like they're in a rush.

"I don't know. I wasn't there when it happened, you know. I just hear the rumors."

"So that's it? That's all you know?"

"Wow, calm down, girl."

"Sorry … I'm just curious."

"Since when do you care so much?"

"I don't know. Never mind," I say.

I don't have the guts to tell her that I'm actually nervous that it might be Hunter we're talking about here. And I'm even more anxious to find out whether it was him that received the beating, or if it was him who was handing it out.

That last thought is making me want to puke.

I can't imagine him doing that to someone. Hunter Bane, planning a fight? No, that doesn't seem like him. He can't have.

Although he looked just like the type yesterday.

"Well, I have to be in here, so …" she says, and she points at the door to her right. "I'll see you tonight."

"Actually … I have to work tonight."

"Oh …" she says, her face turning gloomy all of a sudden. "Okay. Well, put your best foot forward."

I roll my eyes. "Like I ever do anything else."

"Of course you don't. You're perfect, remember?" she winks, and we both burst out into laughter.

"See ya!" I say, and I walk into a different hallway to get to my own class in time.

I sit down somewhere in the middle and start unpacking my stuff. Soon the entire room floods, but my area stays nicely quiet. I don't mind. I mean, I've known for a long time people don't really like to sit next to me. I don't really care about the reason. I don't care at all that they don't want to sit next to me. I like being on my own. I have Evie. Enough friends for me.

As I finish placing my stuff on the table, I notice a guy opening the door. The teacher has already started his class, and seems pissed when the student stands in the doorway.

"Well, come in then," the teacher says, annoyed.

And then I notice it's Hunter.

His face has turned from a colorful palette into a much less noticeable shade of green. Lucky for him he's hiding part of his busted face in his thick vest. He probably only put it on to hide that fact.

I snort as he turns his face toward me and stares at me with his piercing gray eyes like he can see right through me.

I swallow and sink back into the chair. Especially when I realize the only empty space in class is right beside me.

"You're late," the teacher snaps.

"Yeah … Sorry."

"And your homework is shoddy at best."

Jesus, he's really getting it today. I'm starting to feel embarrassed already, and the teacher isn't even talking about me!

"Mister Bane, I don't know if you realize this, but your grades are on the line."

Hunter seems unfazed by the teacher's comment. His face is unmoving but sincere, as if he really cares.

I envy him. I wish I could remain that confident, hard like a brick, when facing a sneering teacher.

Especially in front of the entire class.

"I know, it won't happen again. I'll work harder. I promise."

The teacher squints in silence and looks intently at him for a second. "This is your last chance, Mister Bane. Don't screw it up."

Hunter nods, and somehow that's enough for the teacher to let him off the hook. I don't know how he does it.

When he comes up the steps his gaze is already set on that one empty spot beside me. I'm squeezing my legs together as he sits next to me. My instinct is to scoot far away, but I can't; there's nowhere to go.

I feel watched, which isn't strange, considering his gray eyes are practically trying to penetrate my skin.

Anger is seething inside him; I don't have to look at him to know. I can feel it flowing out of him like a radiator that's burning up.

God, I want to die.

He keeps staring at me, as if he has nothing better to do. My heartbeat is rising, and I'm starting to feel really sweaty. I don't know why he's doing this, but it's freaking me out, and I don't like it one bit.

"Don't you have to pay attention?" I say, avoiding his eyes.

"To you? Yes."

His words make my insides broil.

"The teacher has already started talking." I point to the front, but Hunter doesn't even flinch. His eyes are still on me like a hawk zooming in on his prey.

"I don't care."

I swallow, gathering the courage to turn my head and look at him. The moment my eyes make contact with his I'm drowning. Drowning in amazement. Drowning in fear.

Fear of the unknown.

"But your grades …" I stammer.

He snorts, and a smile curls the corners of his mouth while he shakes his head. "Yeah, right."

And all I can do is stare.

If looks could kill, I would be dead.

He looks so damn handsome when he smiles. It's like

everything around us fades, and all I ever want to see is that smile. It just makes me feel good.

But when the smile disappears, so does my good mood.

The darkness falling over his face unsettles me.

In his eyes I see the hurt, the worries, the insomnia. Sleepless nights have worn down his face, making him look saggy and dull. But I know there's so much more inside there.

Endless stories and an undiscovered world I'm intrigued by.

I want to know what's in there. Inside him. Why he's so angry and sad at the same time.

A sudden overwhelming feeling to grab him and hold him tight takes me aback.

He's having so much trouble in his life right now, even though I have no idea what's going on. I can see there's something wrong. And I want to help him get through it.

But I don't come any closer. I don't move one muscle.

I'm scared. Scared of what he can do. Scared of his power, and his temper.

In my mind I can still see his bloodshot eyes and the hateful look on his face. He was in that fight yesterday, I'm sure of it. The only question is: who was the one instigating it?

I open my mouth, but nothing comes out.

I can't ask him. I just can't get the words to come out. I'm really chicken-shit.

"Something wrong?" he says.

I shake my head.

"Then why are you looking at me like that?"

Hunter inches closer. I instinctively draw back, but he scoots even closer to my side. I'm scared to death he wants to do something to me, and I have no idea what, which makes it even scarier.

A devious smile appears on his face, and it's almost as if

he's enjoying this. Taunting me seems like his way of passing time in class. I don't like it one bit, but on the other hand I'm excited as hell.

He raises his head, and his nostrils flare. I turn my head, my breath hitching in my throat. I can't look when he's doing this, entering my private space uninvited.

It feels as though his nose is close to my hair, because there's hot air flowing close to my ear. And then he inhales.

Holy shit.

Is he smelling me?

I'm frozen in place from sheer panic, my heart beating like crazy.

No guy has ever come this close to me.

He lets out a huge breath afterward and chuckles softly. His breath lingers on my ear, and a shudder runs through me.

"I like it," he whispers.

Oh. My. Fucking. God.

My skin tingles where his hot breath brushed over me. My groin clenches, and my clit thumps.

Why?

His whisper does this to me. Just a whisper.

I've never felt like this before. I think I just died inside.

Hunter muffles a laugh. It's like he can smell my fear.

He takes in a sharp breath and moves back to his usual spot. As if what he did just now was the most normal thing in the world.

I'm still shaken, my body stiff from the encounter. I feel completely naked, and I know he's watching me.

The look in his eyes is like that of a boy who just did something totally against the rules. And it's so fucking sexy I can't stand it.

Still panting, I straighten my glasses. I wait until I calm down before I open my mouth again. "Why did you do that?"

The left corner of his mouth forms half a smile, and he continuous to gaze at me with animal-like eyes. It's his thing, I guess. A 'Hunter's' thing.

"No reason."

"What?" I say, befuddled.

He slumps down in his seat and starts watching the teacher.

"Are you going to explain why you're acting this way?" I ask.

"Nope."

I frown. "Why do you even come to class anyway? Only to torment me?"

He closes his eyes and laughs out loud, making me feel like a fool.

"Leafy, don't take life so serious."

"What's that supposed to mean?"

"You gotta live a little."

"Excuse me, but I think I'm fine without your advice, thanks." I open my books and concentrate on the pages instead. I've had enough of this.

I don't want to be his plaything. I don't want to be made fun of, to be ridiculed, to be laughed at. If that's all he wants from me, then I won't give him anything at all.

"Oh c'mon. Is your life really all that exciting?" he says.

"I don't need excitement," I snap.

"Everyone does something they get excited about. You've got to have something you love doing."

I sigh and close my eyes, trying to wish him away.

"Come on … you can tell me," he says, poking my arm. The moment his finger comes in contact with my flesh I feel weak to the bones.

"Fine. I like reading. Happy now?"

"Reading?" he jests.

"Yes. Books. You know, the thing lying on your table that you refuse to look at."

"You think I'm doing that out of disinterest."

I nod.

"Wrong."

The full stop to our conversation feels uneasy. He clears his throat. "Just because I don't like it, doesn't mean I don't want to. I know it's important. Just like I know it's important to have some fun once in a while."

"Right, because you've seemed so happy these last couple of days."

The uncomfortable mood becomes even more apparent.

Shit. I went a little too far with that last remark.

He knows I saw everything. He knows I've seen the hurt. He doesn't want anyone to notice.

"Believe me, I would give anything to be in your shoes right now instead of my own."

I chortle. "Of course you would." As if my life is so easy.

"Except for the whole monthly women things … you know …" he clears his throat again. What a weird conversation.

"On second thought, never mind. Anyway, you should really start enjoying life more. Might make it a little easier."

"You mean by fighting with people?" I say.

His smile disappears. His eyebrows draw together, and his face turns bitter. His jaw is clenched, and he looks pissed now.

I don't care. I need to know. "Whose idea was it? Yours or his?"

"I don't want to talk about it," he murmurs, and he turns his head away from me.

The teacher puts down his chalk and says class is over. The students around us stand up and start packing their things.

Guess it's time to go.

"Whatever," I say. "If that's your idea of having a nice,

easy life, have fun with it."

I fetch my stuff and stand up. Suddenly Hunter reaches forward and grabs my wrist. "I never said I liked that part."

"Then why do you do it?" I say.

His fingers are warm and engulf my wrist completely. I feel so tiny and fragile right now.

"Because I have to," Hunter says, and he lets me go.

Sighing, he stands up too, and waits. I don't know what for, but he continues staring at me until I'm done packing my things. We walk out of the classroom together while he keeps his eyes on me like a hawk, as if he's afraid I'm going to tell someone.

Suddenly Brody pops up out of nowhere.

"Hey, Autumn," he says.

When he notices Hunter standing next to me, he looks up in surprise. His brows furrow and his lips part, as if he doesn't understand what's going on. "Um … Who's your friend?"

So then I guess he doesn't know Hunter; even though they both interacted with the flowerpot-hairdo guy, they don't know each other. Or they're just trying to fool me.

"Hunter Bane," Hunter says, clearing his throat.

Brody squints at him with a suspicious look on his face, as if he doesn't trust him.

"What do you want?" I say crudely.

"Look, I'm sorry about my friends. I don't want to make things worse, so I was wondering if you'd like to hang out for a while. You're done with classes for today, right? Let's go grab some food."

I stare at him and then at Hunter, who shrugs.

"You should come, too," Brody adds, looking at Hunter.

"What? I uh … no, I can't do that."

"Sure you can. A friend of Autumn's is a friend of mine," Brody says.

I roll my eyes and check my wallet for the little amount of cash I still have left. Hunter rummages his pockets, but pulls them out and shows they're empty.

"Sorry, I'm broke," Hunter says.

"Yeah … me too," I say. "Rain check then?"

"I can pay, no problem," Brody says.

"Oh, no, I can't take that," I say.

"No way I'm letting a dude pay for my lunch," Hunter jokes.

"Besides, I have work in about an hour or so. Don't really have a lot of time," I add.

Brody sighs. "Okay. Well, I'll see you around then. Let me know if you want to do something, okay?"

"I will," I say with a fake smile.

I'm not sure I will. I mean, Brody was my best friend for a long time, but lately we've been drifting further apart. He's changed so much. I don't know if I even want to spend more time with him.

"Yeah, I really have to go," Hunter suddenly says.

When I turn to look at him I see him staring at a bunch of guys near the fence. They're the same guys as last time, one of them the usual flowerpot hairdo. That guy Brody knows, too.

I wonder what Hunter's doing with them. Were they involved in the fight? They must've been.

I don't understand why he's hanging out with them or what they want from him. One thing's for sure, though: nothing good can come from it.

"See ya, Leafy," he says, as he signals the guys.

"The name's Autumn!" I shout after him, but he ignores me.

CHAPTER 8
FIGHT OR FLIGHT

I'm working in a Denny's joint, selling customers sloppy burgers and cleaning their tables after they're done. It's an ungrateful job, with people whining for more sauce and complaining about the taste, which I have no control over, but it pays the bills. And I so need the money.

I work hard to make enough money so I can survive on campus. It's not the most ideal job, but I'm happy I managed to snag it. I need it badly. There isn't any other way to compensate for the lack of funds.

My parents do their best to support me. They raised me well, put all their savings in a bank account and gave it all to me so I could go to college. I can't even begin to explain to them how grateful and happy I feel to have them as my parents.

Even if they're poor.

They tried to give me as much as they could. They did everything for me. And they mean the world to me.

The only way I know how to thank them is by working hard. Their hard-earned money goes into my education, and I want to make sure they did the right thing. I study harder than anyone else I know, and I make sure my grades are top notch.

I don't want to disappoint them. Not ever.

I need to make sure I graduate, find a good job, and make enough money so that I can support them. I want to give them back what they gave to me, and this is the only way to do it.

I want to help them. I want to give back to them.

So I'm glad as hell that I have this stinking job as a waitress in a sloppy burger joint.

Besides, working here lets me think of something other than homework for once in a while.

My hands hurt, and I'm tired, but I won't stop serving customers and cleaning tables. I don't want my boss to fire me, so I do my best and put up my biggest smile as I hand over the cash to one of the customers.

As day turns into night it gets harder to keep my eyes wide open. I have to, though. I've been watching a group of smug guys for some time now. They're sitting in the corner of the restaurant, ordering burger after burger while throwing all their trash on the floor. Scary, nasty bunch.

Some of them have tattoos, others scars, and some of them even have shaved heads. Their clothes are ragged and the shirts they're wearing have murderous phrases written all over them, probably from the lyrics of a song that would make me scream.

Just looking at them makes me feel icky.

When they finish eating they burp out loud and scare away the other customers with nasty jokes. My manager is in the back and doesn't see what they're doing. Throwing around food and wrappings isn't my idea of having a nice time with your friends, but I guess there are real jerks out there who like that kind of stuff.

I stare at the clock and let out a sigh of relief when I realize it's finally past my time. "You can go, Autumn. Thanks for working your ass off today," my manager says.

"Thanks," I say, and he hands me a few dollars.

"For your trouble. I know how hard it is," he says with a wink.

I blush. "Thanks … But you don't need to do that." I want to push it back into his hand, but he clenches my hand together.

"Keep it. I won't take no for an answer." He smiles and I smile back. "I'll close on my own. You go get some rest," he says.

"Thanks. I appreciate it. See you," I say.

I put on my coat and walk into the restaurant. There's only one exit, and it's in the front, so I'll have to pass that annoying group of guys.

As I walk past them, my heart rate elevates, because I feel like they're dangerous. Guys like those are frightening. Too impulsive. Too worked up. Especially when they're around friends.

I don't even look at them when I walk to the door and go outside, but I know they spotted me. I hear them talking as the door closes, and I increase my pace to get away from the restaurant as fast as possible.

Tucking my hands in my coat, I hurry across the street. Behind me is the sound of footsteps. It keeps speeding up, faster and faster, and the noise makes my heart go haywire. They're following me.

"Hey girl, where are you going?" one of them yells.

I ignore them and keep on walking. Just keep walking, don't pay any attention. Maybe they'll go away. Maybe I can outrun them.

But their footsteps come closer, and I can hear there are more with each step I take. They're laughing, and when I turn my head I see it's all of them.

Shit. They're coming after me.

Fuck, what do I do?

I start running, but they do too.

"Come here!" one of them yells.

And then they catch up to me.

One of them grabs my wrist, and I scream.

A tug of war begins between them, my purse, and my coat. Zipping open my purse, I take out the pepper spray my dad told me to carry with me, just in case. But I'm not quick enough, and they snatch it from my hand before I can use it.

They're jerking my coat open, and I fight to keep it on. I clench my arms together and struggle to hold onto my stuff.

Just one large pull is all it takes for them to jerk away my purse. It lands on the asphalt ground and the contents come spilling out. I look around to see if there's anyone around, but the streets are empty.

Nobody can help me.

I'm all alone, trying to fight monsters in the darkness.

A guy shoves the others away and grabs me by the arms so tight I shriek. His breath stinks of alcohol, and the way he smiles makes me want to puke.

"C'mon, little pussycat," he says, and he rips my coat open, tearing apart the buttons. "What are you hiding under there?"

No, no, no! This can't happen. Not like this. I don't want it to be like this.

I scream as loud as I can, so loud my lungs burn.

He puts his hand on my mouth and whispers, "You're a feisty one, aren't you?"

I open my mouth and bite down on his finger hard enough to make him bleed.

"Fuck!" he screams, and he jerks away his hand.

I can still taste his nasty blood in my mouth. The filth sends bile up my throat.

And then his hand comes down upon my face.

My glasses are flung off and land somewhere on the

ground.

The pain of the mark he left on me is hot, burning hot, and it stings on my skin. I can't believe this is happening.

Tears run down my face, and I plead, "Please, don't. Please, let me go."

They all start laughing, and the one I bit is licking his lips. "Not after what you just did."

I scream as loud as I can once the guy starts unbuckling his belt as the other ones restrain me.

Closing my eyes, I pray for safety. I need to be away. Away from here. Away from my mind. I can't see this. I don't want to be here. I just can't.

And as I zone out of this world, I hear a familiar voice screaming his lungs out.

"Get your fucking hands off her!"

My eyes flash open at the sound of his voice. When I see his white-hot face as he storms over to us I think I'm dreaming.

It feels so unreal. Is he really here?

Is he here to save me? Please tell me he is.

"Get the fuck away from her! Right. Now!" he screams as he approaches.

The guy I bit stops fiddling with his trousers and turns around only to be smacked right in the face by Hunter.

He lands a powerful strike on his jaw, and the man staggers and falls down backward on the ground.

"You fucking son of a bitch!" Hunter yells. "Don't you fucking dare lay a hand on her again." He spits on the ground, and before I realize it the guys let me go and go for Hunter.

They jump on him like a rabid pack of hyenas, pounding in on him without restraint.

Hunter tries to fight them off, throwing punches as much as he can. One of them is hit in the stomach and starts puking just because of his hit. Another one is kicked in the nuts and staggers away. But someone else hits Hunter with his elbow, straight in the nose.

"No!" I scream, as I grab my coat and try to pull everything together.

Hunter fights his way through the group of guys, screaming flurries of swearwords at them.

"I'll kill you! You dickhead!" the one lying on the floor comes to and starts pounding in on Hunter, too.

"Stop it!" I scream, tears streaming down my face. "Stop it, stop it!"

But they won't.

They keep fighting each other. Blood is scattered all over the ground and smeared all over their faces. Including Hunter's.

"You motherfucker. Think you can stop us?" the guy yells as he strikes Hunter. "We take what we want, when we want it. You don't get to fucking intervene!"

Hunter barely evades the next punch and makes a quick turn to punch the guy in the side.

He throws out some more jabs, as if he's a professional. His strikes are calculated, fast, and hit the weakest spots on their bodies, forcing them to back up for a second. He goes on like a raging bull, never quitting, never giving up.

"Run!" he screams, his eyes momentarily focusing on me.

My brain tells me to run like hell, but my gut tells me I shouldn't. How can I? I can't leave him. He's fighting because of me. He's the one who saved me. I can't leave him to his fate.

"This is your life now, rookie. Just like it's ours. Get used to it," one of the guys says to Hunter, and he spits on the ground.

"I won't let you fucking hurt her," Hunter growls.

"If you mess with us, you can pay the price with your life," the guy I bit snarls. "We. Demand. Respect."

I stare at the men fighting each other, brutally going at it. I can't even see Hunter anymore, as he's pushed down to the ground. They're going all out. Nobody's going to stop unless I do something.

Some crazy idea in my head tells me to grab my purse and take out the pepper spray, but I notice it's lying on the ground, just like all my other stuff.

It doesn't even take me a second to make the decision.

My instincts take over, and I make a run for it and grab my stuff and the spray. Turning around toward our attackers, I step into the fight and start randomly spraying them until the bottle is empty. It feels good to hear them scream and see the tears in their eyes.

A bitter revenge.

They yell and scream, throwing their arms around in a fit of rage. They're temporarily blinded by the stuff.

This is my chance.

I grab Hunter's arm and haul him up from the floor. He can barely stand, busted by the beating, but I force him to come with me. I can't leave him here. I have to save him, too.

I have no idea how I manage to do this, but I get him out of the crowd and pull him away.

He limps and leans on me, while I drag him to safety, far away from the group. We enter a nearby park and dive deep into the forested area.

His arm is around my shoulder, and I support his back with my arm. His body is heavy, and I can barely help him get to a tree. There, he slumps and sinks down to the trunk.

We're both exhausted, breathing heavily. I sink to my knees and put my purse on the ground, panting.

I feel miserable, sick to my stomach. Those guys were touching me, trying to tear open my clothes. Trying to take away the thing that was mine to give.

The tears start flowing again, and I lower my head and

bury it between my arms. For a moment I just don't want to exist.

And then I feel his hand on me.

He's caressing my head, petting my hair. His fingers are warm and soothing.

"They tried to … they wanted to …" I stammer.

"I know …" he says softly. His voice is hoarse and croaky, and he coughs.

I lift my head. It takes one look at him to immediately feel the pity.

Tears still sting my eyes, but I force them away when I see Hunter's bloodied face. He looks even more miserable than me. His eyes are swollen, his lip is torn, and blood covers half his face. His face is swelling up and turning blue, and his nose seems crooked.

I gasp. "Oh my God …"

Coughing up blood, he tries to move, but winces instead.

"Don't move," I say, and I crawl closer.

Rummaging in my purse, I find a band aid and peel it. He has a wide slash on his left eyebrow, so I cover it up. But before I can continue my work on him, I hear a noise that alarms me.

Voices. Footsteps.

My breath hitches.

It's them.

"Why did you … why did you do that? Why did you help me?" Hunter says. The words come out in a slur, as if he can barely talk.

"Shh …" I say, and I put my finger to my lips. "They can't know we're here."

Hunter never takes his eyes off me as they saunter past the forest, seemingly still capable of walking. I hear them swear and yell, while my heart thumps in my throat.

"Motherfucker! You'll pay for this!" one of them screams.

"See you in the arena."

I wait until they pass before breathing again. "We have to get out of here. Fast."

CHAPTER 9
MENDING THE BROKEN

I don't know for the life of me how I managed to haul him all the way back to campus and to the dorm, but I made it. I'm tired as hell, but I won't give up now that I'm almost there.

Hunter's nose is bleeding, leaving bloodstains on the carpet as we go upstairs. I drag him to the bathroom closest to my room and set him down on the toilet. His face is covered in blood, and it doesn't take long for the bathroom to look like a crime scene.

I snatch a few rolls of toilet paper standing on the table and rip some off. I grab a stool standing in the corner and sit down next to him. Dabbing the cotton against his face, I check if his nose is really broken. He winces when I touch him, but doesn't cry out in pain. He refuses to show me any pain.

How very noble of him.

"I have to call an ambulance," I say.

I turn to fetch my cell phone from my purse, but Hunter grabs my wrist and stops me from moving.

"Don't. I don't want to go there. I can't."

"Why not?"

"Because the cops will be asking questions, and I don't want to answer them." His nostrils flare and he cracks his knuckles.

I smash my lips together out of frustration. "But you're hurt."

"Please …" he says.

He looks genuinely worried. As if he's afraid, or something. And it sounds like he's begging me.

"All right."

He visibly relaxes, his muscles straining less.

I sit back down on the stool and tend to him. He keeps his eyes solely on me, while I inspect his nose. It's not broken, luckily. I clean his face gently, making sure I don't press too hard on his bruises. I open the faucet, poor some cold water over a handful of paper, and wipe the blood from his face.

My vision is blurry, though. I don't have my glasses anymore. They got thwacked off during the fight, and we had to run before I could search for them. Dammit, this would be so much easier with my glasses.

Hunter just sits there, studying me, breathing in and out like he's trying to calm down. His chest heaves, and he coughs again. "God … it's hot in here."

"No, it's not." I put my hand on his forehead and don't feel an unusual temperature. He must still be overheated from the fight.

Then he hooks his fingers under his vest and pulls it over his head.

Oh. My. God.

My pupils dilate as he takes off the top half of his clothes, leaving only bare skin for me to see. I try not to look too dumbstruck when he throws it to the floor and gazes back at me. But I can't stop my eyes from zoning in on his perfect body.

Those thick pectorals, solid abs, and huge biceps draw my

attention like a bee that has found his flower. Especially those V-lines …

My God. I can't stop staring.

My heart is thudding in my chest, and my throat is dry. I swallow away the lump in my throat. I have to fight the urge to touch those deliciously taut muscles.

I've never actually seen anyone this strong and lean before. Well, at least not partially naked.

He lets out a groan as he moves his body to sit more comfortably. The raw, masculine sound sends shivers down my spine.

But when I look at him, I feel bad. He looks busted and bruised all over, and I feel sorry for him.

It's my fault he's hurt.

He protected me. He was the one who saved me. He got into a fight for me.

The least I can do is mend his wounds.

"Be right back," I say, and I rush out of the bathroom.

I make my way to my own dorm room and find it empty. Evie must still be studying somewhere, which means I won't be bothered for some time.

Good.

I need to fix Hunter's wounds and I can't have anyone distracting me right now.

Rummaging through my closet, I find the first aid kit I stocked for emergency cases such as these. I take out the entire box and hurry back to Hunter.

He's leaning forward with his elbows on his knees, holding his own head in his hands.

"Fuck," he says quietly as the bleeding starts again.

"I've got this," I say, and throw all the contents of the box in the sink. It's at times like these that I'm glad my mother taught me all the things I need to know so that I'd be independent.

First I take the bottle of pure alcohol and drown a few cotton balls in it.

When I turn around and sit down again, he stares up at me, waiting for me to do something.

"This'll hurt. A lot," I say before I dab the cotton balls against the wounds on his face.

He hisses. "Fuck! Jesus Christ! What are you doing?"

Slamming his fist against the wall next to us, he lets out a huge breath. I almost jolt up from the noise. He's so aggressive and angry. Sometimes it scares me.

"Cleaning your wound with alcohol."

He calms down once I'm done. I grab a few dressings and cover up his slashes with them. Then I start wrapping a bandage around his head.

"Do I have to wear this?" he says when I'm almost done.

"Yes. You've got a big gash on your forehead. Doesn't look pretty. It needs to heal."

He groans, annoyed.

"How are your knuckles?" I ask, because I know they must hurt after all those punches.

"Fine."

Of course that's a lie. Men and their pride.

He leans back on the toilet, resting his head against the wall. He opens his hands, spreading out his fingers, and gives me access. He looks at me intently as I grab his hand.

The moment my skin makes contact with his, I feel fuzzy and weak, like a meek girl. The way he feels is amazing, so warm, and his hands are almost twice the size of mine. My hand could fit into his perfectly.

If I could ever hold it.

I swallow from the nerves and try not to tremble as I check his hands for bruises and cuts. His hand is tough as leather, and his fingers are so calloused, they make me remember he is a fighter in heart and soul.

I wonder why.

"Thanks," he says when I let go of his hand.

His face isn't doleful like before; on the contrary, he actually seems grateful.

I smile, my cheeks rushing with heat when he smiles too.

"Where are your glasses?" he says.

"I lost them during the fight …"

He chuckles a little, but holds back because of the pain in his chest. "Too bad. You looked cuter with them."

My eyes widen and I gasp for air. My face lights up red hot with embarrassment.

Did he actually just say that?

My heart is pounding. I can't believe this. It feels so unreal. He just said I'm cute.

Hunter Bane thinks I'm cute? Is this real?

For some reason I burst out into giggles. And now I'm even more ashamed.

"What?" he says. He leans forward and stares straight into my eyes. I stop laughing. My muscles tense up and I freeze. He's so close I can feel his breath on my lips.

Sweet, hot, delirious breath.

I want to inhale it. Take him with me and never stop breathing him in.

I want to kiss him.

"What's so funny?" he says. "You think I'm making a joke?" His voice is thick, like a guttural sound, and turns my bones liquid.

I clear my throat. "No. You're just the first to say that."

He leans back, and I can feel my body relaxing again.

"Well it's the truth," he says.

"Others don't seem to think so."

"You shouldn't care so much about what others think," he says. "What *you* think is what matters."

He reaches into his pocket and takes out my glasses.

"Oh my God, you found them! Thank you so much," I say with a gleeful smile on my face.

"Don't mention it. Least I could do for you now that you've nursed me back to health."

I roll my eyes and chortle, while he hands me my glasses. Leaning forward still makes him groan, though.

"Damn … I feel like shit," he says, laughing.

"You look the part."

"I just want to crash on my bed and sleep through the day tomorrow."

He gets up from the toilet and barely stays straight. I quickly put his arm around my shoulder and support him while he walks. We go to his room, and boy, it's not what I expected.

There's nothing out of the ordinary. Just a table, a chair, two beds, a pile of homework and books. It's even clean.

But what surprises me the most is the ginormous bookshelf right beside the door.

I don't have time to marvel at his books, because he limps forward and I have to go with him. I help him get to his bed, and he lets himself fall down on top of it.

Looking at him for a few seconds feels like an eternity. It's so dead quiet in here. Neither of us knows what to say.

"Thanks," I say after a while. "For coming to my rescue."

"I would do it again."

I blush and smile, and the smile he gives me back makes the butterflies in my stomach fly even more.

"Well … goodnight," I say, and I turn around and walk to the door at an awkward pace.

"G'night."

Before I walk out I peek one last time at the wicked fighter lying in his bed.

He looks darn cute and sexy when he tries to sleep.

And then I close the door.

"What are you doing?"

I jolt up and shriek, startled. I immediately turn around. Evie is standing right in front of me, her hands clenched to her waist, and she looks pissed.

"Going to bed," I say with a quavering voice.

"That's Hunter's room," she says, pointing.

"Obviously."

"You just came out of his room." Her eyes scan my face, and when she lowers them to look at my clothes, her pupils dilate. "Oh my God!"

I shush her by putting my finger on her lips. "Don't shout so much."

"But you're covered in blood! Shit. Are you all right?" She grabs my shirt and lifts it, inspecting my tummy where the stain was. "There's no wound."

"That's because it isn't mine." I jerk my shirt loose and lower it again.

She squints, and I can almost see her brain working.

Biting my lip, I say, "It's Hunter's. He got into a fight."

"I knew it! He's the one who was in the fight the other day. People have been talking about him." She gapes at me with furrowed brows. "And you were in there? With that guy, who's got a temper like a stick of dynamite?"

"Shhh," I say. "Stop making so much noise. Let's go to our room. We can talk there."

I push her inside and close the door behind us.

"Autumn, you really shouldn't be around that guy," Evie says. "He's bad news. Big time."

"I had to help him."

"Why? You could've called nine-one-one."

"He didn't want to go to a hospital."

She snorts. "Why not? Afraid of needles or something?"

"I don't know … It doesn't matter. The point is I was the only one who could help him out. What else was I supposed to do? Leave him out there, bleeding to death?"

She sighs. "Well … No, of course not, but …"

"But what?"

"Why were you even there in the first place? I thought you were working at Denny's place. Next thing you know I find you sneaking out of Hunter's room."

"I …" I hesitate. I want to tell her, but at the same time I don't want to speak. Not about that. I don't want to relive the moment some group of dickheads almost raped me.

But I'm so grateful Hunter was there to save me and kick their asses. I owe him. Big time.

How can I explain that to her? She won't understand. Just by looking at her I can see she's starting to hate him, just like almost every other guy she meets. Her eyes are practically burning with fire.

If I say anything, all it'll do is cause her to ask more questions. I'm tired, and I really don't want to talk about it. I want to bury it somewhere deep and never think about it again.

I take a deep breath before I speak. "I didn't see anything, okay. I wasn't there when it happened. I just found him and fixed him up. That's it."

I know I'm lying. And I hate myself for it, but I really want to sleep right now. Maybe I'll tell her sometime later, when things have calmed down.

When I've had the time to calm down.

She sits down on her bed and changes into her pajamas. "Well, I still think it's risky to hang out with him."

I sigh, closing my eyes. "I don't think he's that bad. There's just a lot we don't know about him." I sit down on my own bed and start changing, too.

"Like what? You saw who he hangs out with," she says, crawling under her blanket.

"So? Maybe he has a good reason." I lie down in bed and pull up the covers.

She shakes her head. "Look, I'm just worried about you, okay? After what happened with Brody … I don't want to see you go in the same direction."

I turn around and face her. "I know. And I won't. I promise."

She smiles at me, and even though I can see it's fake, I smile back. I want to reassure her that everything's going to be all right.

At least, I hope it will.

CHAPTER 10
TOO CLOSE FOR COMFORT

I'm only just getting out of bed when someone knocks on the door. Evie springs up from her bed, seemingly already dressed, and opens the door.

"Who is it?" I say, yawning.

I pick up some clothes from the floor and put them on while I hear Evie talking. And then I hear Scarlet's voice.

Frowning, I get up and walk up to them.

"What is she doing here?" I say.

"Evie and I are going to study together today," she says.

My face contorts. I haven't heard about this before. Since when is she making plans without me?

"Sorry, Autumn, I forgot to tell you."

"Thanks for mentioning," I snarl.

"She practically forced me to," Evie says, shrugging.

"No, I didn't," Scarlet says.

"Hold on a second," Evie says, and she closes the door in front of Scarlet's face. She comes close to my ear and starts to whisper. "I bumped into her and Brody last night when you were still at work. They were fighting, big time, and she could really use some girl time right now. She doesn't have any other friends here."

I cross my arms. "Oh, really? And since when are you so interested in doing charity work?"

"I'm not. Look, she offered me some cash in exchange, and I could really use some."

"But you never work! Your parents support you all the way."

Evie shushes me. "Look, I didn't tell you this before, because I didn't think it was important, but they cut me off a bit."

"What?" I gape at her. "Why?"

"Well, you know, ever since …" She purses her lips and rolls her eyes.

It's enough to let me know what's the matter. I've known about her likes and dislikes for ages, but I guess her parents never saw it coming. They don't accept her for the way she is.

"Look, I don't want to go into that right now. Scarlet needs help, she offered me cash, I could use the money … one plus one equals two, right?"

"Right …" I say. I'm still reluctant to say I like the idea, but I don't want to be a bitch either. I don't want to claim her as my study buddy, but at the same time I don't want to lose her either.

"Everything all right in there?" Scarlet yells through the door.

"Yeah, we're fine. Just discussing some things before we go."

"Okay. Let me know when you're done." She laughs awkwardly, and it makes me chuckle.

Evie puts her hand on my shoulder. "You okay with this?"

I sigh and nod. "Yeah."

"You sure you'll be okay?"

"Yeah, I'm fine. Don't worry about me. I can study on my own."

She smiles and then pulls me in for her big bear hug, making me choke. After a while she lets go again and opens the door.

"Ready." Evie turns her head to me again. "See you tonight."

"Yeah, see you later," Scarlet says.

I really have to do my best not to roll my eyes at her. They hurry down the hall, and it surprises me they're not hooking arms yet.

I sigh and turn around, but before I can close the door behind my back, someone pushes it back open.

With furrowed brows I look down at a foot that's jammed in front of the door. What the …

"Got a minute?"

My eyes widen as I hear his voice.

I turn around and stare straight into his fierce gray eyes. Hunter. He looks much better than yesterday. Less blood. Still a lot of bruises, though. But his face is no longer swollen.

However, that smile of his hasn't changed a bit. It still makes me giggly.

I open the door maybe a little too recklessly, because it slams into the wall. I immediately feel embarrassed, and it shows on my skin. Hunter laughs. The sound of it makes me quiver.

"Hey," I say with a chirpy voice.

"Hey yourself." He puts his hand on the door frame, and it makes him even larger than before, even though I thought that wasn't possible. He's so tall and masculine. My eyes feel glued to his skin. It's like when he's around, I can't look at anything else anymore.

"What's up?" I say, clearing my throat. I have to ask something. Otherwise I'll come across like a stammering, drooling chick. And I don't want to lower myself to that state. Although I know I already have, plenty of times.

"Hmmm, nothing. Just thought I'd come visit."

I laugh, but my eyebrows draw together in confusion. "For no reason?"

"Yeah? Why? Can't I come visit the girl who patched me up?"

"That's not it, I just …" I stammer.

He lets go of the door frame and steps forward, so I step back. "You want me to leave?"

"No, no, no," I say.

Each step he takes closer, I step one back, but the moment my back hits the wall, I have nowhere else to go. I'm trapped between the wall and his delicious body that towers above me.

A coy smile appears on his lips. "I think you do. You just don't want to say it. You're scared of me."

He leans forward and puts his hand on the wall beside me. I shudder from the predatory look in his eyes. Those damn mesmerizing eyes that turn me into liquid.

God, I could stare at those for ages.

But at the same time, I want to run.

My heart is throbbing in my throat. He's right. I'm terrified.

"That's it, right?" he says with a voice so gruff it makes my pussy clench. And it's just his voice. Just the sound of it is doing this to me. I don't understand why.

He laughs, but it sounds more like a low groan. It's a guttural sound, turning me into a puddle. For some reason I want to hear more of it.

"Even if you told me, I still wouldn't leave. I always go against the rules." He leans in closer, and my breath hitches in my throat the moment I feel his hot breath against my ears. "That's why you want me."

He moves away again. He steps back, giving me room to breathe, but all it does is make this space suddenly feel very empty. Quivering, I just stand there, as he stares at me with a devilish look on that pretty face of his.

God, I want to jump his bones and kiss him.

Fuck, he's right. I really am attracted to him.

I don't want to be, though.

Shit. I'm seriously glowing for a guy that breaks all the rules, ignores everything that he's told, and goes against everything I was ever taught. He's the epitome of a bad boy; a cocky, confident fighter, who likes to get girls worked up for no reason.

Especially girls like me.

Goddammit, he knows. He knows what he does to me. And still he continues.

"Stop being such a jerk!"

He chuckles. "Me? A jerk? Never."

In a fit, I pick up a pillow lying on my bed and throw it at his face, but he catches it in time. He's still laughing, and it's making me even more pissed. "Stop laughing!"

"I can't. You're too funny when you're mad at me."

"Goddammit, I hate that."

"Hate what? I just came here to talk to you."

"I hate it that you come in here and … and …"

"And what? That I show you the truth about yourself? That you secretly enjoy breaking the rules and don't want to admit it?"

My breath falters, and I close my mouth. I don't know what to say. Part of me wants to shout and tell him to leave. Another part wants to tell him he's right, and that I'm so goddamn into him I can't stand it.

He throws the pillow aside. "Stop being such a snoot and open your eyes. You saw what happened yesterday. That's the real world. You can't hide behind your innocence forever."

The more he says, the more I want to forget about everything.

"You can't shut it out. You have to deal with what happened. Face it head on. It's the only way to stop it from happening again."

"And you think I can face it head on?" I say, crossing my arms, feeling very vulnerable all of a sudden. "How can you say that? You make it sound so easy. Like I should just get over it. I was almost raped last night!" I scream.

It's the first time the world rolls over my lips. Tears well up in my eyes.

He steps closer again, and I draw back into my shell as usual. It's the only way I know how to deal with things. I'm the girl who runs away. Who doesn't even defend herself when she's teased. The girl who hopes things will just go away as long as she ignores them. I'm not a fighter.

He is.

Hunter puts his hands on my arms, and suddenly they're not that tough anymore. He's gentle, and he tugs me closer until I give in.

He pulls me in for a hug. My face presses against his broad chest as I wheeze. Anxiety. This is how my body responds to all the fear and pain that was suppressed after last night. Now it's all spilling out.

I'm crying, my tears making his shirt wet, and he's petting my hair. Shushing me, he caresses the top of my head until I calm down.

"Shit …" I say.

"What?"

"I didn't want to cry."

He muffles a laugh. "Sometimes you have to."

"Do you?"

He sniffs. "When things happen, yes. You've seen it."

Somehow his confession makes this better. It makes me remember that everybody has moments of weakness.

We're quiet for some time. I'm not sure if it's because of our awkward conversation or because he's holding me. Either way, it feels good, and I don't want him to let me go.

I never knew a guy's arms could be so comforting.

"I could help you, you know," he says softly.

"With what?" I say, drying my tears with my hands.

I look up into his face, and he cocks his eyebrows. "Teach you some moves."

I frown. "What … you mean …" The thought alone makes me laugh. "You want me to learn how to fight?"

He grabs my arms and pushes me forward. His grip is harsh and it forces me back into the moment. "Do you want to stop those assholes from taking advantage of you again or not? I'm not always going to be there to save you," he says.

I nod, still wiping the tears from my eyes.

"At least … not unless you want me to." He wriggles his eyebrows, and it makes me blush. For a moment I forget all about the fact that I was just bawling my eyes out.

"Anyway, I know just how," he says. The left side of his lips curls up into a sly smile. "But it'll cost you something." His eyes move down my shirt, and he licks his lips in the process.

Oh my God. Is he checking me out?

My panties are already getting wet just from seeing his eyes skim over me like I'm worth looking at. As if I'm sexy.

But then I realize what he just said.

"I'm not some kind of—"

"Bookworm?"

"Excuse me?" I stammer.

"That's what I need."

"You. You need me?" I say, befuddled.

A short, cute laugh comes out of his mouth, and he wipes his finger along his lip. Oh, how I wish I could be that finger.

"Help me with studying."

My jaw drops. I'm shocked. He wants to study? Hunter Bane actually cares about his college degree?

"Well … this is new," I say.

"Don't look so surprised. I told you, I think it's important, but there are other … things in my life right now that make it … difficult, to say the least." He clears his throat. "So, are you in or not?"

"Uh … Yeah, sure."

Hunter grabs a book lying on my bedside table and dangles it in front of me. "If you help me with this, I'll teach you how to defend yourself."

"All right. Deal." I try to snatch away the book, but he skillfully avoids me.

With a devious smile he turns around and starts walking toward the door. "Great. Then let's get started."

CHAPTER 11
INFATUATION

I walk after him like a puppy dog, and we go into his room. He puts my book down on his desk and turns around.

"We've got an hour or two. My roommate will be back by then."

"What does him coming back have to do with us studying?" I say, peering into his room.

He sits down on his bed. "Can't have him see me read a book."

I gaze at him, and the serious look on his face makes me burst out into laughter.

"What? Are you serious?"

"I'm dead serious."

"It's just a book." I use the table to lean back.

"Not to them. They'd kick my ass if they saw me trying too hard. Nah, I gotta fit in."

"With who?"

"No one."

So, he refuses to talk about it. I'm still going to want to know. I won't stop asking about it.

He clears his throats and pats the bed. "Sit down."

It sounds more like a command than a question. Still, I do as he says. Those eyes of his are luring me, coaxing me to come. My body wants to do whatever it takes to get close to him.

I'm not so sure anymore what my brain has to say.

As I sit down, I look at his bruises and the scabs on his wounds. "It's healing quite nicely."

"Yeah, about that, do you think we could take off the bandage? I don't really want to go out into the world looking like I have a war wound."

I chuckle. "Sure. I didn't know you were that insecure."

"I'm not. I just don't want them to ask any questions."

I have no idea who 'them' is, but I think it has something to do with the guys he keeps hanging around with.

Squinting, I start peeling off his bandages. His eyes are on me like a hawk, checking my movement. I have to twirl it around his head to take it off, so I lean forward. Sometimes I catch him flashing a glance at my boobs. My entire body zings from seeing it. Like I want him to see me. Almost as if I'm prepping to be touched.

I clear my throat once I'm done, and check the remaining scar to see if it's healing well enough.

"Are you afraid they'll ask you why you were in a fight?" I say.

He snorts. "Oh, no. They know already."

"Then what? You're afraid to look weak?" I say.

When he doesn't answer, I know I made the right guess. "What does it matter what they think? You were the one who told me that the only thing that matters is what *you* think of yourself."

His eyebrows tighten and he looks down at the floor. "I said that because it's true, but my situation is a little more complicated than that. I need to be fit and ready, at all times."

"For what? Fighting?"

He sighs, which sounds more like a dragon's breath, and reaches over to his fridge, taking out a bottle of water. He holds the plastic bottle against his swollen face, the coldness of it probably soothing to him.

"I fight because I have to."

"Why?"

"Stop asking so many questions. I saved your ass. That's the only thing you need to know."

I swallow and sit back. I feel I overstepped his limits a bit. "Thank you for helping me back there. If it wasn't for you, I'd be …" I push away the word again. "How come you were there anyway?"

"I was watching them. Still pissed I didn't spot them leaving the joint. Otherwise I would've been there way quicker."

"You were watching them?" I say with a voice that makes me sound like an interviewer.

He shuts his mouth and just stares at me.

Okay … I guess even that question is too much for him.

I wonder what in the world he's hiding.

"Well, your wounds look like they've healed quite nicely. Should be no more than a couple of days before the scars are completely gone."

"Too bad. I kinda liked the idea of looking like a pirate." He leans closer, makes a *yaarrghh* sound, and forms hooks with his fingers.

We both burst out into laughter.

We spend the next hour going over his homework and outlining what needs to be done in order to catch up. He's behind schedule by quite a bit, and it worries me to see him struggle this much. I didn't know he had so much trouble coping with college life.

When he throws the book to the other end of the room, I

sigh.

"Enough for today. I'm fucking tired already," he says, yawning.

"But we haven't even started yet."

He shrugs, and I stand up. I pick up his book lying next to the book shelf, and when I come back up I can't help skim over the many books inside. It's like a treasure chest to me. I wish I could just grab a bunch of them, sneak out, lock myself in my room, and read all day.

I hear footsteps behind me. Then I feel his chest press up against my back.

I shudder. His pecs are pushing against my back, and I love how it feels. My whole body clenches with need.

"I used to read a lot when I was little," he says softly.

"I can see …" I say.

"You like books a lot, don't you?" he says, and he lowers his head so he can look into my eyes. I don't dare turn my head. I'm much too excited. Electrified by his proximity.

And then my eyes catch a peculiar book. *Harry Potter and the Sorcerer's Stone.*

I gasp. "Oh my God! You've read *Harry Potter*? God, it's been ages since I last saw that book."

He chortles softly, so close to my ear it's making me shiver.

I turn around within his arms and find myself gazing into his hypnotizing eyes.

"I told you, you shouldn't judge a book by its cover. Reading is … difficult. But if I have the patience, I enjoy it." I don't even hear the words he's saying. All I can see are those rugged lips as they separate. How he licks his lips in between and squeezes them. How I want to kiss him.

He inches forward. The intoxicating scent of his aftershave arouses me. His arm reaches past me, and I'm still amazed by the size of his muscles as they move beside me. I gulp when I see them flex. He takes out the book and holds it in front of me.

"You can have it."

He waits until I hold up my hands and gives it to me. "I … I …" I stammer like a dribbling, love-struck teen.

When I look at him all I see is hotness. Power. Masculinity. He radiates sex. Oozes it from his protruding veins. Screams it through his magnificent eyes.

And it's such a turn-on, I can't stand it.

All I want is for him to be closer, to touch him, to have his hands all over me. I'd like that.

Suddenly he moves back and clears his throat. "Well, I guess we should call it a day, for now. Let's continue tomorrow." He opens the door for me.

I smile and draw in a much-needed breath. "Yeah, sure." I walk to the door, clenching the book firmly against my chest.

"Cool," he says as I walk out. "See you tomorrow then?"

I nod, and he nods, and then a moment of very uncomfortable silence follows.

"See ya," he says, and then he closes the door in front of me.

I just stand there, staring at the wood. My heart is beating like crazy. My breath is crazily fast. I want to jump up and down from all the tension that's been building up inside me.

God, I could squeal forever.

I have to tell someone. I really have to talk to someone, right now. This has got to come out.

I think I'm falling for Hunter.

But Evie's not around, and I have no idea where to find her. Sure, I could go looking, but that would take me ages, and by that time it'll no longer be fresh.

Maybe I could tell Brody.

It's not such a bad idea, actually. I mean, he was my best friend, before I had Evie. He can't have changed *that* much, can he? I don't want our friendship to disappear. Maybe if I tell him some good news he'll cheer up.

Before I realize it, I'm already standing right in front of his door. I try not to be overly enthusiastic as I open it.

"Brody, I …"

My voice stops working.

Brody's behind his desk, fidgeting with plastic bags. He's putting some white powder inside them.

My eyes widen as I see him doing the thing I never imagined. He's preparing drugs?

He turns his head the moment I burst in and covers his stuff with his jacket. "What are you doing here?" he snaps.

He gets up, and I immediately step back as he comes toward me. "I don't have time right now," he says, and he slams the door shut.

It takes me a while to realize I'm not even breathing.

I take in a sharp breath. If what I saw there was real, Brody is a … drug dealer?

My God … Why?

"Brody," I shout. "Open the door. We need to talk."

No response.

I start banging on the door, but he doesn't open. "Why are you doing this?"

I'm asking questions I know the answer to already. But I don't understand why he couldn't think of any other way to make enough money. I know we've always been a bit poor, but that doesn't mean he should stoop so low and just go the criminal route.

This can't be real. It just can't. Never in my life would I have imagined him dealing drugs. And yet everything he's done the last couple of days suddenly makes all the sense in the world. He's changed so much, I don't even recognize him anymore.

And that's when I realize he's no longer my friend.

CHAPTER 12
TUG OF WAR

I love sitting under a tree, reading a book. With the warm sun on my face and a light breeze it's the best thing in the world. Nobody to disturb me or tear me from the pages of my book.

The word 'my' makes me gloat. It's not actually 'my' book. It's the book Hunter gave me yesterday, and it still smells like him. Well, more like his room, but still, anything that reminds me of him makes me giggle.

I twirl my fingers through the grass as I hold onto the book with one hand. I'm lying on the ground on my belly, making sure my clothes don't get dirty by placing a blanket underneath. When Evie's still in her classes, I like to spend my time reading and pining over boys I will never have. Gotta do something.

Besides, I don't have Brody to hang out with anymore.

Even if he wanted to, I'm done with him.

I've been forcing myself not to think about him since yesterday. He doesn't deserve it, and it would only make me cry. I don't want to cry over something so pathetic.

I should just forget about him.

Suddenly, a shadow is cast over the pages of my novel. The sun is blocked by something … or someone.

As I peer up with furrowed brows, I see it's Hunter, and my annoyed look turns into a cheerful smile.

My eyes light up the moment I see him. He's towering above me, wearing ragged pants and a flimsy tank top, which barely covers his broad chest. I gulp at the sight, especially because his black jacket makes him look so tough.

He's like a motorcycle rider, only he isn't. He just looks like one.

Hunter goes to his knees and snatches away my book.

"Hey!" I snap. "I was reading that."

"Yeah, 'was.' And now you're not." He holds out his other hand. "Get up."

I grab his hand, and the moment my fingers touch his it sends electrical shocks through my entire body. He's so strong, he can lift me in one go without my help. My boobs bounce from the way he jerks me up, and I see his eyes flick to them for only a fraction of a second.

I gulp, and a flush spreads across my face as I pull my shirt up higher.

"What's this for?" I say.

"Time for some training." He leans forward, grabs the blanket, and folds it up.

"What, now?"

"Yes, now. My classes are finished, and by the looks of it so are yours. We don't have much time, so let's make the best use of it."

"B-but I have to study and—"

"But, but, but," he mocks, making a pouty face. "If you wanna learn how to defend yourself, you gotta put in the effort."

I frown. "I was busy. You think I'm just going to adjust to your schedule?"

"You can read a book anytime you want. I can't do this with you anytime I want. If I could, I would, trust me," he grunts with a thick voice that makes me shiver.

My pupils dilate when he says that, and my core heats up. Damn, why does he always do those things? And why do I find it so goddamn attractive?

He steps back a little, putting on a cocky smile as he throws my … his book in the grass. Then he throws the blanket on top of it. Grinning, he takes off his jacket. The lines of his muscles show clearly through the thin fabric of his tank top, and my heart is already beating in my throat just seeing it. His biceps bulge and for a second I think he's flexing them.

"C'mon," he says, rubbing his hands together. "I'm ready for you."

One of my eyebrows lifts up. "What? In these clothes? I'm not dressed for sparring."

He snorts. "You won't be dressed for it when they attack you again either. Now c'mon." He signals to me with his fingers, lifting his eyebrow only a little to taunt me.

I take a deep breath and place my hands on my waist. He's gawking at me from a distance, bending through his knees like a professional wrestler. If the look on his face wasn't so goddamn sexy, I would've shaken my head and walked away, but I can't.

For some reason I'd love nothing more than to tussle with him.

"Well? Are you going to come at me or what?" he says.

Swallowing, I fling my arms and legs to shake some life into them after sitting for so long. I take a deep breath and a good look at him. His tan muscles are already primed, ready to go. He looks like a football player waiting for the ball to be thrown into his hands so he can race off.

"Don't make me wait … I hate it when girls make me wait."

I chuckle. "Oh, really? What then? Are you going to kick a wall again or something?"

He muffles a low laugh. "I'll come after you myself if I have to. And things get rough with me pretty fast."

There's some sexual innuendo in there, I'm sure of it. The way he groans makes me want to bite my lip.

God, he's so hot.

Goddammit, I have to stop thinking like that.

No way a guy like him would ever fall for a nerd. He could pick any girl he wants. Who'd want to pick me?

Clearing my throat, I say, "Okay. Here I come."

After taking a quick breath I bolt toward him. I put all my strength into it, but he still manages to stay upright as I crash into him. He's like a rock in the ocean, forever unbreakable, and I'm the fish slapping up against it.

I try to tackle him, but instead I'm the one falling on my ass.

"Ouch!"

He laughs, so loud it makes me feel embarrassed. Everyone can hear him.

"Why are you announcing you're going to attack? That's like playing right into my hands," he says, and he holds out his hand.

I grapple him and try to pull him down, but he remains as balanced as ever. Shaking the finger on his free hand, he says, "You think it's that easy to bring me down?"

"I'll make it happen. Eventually."

He chuckles. "I like your spunk." He takes a few steps back. "Try again."

I clean the dirt from my legs and bite on my cheek while thinking about a tactic. If I could only get him to move, then I could take him down. I thought he was going to teach me something, but instead I'm charging into him. Not my idea of learning self-defense.

"C'mon. I can take you, Leafy," he says, biting his lip.

That name he has for me … God, I hate it. Why can't he just call me by my real name?

I've had enough of his provocations. Maybe I'll just kick him in the balls instead. That'll show him not to mess with me.

I know it's below the belt. Literally. But at least I can try to win this way.

God, I've changed, too.

I charge forward without warning this time. As I lift my knee he deflects my leg by pushing it down with his free hand. With the other, he grabs my lower arm.

"You're getting dirty." He squeezes my wrist, hard, and makes it impossible for me to escape. "I like it," he murmurs.

With clenched teeth I fight to get loose, but he won't release me.

"Put a little effort into it," he says. "Nobody's going to be nice for you. I'm not either."

I slam his arm with my free hand, but he still won't let me go. It's like he doesn't feel anything. Nothing. Nothing at all.

Damn, is he some kind of brick wall?

He chuckles. "C'mon, hit me." At first it sounds like he's pushing me, but after a while it becomes plain mean. "Hit me!"

"I'm trying!"

"You're a wuss. A boneless nerd. You can't fend for yourself. Can't live in the real world. Not even one day."

"Shut up!" I gather all my strength and punch him so hard in the gut his stomach retracts, and he takes one step back. His grip on my wrist loosens, and I jerk myself free.

"What the fuck is wrong with you?" I say, my eyes welling up with tears again. "You're being an asshole, and you know it."

"Damn, that was a good jab," he grunts.

"Who cares? You're a bully."

He laughs and steps forward. When I try to hit him again, he grabs both my wrists and comes to a halt right in my face. "I'm helping you."

"Helping me? You're insulting me, belittling me, and making me feel like a pile of crap."

"And those guys didn't?"

"What do they have to do with it?" I snap.

I try to jerk my wrists free, but he won't let me go.

"Anger helps you fight. It fuels you." His lips quirk up into a devilish smile. "Guess this is your first time finding out about the power of rage."

"Whatever."

"C'mon. You know I didn't mean any of it. It's just to get you worked up."

"Let me go," I hiss.

"Make me," he says jokingly.

I'm so pissed, I kick him against the shin so hard I think I'm going to snap bones.

Instead, I break his stance, and he slips. I see him tumble down to the ground, but not before he grabs my leg and pulls me with him.

I squeal as I land right on top of him.

I'm staring into his face, my body resting on his body.

Oh. My. God. I can't believe this.

I think my heart has stopped beating, because all I hear is his breathing. My body tenses up, feeling his skin against mine. I want nothing more than to press my body closer to his.

His chest moves against mine each time he inhales, and these few seconds feel like an eternity.

His hand lifts. When it reaches the top of my head, I swear I'll fall to pieces right here, on top of him.

Something tickles, and then he retreats. In his hand is a leaf, which was probably stuck in my hair. He releases it and lets it drift away with the wind. Then he stares at me, his eyes suddenly showing a little hesitance. His lips are parted and perky, and all I want is to press mine against his.

And then smack him again.

He's breathing against my chin, and I feel my groin heat up. I'm getting all wired up because of him.

Shit.

I scramble off him with a face that's probably as red as a beet. He's not smiling anymore, and he looks uncertain of what to do. As if he realizes that I like him and that he can't give me what I want.

My smile disappears with that thought, too.

He gets up and pats his pants to shake off all the excess grass.

"Jesus, what are you guys doing?"

I turn around at the sudden sound of Evie's voice.

"Hi!" I say, a little too perky. "Uh … we were just training."

One of her eyebrows goes down and the other goes way up. "Training? For what? The dirty Olympics? You guys look nasty. And sweaty too." She waves her hand close to her nose.

Hunter coughs. "I'm teaching her self-defense, and she helps me with my homework."

"Oh, really?" Evie says, squinting as if she still doesn't trust him.

"Yes," I say.

"Uh … Look, I'll see you around, okay?" Hunter says, and he picks up his jacket and puts it on again.

"Yeah, see ya," I say as he walks away.

My mind drifts off into weird corners when I see him walk away with that firm butt of his. I'm still a little flustered by what happened just now. I almost kissed him.

Evie snaps her fingers and jerks me out of my daydream.

"Earth to Autumn. What are you doing with that guy?"

"He just told you."

"Duh, I know. That's not what I mean. Why are you hanging around him? You *know* he's a troublemaker."

"He's not *just* that." I walk toward my blanket and start picking up my stuff.

Evie walks after me. "You have no idea what you're getting yourself into. For all we know he could be hanging out with ex-cons and juvies. Wouldn't surprise me."

"Evie …" I say, sighing. "I know you're trying to protect me, but you gotta trust me on this. I think he's a good guy."

She rolls her eyes, but I continue anyway. "You have to give him a chance."

She closes her eyes and sighs. "Fine. If you want to. But I'm still going to watch him, make sure he doesn't do anything dirty."

I laugh. "That's going to be kind of difficult when Hunter and I are sparring together. Can't *not* get your hands dirty, if you know what I mean."

"Yeah, yeah, I get it. You want some independence and to kick some ass at the same time. Now let's get back inside and put you under the shower, because you smell like hay, and it stinks."

CHAPTER 13
INCH BY INCH

Evie's out to dinner with her parents, who swung by for the weekend. I'm sitting here, alone, reading my books. I'll always be reading books. I don't care whether it's fiction or educational, I gobble them up like muffins. It's more like brain food, and not unhealthy for your body, unlike muffins.

Although, I would never say no to those either.

I don't have the time or the luxury to go out to dinner with my parents. Heck, none of us would have the money for it anyway.

I'm behind on my homework schedule and fervently writing down notes as I skim the books in front of me. I'll read them thoroughly later on.

When someone knocks on my door, I don't even look up before yelling, "Come in!"

"Do you ever do anything else?" Hunter chuckles as he opens the door.

I turn around and see him standing in the doorway with a coy smile on his face.

"I need to get this done in time," I say.

"Oh, c'mon, you can work me into your schedule."

I hear him stomp as he walks inside. "Sorry, but I don't have time for sparring today."

"I'm not talking about sparring."

He's right behind me. I know because his body creates a shadow on my work, and I can't really see what I'm doing anymore. He reaches forward and grabs my book.

"Hey!"

"Chill. I'm just putting it away. See?" He puts the book back onto my shelf. "You really need to relax sometimes."

"I am relaxed," I say.

And then he places his hands on my shoulders. His fingers squeeze my flesh, and he starts pressing. Soft and hard, pinch and release. He's massaging me.

"See? All tensed up. Can't be good."

I struggle not to moan from his touch.

"Tell you what, why don't we go hang someplace today? Takes your mind off things for a while."

"But it's almost evening, I can't—"

"Because it's evening?" he jests. "C'mon. You gotta give me a better cop-out story than that."

"I need to get this done."

"Homework can wait. You need to have some fun once in a while."

"But …"

"I'm starting to think you're just making up excuses so you can avoid having to hang with me. Are you afraid?"

He leans forward and gazes into my eyes with a playful look on his face. I can't deny that he looks so goddamn cute when he does that cheeky smile.

"No, of course not," I stammer.

"Do you want me to drag you out of that seat then? And that's not an empty threat."

His words stir my insides, heating them up.

"Oh, all right," I say. It's impossible to say no to him.

"Awesome, let's go."

Hunter turns the chair with one hand, spinning me around. He grabs my hand and pulls me up.

I almost squeal as he drags me along the corridor and out of the dorm.

♥♥♥

We walk through the city for about thirty minutes before Hunter stops on the corner of the street. He peers up at the movie theatre just ahead and then points at it.

"We're going to the movies?" I say with my eyebrows raised.

Hunter's eyes scan the area, as if he's checking whether the coast is clear. Then he nods.

"I can't pay for that, you know," I say.

"Don't need cash to have some fun," he says, and he grabs my hand and pulls me to the rear entrance.

"What? You want to sneak in?"

He puts his finger to his lips and shushes me. "Do you wanna get caught?"

I shake my head as he opens the shoddy door. "I can't do this."

"C'mon, live a little," he says softly. "We won't get in trouble if you keep your mouth shut. It'll be fun. Trust me."

He pulls me through the door and checks the hallways for any guards. My heart is beating in my throat as we barely pass an employee on his break.

"This way," Hunter whispers, and he pulls me to the side and into another door that says 'SERVICE ONLY.'

We come out in a room with booming sounds, filled with

red chairs. A movie is already playing, and there are people who are watching it and are unaware of our presence.

"Quiet," Hunter whispers into my ear, and it tingles against my skin.

We go to the back row and slump down on the seats, hoping nobody will notice us. My heart is still going crazy, and it surprises me that Hunter's relaxing already, putting his arms over the arm rest. I get the feeling this isn't the first time he's done something like this.

"Do this often?" I whisper.

"Sometimes."

"But if we get caught, we'll be in major trouble."

"I've done this often enough to know how not to get caught," he says, staring at the screen.

We watch the movie, and after a while I settle in more. I'm getting used to the idea we're doing something totally against the law. The only way I can make this okay for myself is by telling myself I won't be doing this again anytime soon.

But damn, it's exciting.

I never expected going against the rules was so freaking thrilling.

"You're enjoying this, aren't you?" he suddenly says.

"What? The movie? Yeah … it's fine," I say.

"No. You're starting to like being a lawbreaker."

"I am not!"

He laughs, and it's a low, husky laugh, making my heart skip a beat. "Of course you are." He leans forward in his chair, coming a little too close for comfort. "You pretend you're a proper schoolgirl, but you feel caged by it." His hand drifts to my hair, and I freeze. I can't breathe. "On the inside you're begging to be released." He tucks one of the loose strands of hair behind my ear and chuckles when it doesn't bend to his will.

"I … have to go to the bathroom," I say, my voice

changing in pitch with every word.

I'm chicken-shit. I can't handle this. Whatever it is. I have to get away right now.

As I spring up from my seat, he leans back again. I try to pass his seat, but his feet are in the way. He doesn't make any effort to move them, so when I try to walk past them, I stumble.

And land right on his lap.

My eyes widen as my butt presses down on his firm legs. I want to squeal, but at the same time my mouth feels sewed together. I'm sitting on Hunter Bane's lap, just like in my dreams.

And then I feel his legs stiffen.

Something's growing in his jeans, poking me in the flesh.

Oh. My. God.

I panic and jolt up from the seat in an uncomfortable manner, grasping the arm rests. Clambering out, I run through the room like a headless chicken and race out the door.

My eyes scan the hallway for any employees that might catch me before I bolt toward the nearest restroom.

Inside, I jam my foot against the door and sink down to the floor.

My God. I can't believe it.

I was on him. I could feel his muscular legs. And something else.

Just the thought of his cock makes my pussy clench with need. Especially when I imagine it hard. I don't even know what he looks like. I don't even know what any guy looks like.

I don't have any experience with this.

That's why it's freaking me out.

I have no idea what to do with this. Is he into me? Or do guys always get a boner when a girl sits on their lap? Both questions make me squirm.

I wish I had done more in high school than just kiss some

boy, but that's all I got, unfortunately. I was way too busy studying back then, but now I'm not so sure it was the right thing to do.

What if Hunter really is going after me? What do I do?

I have no idea what boys want, or like, for that matter. All I know is that I felt his cock and that I can't forget about it. I loved the feeling. The moment my butt made contact with him, I wanted much, much more than just *that.*

And it terrifies the shit out of me.

Hunter Bane isn't just 'some' guy. Not like the ones I made out with in high school. He's like the predator of predators. If he ever got his hands on me, I'm sure he'd devour me whole.

That's the thing that scares me the most. That he wants a lot more from girls than I can handle.

God, what have I gotten myself into?

I wipe the sweat from my forehead and get up from the floor. I stumble to the sink and stare into the mirror. My hair is a giant spider's nest, and I'm startled by my own reflection. I look horrible. How could any guy want this?

Opening the faucet, I put my head under and drink straight from the tap.

Suddenly, the door opens, and I shoot up and almost bump my head into the faucet.

"Sorry, thought this was the guys' room," a guy says.

When I look up at him, I stop breathing.

I'm even almost pissing myself.

It's one of those guys from the restaurant. One of *them*, the ones who tried to …

I'd recognize his tattoos anywhere.

Of all the places to run into him, this is where he shows up? Do I reek of bad luck?

He frowns and squints at me, and then his eyes widen. It's like a moment of realization where he notices it's me. The girl he tried to …

"Wait a minute …" he mumbles. "What are *you* doing here?"

I grab my bag and don't wait another second. With one big sling I slam it into his face.

He stumbles back into the hall, and I make a run for it.

"You fucking bitch!" he yells.

My heart is pounding in my chest. I have to get away as fast as possible. Away from here. Anywhere.

Then I see Hunter stepping out of the theatre. His eyes are perked up like a Labrador, as if he heard something that caught his attention immediately.

My squeal.

It takes him one look at the guy to notice who it is.

"You …" he growls.

Then he charges at him and punches him straight in the face.

The guys go at it, and I look around, panicking, not knowing what to do.

"Hunter," I say, as I see a guard approaching from the back, probably drawn to all the ruckus. "Hunter!"

He roars at the guy and punches him a second time before getting up on his feet again. "I'll kill you if you ever show your face to her again."

I pull Hunter's shirt so much it's almost ripping. After blowing off some steam by flaring his nostrils at the guy for a couple of seconds, Hunter turns around and looks me straight in the eye.

"Did he hurt you?" he says.

My eyes widen as I notice the guard has spotted us.

"Hey!" the guy yells.

"We gotta run!" I say to Hunter, and I grab his hand and push him back into the theatre.

"No, I want to know if he touched you!" Hunter screams as we run across the room to the service entrance we came in through.

"Not now," I say, and now I'm the one dragging him through all the corridors until we reach the exit.

Breathing in the fresh air as I open the door is a welcome change to the indoor mugginess. I'm so glad we managed to escape before the guard caught us.

And I'm glad Hunter was there to kick that guy's ass before he tried something on me again.

Suddenly, Hunter punches a wall, and screams. "Fuck!"

I'm still panting, trying to catch my breath, but Hunter's going mental. I turn around, still gasping, but then I see his bloodied knuckles.

"Your hand!" I say.

"It'll heal," he snarls. Then he grabs my arm and turns me around. He holds me tightly, staring straight into my soul. "Did. He. Hurt. You?"

"What? No … No, he didn't have the chance," I stammer.

He snorts, and his nostrils flare again. "If that guy EVER comes near you again, I swear I'll—"

"You'll what? Pound in on him again?" I sigh. "You can't keep doing this, Hunter."

"I will NOT let them have their way with you," he growls. "They wouldn't just rape you. They would kill you."

A cold shiver runs down my spine hearing him say those words so harshly.

"You don't know what those guys are capable of," he says.

"Oh, and you do? Is that what you're trying to say? Tell me, Hunter, what fucking thing are you involved in?"

He frowns, grating his teeth. "It's none of your business." He turns his head away, but I cup his chin between my index finger and thumb and force him to look at me. I've never been this brazen in my life.

"It *is* my business. If you're involved with these guys then …"

"To hell I am," he says.

"Well, you made it my business the moment you stepped into my life and tried to change me for whatever reason."

Hunter grasps my wrist and tears it away from his face. We're bumping chests now.

"Whatever it is that you're doing, it's not good," I say. "I'm telling you, as a friend, that you have to stop this."

Suddenly, he pushes me against the wall with my wrist behind my back. He's trapped me inside his arms. I can't escape.

"Is that what you think I'm doing? Befriending you? Trying to change you?" he hisses.

I shudder from his proximity. His lip is quivering, and my heart is thudding in my throat. My nerve endings are on fire because his hands are holding my arm tight.

"You have no idea, do you?" he snaps.

I shake my head, my lips smashed together.

He snorts. "Of course you don't. You have no idea how fucking hard it is to do this. I don't *want* to be in this shit, but I am, and I can't change that."

"Yes you can! You can do everything. You're Hunter Bane for crying out loud! You'll fight your way out of it." The words slip out of my mouth before I realize it.

He looks up at me with those hawk-like eyes again, squinting, as if he can't believe his ears. "You don't have a fucking clue. You and everyone else on campus all think you know what you see, but you don't. What I do, I do for a reason. I need to do it. There is no other way to …"

"To what?" I say.

He sighs. "To save him. My brother."

Hunter closes his eyes and comes closer. I freeze in place

as his head bumps into the wall next to me. He's pushed up against me, resting his forehead against the wall. Then he lets out a groan.

I didn't know the extent of his problems, but now that I've seen a glimpse …

Wow.

He looks so weighed down by stress. I can't help but feel pity for him.

No wonder he wanted to do something fun today. He's trying to escape.

I wish I could say something, but I have no idea what to say. Nothing would help change anything for him. He's trapped in some kind of shady business, fighting, trading, just so he can save his brother.

Shit. This is getting more complicated by the minute.

All I know is that he's trying not to fall apart here. I can see it from the way he's slumped over against me, clinging to the one thing that's at least a little good in his life. Me.

My free hand goes up on its own and starts caressing his back.

Hunter lifts his head and looks at me from the side. His eyes shine with sadness and unexplainable fury. His plump lips are parted and the moment I look at them, all I want is to feel them on me. To comfort him with my love.

Because I want to give it to him.

I've really fallen for him.

For a second he hovers close to my face. He inches forward. Not for a moment do his eyes leave mine as he takes in a sharp breath.

He's so close to my lips, all I have to do is lean in and kiss him.

Suddenly the back door opens, and Hunter leans back. A guard steps out.

"You!" he yells.

"Shit!" I say.

Before I know it, Hunter's already grabbed my hand and we're running.

CHAPTER 14
UNRAVELING THE SECRETS

Hunter and I go our separate ways when we reach our dorm. I'm still a little shaken by everything that happened. Breaking into a movie theatre. Bumping into one of those guys that scared the shit out of me. Hunter and his brother. Our almost kiss.

It's not that I'm afraid. It's more like a jittery, butterfly-like feeling.

I want to jump and dance, grab Hunter and just kiss him already.

But I can't. I'm such a freaking wuss, I can't even stand the idea of feeling his cock underneath me.

Well, that part was a bit shocking. Not sure if it was positive or negative.

Scary as hell. But a compliment, too … I think.

Still, I'm like a frolicking girl when I run upstairs and storm into my room.

"Oh my God," I scream as I enter the room.

Evie jolts up from her bed and looks spooked.

"Jesus! You almost gave me a heart attack there," she says.

"I can't believe it," I say, and I slam the door shut behind me.

"What?"

"Hunter and I went to the movies."

"So that's what you were doing. I was already starting to think you'd never come back, and … Hey, wait a minute. Did you just say 'Hunter'?"

I sit down next to her and squeeze my own hands together out of pure delight. "Yes, Hunter. We snuck inside, and it was totally against the law, and I loved every second of it."

She just gapes at me, her eyebrows askew.

"Holy shit, I almost kissed him," I say.

I flop down on her bed and slap my hand across my mouth out of disbelief. "This is so unreal."

"Hold on. You went with him without buying a ticket?" She turns around and looks at me. "Autumn Blakewood went to the movies without paying? You? I can't believe my ears."

"I know, right … And the weirdest thing is that I liked it, too! Now I get why people do stuff that's against the rules. It's so freaking exciting!"

I start rolling around in the bed because I have too much energy. I try to pull Evie with me, but she won't budge.

"Are you serious? The real Autumn would never do that."

"It was only one time," I say. "Don't worry about it so much. I had fun. That's important."

"Hunter's changing you. Can't you see? Before you know it, you'll be just like Brody."

I snort. "No. I'm not a pot smoker."

She chuckles and shakes her head. "Well, I still think it's not a good idea to hang out with Hunter."

"I … I think I'm starting to fall for him," I say softly.

Her confused face turns into an angry frown. "What? You've got to be kidding me."

"I'm not." I sit up again and grab her hand. "I know it

when I feel it. I like him, Evie. I really, really like him."

She jerks her hand away. "Please tell me this is a joke."

I get up from the bed and change into my pajamas. "No … I'm serious."

She sighs and gets under the blankets without speaking another word.

"I don't get why you're acting like this," I say, trying not to sound harsh.

She just shrugs and buries her head in her pillow.

"Evie …" I say, as I crawl into my own bed.

"I don't want to talk right now," she says softly.

"Okay."

I really don't know what else to say. I don't get why she's so mad at me. Does she really hate it so much that I'm hanging around Hunter?

Why can't she just be happy for me?

"Good night," she says.

"'Night," I say, and we turn off our lights and go to sleep.

♥♥♥

The next morning Evie's already gone when I wake up. She's never an early bird, and it surprises me she managed to get out of bed without my help. On her bedside table I find a note with a scribbling on it.

A.

I'm hanging with Scar today. She's payin' up today, plus I'm getting extras if I stay longer, so …

See you tonight, I guess.

E.

The note crumples in my hand. I know what this is. She's

really avoiding me.

Reading this makes me so goddamn sad, I could cry.

Someone knocks on my door, and I immediately brush away the single tear dripping from my eye.

I turn around with the note clenched firmly between my fingers. It's Hunter.

"Hey," he says. At first he looks confident, but then his gaze turns compassionate and worrisome. "Everything okay?" He glances at my fist that holds the note.

I briefly close my eyes and sigh. "Not sure."

"I was gonna ask you to be my study buddy today, but if you're feeling crappy, I can come back another time."

He's already turning around, but I walk toward him and grab his hand. "No, wait."

He turns back around, and only then do I realize I'm actually holding his hand. A flush spreads across my cheeks, and I quickly release him from my grip. "Um … I could use some distraction."

He smiles. "You sure? I mean, studying isn't really a distraction, more a bore."

I shake my head and laugh. "To you it is. I think it's fun."

Chuckling, he walks back to his room, and I follow him. "I can think of a few more things that are way more fun to do …" The low, intimate tone of his voice gives me the shivers, because I always hear these sexual innuendos in his sentences that I just can't ignore.

Maybe I'm imagining things.

"Like having girls on my lap."

Or maybe not.

I don't think my temperature can get any higher. It's so hot, I'm practically swimming in my clothes right now. And I know it's not a heating problem; it's me.

There are books spread out across his bed, but they're all

closed. It makes me think he just put them there so I'd see he's doing his best. Or at least trying.

Grabbing one of the books, he sits down on his bed and flips through the pages. "I tried this morning," he says.

I sit down across from him, on his pillow, and can still smell his scent drifting in the air. It's such an intoxicating scent, I just want to sniff and take it in. It's a mix of aftershave and his body, but I love the two mixed together. I just love smelling him.

God, I feel so stupid right now for thinking about how he smells. As if that's all that matters. As if I can't resist his presence, in any form.

I hate to admit it, but I really can't.

"Could you tell me how you do it?" he says, holding up the book.

I wake up from my trance and look at him. "Yeah, of course."

We work on his homework for the next couple of hours. Now that I'm spending so much time with him, I can clearly see why he was cheating the other day. He has so much trouble remembering things he reads. And not only that; reading itself is hard for him to do, too. It amazes me he went through all those Harry Potter books with his reading skills. It must've cost him a lot of perseverance.

He keeps insisting he tries it, though. He doesn't want me to tell him the answers, even when he tried peeking at my notes before. He's too stubborn to admit he can't do it on his own. Or just too embarrassed by the fact that he fails every time.

It takes him such a long time to find the answer, but he keeps trying, never giving up. I admire his tenacity. His willpower. I admire a lot of things about him.

"I can't do this," he says after a while. He puffs and throws the book aside, dropping his head between his arms.

I pat him on the back. "Don't say that. You'll get it eventually."

"No, I won't." He looks at me with sad eyes, ones that make me want to hug him tight. "Goddammit … I tried everything. Asking you to help me out was one of the few things I thought would help."

"But it can, if you give it some more time. It takes a little more effort to really get the hang of how to do it fast."

"No! You don't get it. I …," he stammers.

It's unusual for him not to know what to say.

"You what?"

He shuts his mouth and starts grating his teeth again. Seems like he's hiding something again.

"What, Hunter? You can tell me." I lower my head so I can look at him. Only peeking a few times, he's hesitant to look back at me. After a while, he lets out a huge breath and opens his mouth. "I think I have a learning disability. Trouble with remembering …"

My mouth drops open. I don't know what to say, but I linger on the words 'I think,' which he said.

"Are you sure?" I say.

"Yes, I'm sure," he says, sighing. "I just can't prove it. That's why I can't use it as an excuse."

"But how do you know then?"

He frowns. "I'm not really in the mood to tell my entire history, all right?"

I bite my lip. "Sorry … I didn't mean to be so pushy. I just …"

"I know …" he says. "You want to help me. You think it's pitiful, and that's exactly why I do *not* tell anyone. Ever."

I swallow. I can't believe he's telling me this.

However, I feel flattered. It sounds like something you'd keep to yourself. Especially in college.

I understand what he means, though. I hate it when people do the same to me. Feel sorry for me because I've been teased. And then they want to help me like they can magically make all the hurt disappear.

It's more of an insult to the injury, really.

So I won't do that to him. I refuse to be like that. I will not make him feel bad for having this condition by feeling sorry for him.

"I don't think it's pitiful. It doesn't make you weak. You have to work twice as hard as anyone else to memorize the same material," I say, smiling. "The only thing it does is make you more powerful, because you have to overcome this and become stronger in order to survive."

It's quiet for a few seconds. Then he opens his mouth. "Thanks."

The smile he flashes back at me makes me blush so much I feel too embarrassed to look at him. Turning my head, I notice a framed photograph standing on his desk. It's a guy with the same hair, only much longer. He looks older than Hunter, but they share so many features, I wonder if they're related.

Before I realize it, I've already leaned forward and grabbed the photo.

My fingers drift over the face that looks so recognizable, even though I've never seen it before. Must be …

"My brother, Jessie," Hunter says, his voice switching in tone.

"You two really look alike."

Hunter chortles. "You're not the first to say that."

"He looks nice."

He muffles a pathetic laugh. "You wouldn't say that if you knew him."

"Why not? Does he fight everyone he meets, too?" I say, putting the frame back on his desk.

He squints, carefully assessing my movements as if he's not too sure what to say. Or not too sure if he can trust me.

"Something like that."

"Worse?"

"Way, way worse."

I purse my lips and nod in bewilderment.

"He's in jail."

And now my jaw drops, too.

"I told you I'd love to trade my life with someone else," he says.

"But I thought you said you had to save your brother, Jessie?"

"Yes, I have to get him out of jail." He frowns and cracks his knuckles. "But it's fucking difficult to get it done, and it's fucking hard to deal with right now."

"Wow … What did he do?" I say, too curious not to ask. I shouldn't actually be surprised about this, considering Hunter's shady behavior, but I am.

"Does it matter? I just want to get him out of there as fast as possible. You don't know how terrible it is in there." He gets up from the bed and starts pacing around.

"But … if he's in there, he's safe, right?"

Now his nostrils start flaring again, and I'm feeling antsy already. Shit. Maybe I shouldn't have said that.

"No. Life in prison is hard. Especially if you don't deserve it." He's breathing quite loudly now.

Suddenly a roar comes from his mouth. "Fuck! He's my fucking big brother, and he's fucking locked up with murderers just because he tried to take care of me."

His fists are so tensed up he's holding them up in the air. And then he slams them into the wall.

"Don't!" I say, and I almost come up from the bed until I see the vicious look on his face.

"Goddammit!" he screams, and he smashes his hands into the wall a couple more times. "It's so hard without him. I just can't …"

When he finally calms down, his body rests against the wall, and he sinks down to the floor after a while.

My heart is beating fast, but I can't just keep watching him from a distance, even if I'm scared.

He needs someone. I want to be there for him.

I crawl up from the edge of the bed and walk over to him. I put my hand on his shoulder and sink down to the floor, too.

"He's the only one I have. The only one. There's no one else. And now he's gone, too."

I shush him and pat him on the back, trying to get him to stop fuming.

Suddenly, he turns around and pulls me toward him. My eyes widen as he buries his face in the nape of my neck, sniffing.

My thighs squeeze together in anticipation, because I can't handle him touching me. It heats me up so much, I feel it in my core. And I feel terrible that I'm feeling this way right now.

"The day I got the phone call I was so mad I smashed it to pieces," he mutters.

So that's what was going on the day he kicked the wall … Now I get it.

I'm overwhelmed with the feeling that I need to care for him. "It's okay," I say. "I'm here for you if you need me."

I didn't know it was this bad. If I had, I would never have asked about it. I don't want him to be reminded of something this horrible.

I can't imagine what it's like to have your last family member behind bars. What would I do if I had nobody else?

I'd turn into a nervous wreck and pray to God someone saved me and my family.

Maybe he's doing the same. Maybe he's fighting his way

through his misery, trying to make sense of it all. I don't know what the reason behind all of it is. All I know is that he's put up this barrier to protect himself, and that he's breaking right here, right now.

"Look at me," he says, sighing. "Spilling all my beans to some girl on campus." He lifts his head to look at me with his adorable gray eyes.

"I'm not some girl," I say, winking. "I'm *the* Leafy."

He chuckles, and I'm glad his mood has improved. "Sounds better coming from your mouth."

He takes a deep breath and stretches, his muscles straining to the limit, making me gulp. "God, if any one of the guys finds out about this, I'm dead meat."

"Why?"

He laughs as we get up from the floor. "The guys I hang out with aren't as innocent and sweet as you are, Leafy," he says jokily.

"What do you do with them anyway?"

"Nothing good," he says.

Suddenly the door opens.

Immediately Hunter and I let each other go and stare at the person standing in the doorway.

"Crap, sorry," the guy says.

The moment he catches my eye, my heart stops beating for a second. It's that guy with the flowerpot hairdo, the guy who hangs around Hunter a lot. The guy Brody talked with.

So this is the guy who they both know.

"No, it's no problem, dude," Hunter says, clearing his throat.

We both get up and Hunter signals to me. "That's my roommate."

"Jaret Paxon."

"Autumn Blakewood," I stammer.

We shake hands, but soon he diverts his attention back to Hunter.

"Sorry, dude, but I don't have much time for small talk. I've got another delivery for you to make, and something else."

A darkness looms over Hunters face, and it sends a cold shiver down my spine.

"Now?"

"Yes, the boss wants it done today."

The boss? What the hell?

Hunter sighs as Jaret walks out again. "Fine. Let's go."

"Huh? Where are you guys going? What's going on?" I say, terrified of the answer. Is this the part where they beat up some dude? And what do they mean by 'delivery'?

When Hunter said he had a roommate, I didn't expect him to be part of this.

I don't like this Jaret guy. Not one bit.

Before I have a chance to make them answer, they're already running down the stairs.

Well, Hunter's wrong if he thinks I'm going to let him leave me like that. Not with all those questions. Not that quick. No matter if I know about his brother, it doesn't mean he can just go around beating people up for God knows what reason.

So I grab my things and bolt after them.

CHAPTER 15
OUT WITH THE OLD, IN WITH THE NEW

I make my way down the stairs, trying not to produce any sound. Hiding behind a wall, I check if the coast is clear. I don't want them to see me. They have to feel secure enough to go about their business, so I can finally find out what they're really doing. What Hunter is really up to all those times he's with them.

What kind of shit he's gotten himself into.

Lurking behind a pillar, I watch them walk into an alley behind the building. I run after them, making sure I don't get seen. There's a guy in the alley, and they're shaking hands.

"Got the stuff?"

"Yeah." Hunter fishes in his pockets and takes out a tiny plastic bag filled with some white powder.

Images of Brody organizing those exact same plastic bags flash through my mind.

"How much?" the guy says.

"How can you do this?" I scream.

The guys turn around, all looking like they've seen the chief of police. When Hunter notices it's me, his eyes fire up with anger.

"What are you doing here?" he yells.

I storm over to them, and the guy who they were talking to runs past me, scared he'll get in trouble, probably.

"What the fuck is wrong with you?" I frown and stare at Hunter towering above me. I'm no longer afraid of him. He can do with me whatever he wants, I don't care. He needs to hear this.

"I told you it was none of your business. Why can't you just leave it alone?" he growls.

"Of course I won't leave this alone! You're selling drugs! How can you do this? " I say. "And you, you got him into this!" I point my finger at Jaret, who starts shaking his head.

"No, I'm in this as deep as he is. I've got no part in him getting into this," Jaret says.

"I can't believe this! Goddammit, all this time you've been doing this, haven't you? What would Jessie say?"

Hunter steps forward, pushing me against the wall. "Leave my brother out of this. I will do whatever the hell I need to do to survive."

"It's wrong, and you know it."

"I don't care," Hunter says.

I purse my lips together and frown, pushing back the tears. "Fine. Suit yourself."

Fuming, I storm off, leaving the guys there dumbfounded.

♥♥♥

Back in my room, I've been reading the same page for minutes. I can't seem to even finish one chapter today. The only reason is Hunter and what I caught him doing.

I still can't believe he's selling drugs.

Brody must be involved.

He was making the bags, and now Hunter's selling them. They're all part of the same group. Is it a gang? I have no goddamn idea, but it freaks me out knowing this is all happening at my college, and nobody else seems to know about it.

Opening my drawer to take out a different book, I notice something lying on the bottom. A note with handwriting on it.

I take it out and feel something attached to the bottom. Fiddling with it, I rip it off. It's a tiny bag filled with only one white pill.

Hey Autumn,

I'm sorry for being such a dickhead the last couple of weeks. We're both working hard, but I know that's not an excuse. You've been studying so hard, and I think you could use a little boost.

I hope I can trust you with this.

Cheers, Brody.

With trembling fingers I rip open the packet and inspect the pill. Shit. Is this really what I think it is? How can he give this to me and treat it like some kind of peace offering?

The nerve …

And to think he's even asking me if he can trust me. *Him*, of all people. The irony.

With furrowed brows I throw the tiny bag back inside my drawer and slam it shut.

Someone knocks on my door, and from the heavy thumping sound of it I can clearly hear it's Hunter. He doesn't even wait before inviting himself in.

I don't want to look at him right now.

He stomps forward with his heavy feet, coming closer to

me. I'm shivering behind my desk, but I don't want him to see my nervousness.

With a thwack he throws a book in front of me, and I jolt up from my chair.

"You left this on my bed," he says, leaning sideways as much as he can so he can look at me.

He puts his hand on the table, waiting for me to answer.

"Thanks," I say, after his fingers scrunch up my papers.

And then I notice his knuckles. They're all bloodied up, scratch marks all over them.

My eyes widen, and I look up at him. A black eye marks his face.

"You're hurt!" I say, and I grab his hand and check his wounds.

He only growls and just stands there, saying nothing. His rough fingers lie limp in my hands, as if he's giving me complete access to fix him up.

Frowning, I throw one angry look at him, but he just looks back at me with those piercing gray eyes like there's nothing wrong.

"You got in a fight again," I say as I grab some tissues.

Wiping his wounds clean, I glance at him, but he refuses to answer. I'm so mad at him for selling drugs, but at the same time I can't let him stay all bloody like this. I have to help him out, even if my first instinct is to tell him to leave my room.

I don't want to see him hurt.

"Was this the other thing they asked you to do?" I say, looking him straight in the eye. He just stares back.

I stand up and grab an ice pack from my fridge. I also fetch a stool and put it down in front of my chair. "Sit."

He groans, annoyed, but sits down anyway. He looks pissed, probably not used to having girls tell him what to do. Well, if he wants help, he'd better do as I say.

I press the pack against his black eye and put his hand on top. "So, you want me to fix you up, but you don't want to tell me why you're busted up?"

"It's not going to change anything," he says, keeping a stone-cold face as if none of this is even remotely bothering him.

"Yeah, well getting into fights isn't going to change anything, either. I don't understand why you always have to do what they say."

I open my drawer and take out a package of bandages, but before I can close it again, Hunter pulls it back open. He puts his hand inside and fishes out the plastic bag with the pill.

His eyes become viciously big, and he makes a fist with his bruised knuckles. "Who gave you this?"

"Does it matter?"

He slams his hand on the table, and I almost spring up from my chair. "It matters if I say it does!"

"And you think that by yelling I will just go ahead and tell you? Just like you told me why you're dealing drugs and fighting people?"

His nostrils flare and his nose twitches. "Whatever. As long as you do *not* use it."

Snorting, I say, "Why do you care? You're the one who's handing out drugs to people. It shouldn't matter to you."

He grabs my hand as I'm busy with the bandages. "*You* matter to me."

Frozen in place, I hesitate. My face heats up, turning my cheeks pink. I can't even look at him.

"W-well," I stammer, "I don't think you're the one to tell me what to do and what not to do." Seeing the drugs in his hand and his bruised face makes images of the day in the cafeteria flash through my mind. He looked so drugged up back then.

Now I know why.

"You take them yourself. That day you showed up in the cafeteria you looked like you were beaten up quite badly, and you had red eyes. Don't deny it. You've done it yourself."

The bag with the pill is crushed in his hand. "And you think I wanted to do that?" he hisses.

"You tell me," I mutter.

"I hate it. I hate the fucking stuff so much, you can't even begin to imagine. But I had to. There was no other way to …"

"To what? You had to use drugs to do what?"

"To forget. To feel a little better. And because they told me to," he says, sighing.

I knew it. He's really under their thumb.

I swallow, wrapping the bandage carefully around the slashes on his knuckles. He doesn't look as broken as last time, but it still isn't a pretty sight. I wonder what he'd do if I wasn't here. Would he go to the hospital? Or would he just leave his wounds and let them get infected?

However, now that I've seen the extent of his problems, I totally get why he wouldn't want to go to the hospital. If you're there, and you've been in a fight, the cops are immediately involved. With his history I don't blame him for not wanting to have anything to do with law enforcement. They robbed him of his brother.

"Tell me you won't use that stuff … please." His voice is croaky, and it sounds like he's begging me. "Not ever," he adds.

I snatch the pill from his hand and throw it in the garbage bin next to my door. He visibly relaxes, seeing it disappear.

"I won't. But why do you?" I say, and I fasten the bandage around his hand with a clip.

"Because I have to."

"Why can't you just tell me why?" I say. "Are you afraid I'm going to spill your secrets or something? Don't you trust me?"

"Because I don't want you to get hurt, all right?" he bursts out.

I'm dumbfounded by his sudden explosiveness, but also because I'm flustered. I don't really know what to say to it, because it feels so unreal. I don't even have the guts to look him in the eye. My heart is pounding in my throat.

His free hand reaches for my face, and I freeze. My nipples tighten when his fingers touch my skin, and my nerve endings are on fire. I burn on the inside, wanting more of his touch. His thumb skids across my cheek, gently caressing my soft skin with the rough pad of his thumb.

My breath hitches in my throat.

I can't believe it. He's really touching me.

It feels so good, I just want to nudge my head into the palm of his hand and let him touch me everywhere. It sets my heart on fire.

When he stops, I shudder.

He chuckles a little. "I told you you're afraid of me. I knew it."

I bite my lip, my cheeks burning up, feeling very exposed. "I'm n-not," I stutter.

"Yes, you are. You're terrified of me. Just a touch from my hand makes you shiver." The grin on his face is making me feel both embarrassed and hot and bothered.

"Why are you so afraid? I'm not going to hurt you," he says with a cocky voice that makes me want to give him a second black eye.

"Because I've never had a boyfriend before, okay?" I say, sighing. "At least not past the kissing stage." There. It's out now. I've said it. And I feel completely stupid for blurting it out.

For a second Hunter just stares at me with a blank look on his face. Then he bursts out into laughter.

"Is that it?" he says, in between laughs.

Frowning, I make a fist with my hand. "Yes. Stop laughing."

I pound him on the shoulder, and he inches back with a wince. "Ouch. Damn, your punches have improved."

Shaking my head, I snort. "You're an asshole, you know that? Laughing at girls because they're not experienced."

Suddenly Evie walks into the room and stops in her tracks when she sees Hunter sitting there.

I clear my throat. "Hey," I say.

"Can we talk?" Evie says, looking fazed.

Hunter looks at her and immediately gets up from his stool. "I'll get going."

"Yeah, I'll see you tomorrow for training then?"

"Sounds cool," Hunter says, and he smiles. "Thanks."

Then he passes Evie, who's still standing in the doorway.

I clean up all the mess that's left on the desk, while Evie just holds herself, standing there, looking at me. I don't really know what to do or what to say. She's mad at me, that's for sure. Ever since I told her I was falling for Hunter she's been acting strange.

Does she really hate him that much?

"Do you have time?" she says.

"Sure," I say, and I turn toward her.

She sits down on her bed and stares at me from a distance with a scared look on her face.

"What's the matter?" I say, getting up and sitting down next to her.

"I … I just can't deal with this. Seeing you and Hunter together all the time …"

"Why? I mean, he's nice. You should really get to know him first."

"That's exactly what I'm afraid of."

Frowning, I look at her. I don't get what she's saying. Her

lip is quivering, though.

"I've been afraid to tell you all this time … and that's why I've been hanging out with Scarlet for such a long time. She's actually quite nice, if you get to know her."

Wow, it surprises me that Evie's actually saying this. I never expected her to see past her initial opinion of Scarlet, but she's done a complete turnaround now. Weird.

"Anyway … She's been helping me out a little, and I've been helping her in return."

"That's nice. I'm glad you found another friend. Now I'm not the only one," I say, and I grab her shaking hand and squeeze it.

I want to show her that I'm here for her, no matter what she's going through. I don't care if she got mad over Hunter; I just want us to be friends.

"She told me to just tell you."

"Okay? What do you want to tell me?" I say.

She turns around to look at me, her lips parted. She licks her lips anxiously.

Suddenly she leans in and kisses me right on the mouth.

I panic, open my mouth and draw back. What is she doing?

A flush spreads across her cheeks and she looks in pain just from seeing me react.

Shit. Brody was right all along. She likes me.

Oh God. What have I done?

"I … I'm sorry," I say. "I don't feel that way."

I should've known. I should've realized it sooner.

I've been flaunting Hunter and my feelings for him in front of her face all this time, and she's been pining over me instead. I can't believe I've been such a jerk to her. Now I understand why she dislikes him. She hates that he stole me from her.

But I can't do anything about that. I don't want to lose Hunter.

But I don't want to lose her either.

"It's okay," she says, her smile fading. "I know. I've known for quite some time, but I was ignoring it. I wanted it to be different. I didn't want to be 'just best friends.' I wanted more."

"I'm sorry," I repeat.

She chuckles lightly. It sounds like she's embarrassed. "No harm in trying, right?"

Her eyes are getting glossy, and she's swallowing away the tears. Just looking at her makes me feel sick to my stomach. I've been blind to the truth. She's into me, but I can't offer her the same love in return. Not like that.

"But … I'm not," I stammer.

"I know …" she says, nodding, biting her lip. "I just wanted to let you know."

I look down at the sheets, unable to think of what to say.

"I don't think I can stay here any longer," she says.

My eyes jolt up to her again. "What?"

"I can't do this anymore, Autumn. I can't watch you with Hunter, knowing what I'm missing. Knowing what I can never have. It's turning me into a person I don't want to be."

"So you're leaving?" Now tears are forming in my eyes, too.

"Scarlet offered me her room for a couple of weeks. Her roommate left, so … At least I can crash somewhere." Evie stands up and packs some stuff into her suitcase.

So it's really true. She's leaving because of me. Because she has feelings for me I can't give her in return.

"But you barely know her," I stammer.

"I think I can manage," she says, zipping her suitcase shut. "I like you, Autumn. Too much. I need to be alone for a little while, so I can overcome that. Maybe stop thinking about you every second of the day."

I smile, feeling embarrassed by the idea that she thinks of

me the way I think of Hunter.

Damn, this is complicated.

"Well … bye," she says, and she gives me a gentle peck on my forehead. A tear runs down her face as she grabs her suitcase and stumbles out the door, glancing at me one final time before leaving.

CHAPTER 16
HUNTERS GONNA BE HUNTERS

I can't close my eyes tonight. The tears just keep coming, making my entire face wet. Eventually I just give up and started reading instead. Not that it proves much of a distraction. Evie and her confession play over and over in my mind, and I keep thinking about what I should've done differently.

It's too late to change it now.

Getting out of bed is hard, but I manage. I don't want to lie down if I can't sleep anyway. Better do some homework instead.

It's dark outside, and when I look at Evie's bed the emptiness makes me feel hollow inside. I feel like I just lost my best friend, which is absurd. She's only a few dorm rooms away. Still, I'm feeling blue today.

Just as I'm about to sit down at my desk, someone knocks on my door.

I open it and am baffled. Jaret is standing there in a fine suit with a glittery hat on.

"Wow," I say, squeezing my eyes shut because of all the shimmers. "Going somewhere?"

He chuckles. "It's the hat, right? I thought it looked cool."

"I'm jealous," I jest. "So, what's up?"

"Well, there's this party going on at a secret location, and I wondered if you'd like to come?"

"What? Me?" I say. "Secret parties?"

"Hunter's there, too. I'm surprised he didn't bring you. Maybe he forgot. Anyway, since you're his girlfriend, I figured you'd want to come."

"I'm not his …" I've already stopped talking before the entire sentence comes out. I'm not his girlfriend, I think. Just the thought makes me blush like crazy. But maybe if he believes I'm Hunter's girlfriend, I can get inside and figure out what he's doing at that party.

"Sure, I'd love to come," I say with a big, fake smile.

Maybe this will be a good thing. Sitting here and thinking about Evie all night long clearly isn't doing me any good.

"Cool. Thought you could use the distraction, seeing all that homework." He glances at the stack of books on my desk.

"Thanks," I say. "It's nice of you to ask me."

He smiles proudly. "No problem. So, you ready to go like this or do you want to put something else on instead? I recommend short skirts, especially if you want to be let inside," he says with a wink.

Squinting, I say, "Yeah, okay. Hold on a sec. I'll go get dressed."

"I'll wait here."

I close the door behind me and immediately rummage through my closet, looking for the perfect outfit. I'm not good at this at all. The last time I went to a party was in the third grade, and it was a sleepover. I don't know if you could even call that a 'party.' I have no idea what to wear, so I just grab the sexiest clothes I have, which is a short black dress and heels to match.

After fixing my hair, putting on some mascara, and putting on some earrings I open the door.

"Wow, good job. What a transformation," Jaret says, astonished.

"Let's go," I say, and I walk past him.

"Uh, sure. Let's take my car then."

Maybe I'm rushing a bit too much, but I want to get there as fast as possible. I want to find out more about Hunter and what he's doing with those people, and I think this is the perfect way to find out. Since Jaret's going there, too, and they're both into the drug-dealing thing, I'm pretty sure this whole party will be flocking with the same kind of people.

That's some scary shit.

Jaret points us to his car, which is a low convertible. My eyeballs almost pop out the moment I see it. There's some real money to be made with what they do. No wonder they're so hung up on it.

I swallow away the lump in my throat as I get inside and close the door. Putting on my seatbelt, I say, "Nice car."

"It's my baby," he says.

I nod in awe as he starts the car and steps on the gas, making a lot of noise. Pushover.

Normally, I would never, *never*, go with types like him, but this time's an exception to that rule. I'll break my own laws if I have to. I'm way too curious to find out more about Hunter.

"So, you guys do a lot of dealing then?"

Jaret holds his breath and gazes at me with widened eyes. "Don't tell anyone, 'kay? I know you're Hunter's chick, and I hope I can trust you, because otherwise …"

I hold up my hands as a peace sign. "I won't, I promise. I'm just curious. Why are you even in school if you make so much money? No need for a job, right?"

He chortles. "I'm here because my parents want me to be.

I just want to party, have some fun. I'm more of the gambling type." He reaches into his collar and takes out a necklace with a die as a bangle.

"Cool," I say, as he shows it to me and tucks it away again. It's not even remotely interesting. I just pretend I think it is.

"My lucky charm."

"Must bring a lot of luck if you're driving this car and raking in so much cash." I keep going back to the same topic, because I want to know more about what they do, and I think Jaret is the perfect person to spill it.

"Nah, I'm just lucky I found the right … 'job.'" He winks, and he jerks the steering wheel so hard I'm almost flung against the window.

"So do you take them sometimes too? The drugs, I mean."

"Sometimes. Takes the kick off things, you know."

"Why do you do it? The trading? Just for the money?" I ask, as we shoot through the streets.

"Mostly, yeah. The other part is because they'd kill me if I stopped now. I don't really have the luxury to do what I want. On the other hand, who am I to complain?" He laughs it off like it's a joke or something, but the air in this car suddenly feels too thick to breathe in.

Words like 'kill' and 'drugs' are being thrown around like they're common goods, and it's freaking me out.

"We're here!" he says as he parks the car like a lunatic, occupying several spots. I'm gazing outside at a gigantic house filled to the brim with people. It almost looks like a tidal wave of people will soon come crashing out.

Lights are turned on, loud music is playing, people are screaming and yelling, having fun with God knows what. There's not another house within a two-mile radius, so it looks like an out-of-control party.

We get out of the car, and I feel dizzy because of the ride, but I don't get any time to regain my composure. Jaret hooks his arm through mine and takes me to the house.

My heart is going bonkers inside my chest as we walk up the steps. The lawn is littered with plastic cups, and toilet paper, for some reason. There are panties hanging from the tree branches, and a couple of shoes. I hear lots of giggling, and I'm thinking there are dirty things going on here I don't want to see.

I'm scared to death to enter that house.

But I do it anyway.

It's not like I have a choice with Jaret practically dragging me inside.

As the door closes behind us, I'm almost going deaf from the loud music.

"You can find Hunter on your own, right? I really have to play some cards," Jaret says, his eyes flicking to the poker table and back to me.

"I guess," I stammer.

"Cool, see you around!" he says, and then he walks off through the crowd, leaving me alone at the door.

Shit.

Now I'm on my own. What the fuck do I do?

I'm getting a panic attack already just by looking at all these people dancing, drinking, smoking. It stinks in here, and the air is filled with toxic fumes that make me cough. Some are smoking pot on the couch, others are sniffing up coke lines from the table. I'm disgusted by the mere sight of it, and I can't believe I'm actually here, watching it.

What the hell am I doing here?

I want to turn around and run, but at the same time I can't just leave either. Jaret's my ride, and he's left me alone. I don't even have an idea how to get home.

Besides, Hunter is here. I should try to find him, see what he's up to.

In the corner is a bowl of punch, and I make my way to the table. I grab a cup and fill it to the brim. Under normal circumstances I won't just drink for the heck of it, but I really need something to take the edge of this anxiousness I'm feeling. I can't go around this house looking like a scared little kid. That'll only generate suspicion. No, I need to blend in. Fit in with the crowd. Act like them.

I down the punch in one go, and then follow it up with a jello shot. It's already dazing me, and I feel wobbly on my legs. Whatever they put in these drinks can't be good, so I decide this one is my last.

'Uprising' by Muse is playing, and I'm suddenly in the mood for dancing, so I push my way through the crowd.

Peering around the room, I see Brody hanging on the couch with a couple of girls. My eyeballs almost pop out of my head seeing him subjected to women's hands. They're groping him, running their fingers through his hair, handing him drinks and smokes. Disgusting.

Desperate to ignore him, I turn around and walk in the other direction. When I spot Hunter, I stop in my tracks.

Leaning against the wall in a corner of the giant mansion is Hunter Bane. In his arms is a curvy blonde girl, squirming up against him.

Chills run through my body. I feel cold and dead inside as I stare at the two. I can't believe what I'm seeing.

She's smoking a joint, and they're whispering words into each other's ears. Hunter's lips quirk up into a lopsided smile as he reaches into his pocket and takes out a plastic bag with white powder and hands it to the girl.

The moment she turns to give him a small kiss on the cheek, I realize it's Scarlet.

What the fuck?

What is she doing here? And why is she smoking pot and

getting drugs from him?

Why does she have her hands all over him? She's supposed to be with Brody!

I'm furious. All I want to do now is punch her in the face.

And then Hunter's gaze shifts toward my position. When he sees me, my heart shatters.

His eyes are dark and full of contempt. He doesn't seem even slightly surprised to find me here. Doesn't even look scared or sorry. He only gives me a fierce, stone-cold stare.

Tears sting my eyes, and I struggle not to run over there and hit him in the face.

Instead, I turn around, push through the crowd, and run outside.

Brushing away the ones that have rolled down my cheeks, I force back the rest of the tears while bolting down the steps.

Suddenly, someone grabs my hand and holds me back.

"Let me go!" I scream, kicking and jabbing.

"No. Not until you listen to me," Hunter says with a low voice.

Somehow one of my backward kicks hits him in the nuts, and his grip on me loosens.

"Wow, nice kick. You've learned a lot," he grunts.

I don't wait one second before making a run for it. My feet take me as far as they can through the parking lot before Hunter catches up to me.

"You wanna play catch? I can do that." He muffles a deep, guttural laugh that alerts all my senses. "I'm Hunter. Seizing innocent prey is what I do best. You should know better."

Darkness surrounds us. I'm running past the cars to ditch him. It's scary, but thrilling to the bone, too.

When I stumble over a ridge, I barely manage to catch myself before falling. I try to get up as fast as possible, but Hunter's already caught me. His fingers clench firmly around my wrist as he pulls me up from the street.

"Let go of me!" I squeal.

"No," he says crudely.

"Fuck you!" I say. "You can't keep me here forever. I'm leaving."

"Oh, no, no, no." Hunter flings me around and traps me between his sculpted arms. I fight to free myself, but it's no use. He's too strong, and I'm at his mercy. I don't want to be, though.

"You're not going anywhere."

"Let me go or I'll—"

"You'll what? Scream? Yeah, nobody's going to react to that. Not here," he says with a chuckle.

"I want to go. Now," I say.

"Go where? Home? Good luck. Your driver is wasted, and there's no way I'm going to let you go on your own. It's too far to get to the dorm, you'll never make it on foot."

"I'll call a cab," I snarl.

"With what money?" he says.

"You're a fucking asshole, you know that?" I hiss.

He chuckles. "Why? Because I give girls what they want?"

I bite my lip, feeling the tears well up again. I get the urge to smack him, but can't, because he's holding me too tight against him.

"Let's face it, you thought I was a sweet, troubled guy, who just needed a friend. And now you find out how wrong you are about me."

Refusing to speak, I just stare at him in blind hatred.

I hate him. I seriously hate his guts.

"You can give me the silent treatment all you want, but we're going to talk. Eventually. I can wait."

"Fuck you! I saw you in there … Pathetic. Scarlet's with Brody. How could you do that?" I'm fuming, and I feel like a dragon spitting fire. I just want to shout swearwords at him all day long.

He chortles. "Brody was right there with us. Do you think he'd be relaxing on a couch with a bunch of girls if he minded?" Hunter shakes his head. "You've got it all wrong. Scarlet's the one in pain. She was just looking for some distraction."

"Whatever." I turn my head so I don't have to look at him anymore.

Hunter squints, carefully assessing my reaction.

"Regardless, I'm not going to let you just walk away from here."

"And you think you can stop me? Not a chance." Now I'm squirming again, twisting in his arms.

He muffles another laugh and grabs me by my arms, leaning in. "Want to test out that theory?"

There's a sly half-smile on his face, and all I can do is purse my lips together and boil in my own anger.

Hunter puts me down in front of him, grabs my hand and drags me to a car. Protesting isn't of any use. His strength is triple my own. He opens the passenger's side door and points inside. "Get in."

"Since when do you have a car?" I say.

"Borrowed it. Now get in."

"I don't want to," I snap.

"Do you want to stay here all night? Or do you want to go home?"

"I don't care."

"Get. In," he says crudely.

"No."

"Goddammit, get inside or I'll lift you up and lock you in myself."

He looks so determined it's intimidating.

Swallowing, I take a deep breath and step inside the car.

"Stay there," he orders, as he walks to the other side of the car and gets in.

My arms are crossed as he starts the car. The engine rumbles, and Hunter gives me a piercing glare before the car races away with screeching tires.

CHAPTER 17
SEDUCTION

Chewing my cheek, I stare out the window. Rain is pouring down, blocking my view, but I will not turn around. I try not to even glance at him. I don't want to give him the satisfaction of making me look at him.

I don't want to peek at him for even one second. Not anymore.

"Before I take you home, I need you to do something for me."

Snorting, I shake my head and refuse to answer.

"Talk," he says.

It's quiet. I keep my mouth firmly shut as Hunter switches up the gear. We race through the streets as if it's a racing track.

"You're really mad, aren't you?" he says.

"Damn right I am," I snap.

Shit, I broke my own promise of not talking to him.

He chuckles. "You're getting worked up over nothing."

"You were trading drugs again! I wouldn't be surprised if you took some yourself, too."

He laughs, and it's a deep, husky sound that turns my

insides to mush. I don't want to feel that way, but I still do.

"I only sell it. I don't take it. I told you, I hate that stuff. I would never take it unless they forced me to."

"Well, you were at that party, which is already bad enough."

"You were there, too," he scoffs. "Quite a surprise to me. I can't believe you showed up there. Do you even know how fucking dangerous that is, huh?"

"I was looking for you. Jaret brought me. It was his idea."

"Yeah, and I'm going to thoroughly thank him for that later." He furrows his brows in an annoyed manner.

"Don't blame it on him. I didn't say no. I wanted to see what you were doing, and I was right all along."

"Oh? So now you're the one watching me?" One of his eyebrows lifts, and on his face is a cheeky smile.

I just want to give him a smack on the head.

"You're following me, checking what I do. You went to a party in *that* dress, just to keep up with me."

His eyes swipe over my body, and my pussy clenches with need I don't want to feel, but do.

"You've changed, Leafy."

"Don't call me that," I snap.

"Why? You think it's a bad name?" The smug smile on his face makes me roll my eyes.

"You're laughing at me."

"No, I'm not."

"Yes, you are. You always do that."

"No. I just like to see you riled up."

I sigh. "Whatever."

He steps on the gas, making the car go even faster. It's scaring me a bit. There are puddles on the road and the windshield is spattered with rain. We might slip if he makes a turn here.

"Can we go slower, please?" I mutter.

He ignores my question. "You know what I think? I think you're jealous."

"W-what?"

"You heard me. Scarlet was all over me, and you hate that."

Pursing my lips, I snort, trying to show him that I do *not* care. I definitely don't care. At all.

Okay, maybe I do.

He ripped my heart out. I don't want to admit it, however.

"You don't have to say it. I already know you like me."

A flush spreads across my neck and cheeks, and I try to hide it behind my hair.

"You wished it was you purring up against me instead of her."

"Shut up!" I say, and he chuckles. "Just stop it."

"Oh, I'm only getting started."

"Can we just go home?" I mutter, sighing.

Suddenly the car starts to rattle, and smoke rises up from the engine.

Shit. Now this.

I can't believe what a disaster this night is turning into. First I find out my best friend is in love with me, and now she's avoiding me. I find out Hunter's a drug dealer for some shady guys, and he gets into fights because of the same people. And I thought Scarlet and Brody were a couple … guess that's a thing of the past, too.

Seeing her put her fingers on him makes me so goddamn angry, I could scream.

What a night.

"Fuck," Hunter mutters, as we go slower and slower.

The car starts to sputter, and the engine stops running after a while. Then we come to a halt.

"Yes. We're fucked," I say.

Dammit. I just want to go home, lock myself up in my room, and sleep. I don't havc time for this.

Fishing his phone out of his pocket, Hunter steps out of the car and starts dialing some number.

He's just standing there, calling, in the middle of a rainstorm.

However, I don't want to wait for him to call someone and get us some help. Maybe I can see what the problem is. I'm not a champion when it comes to cars, but I can at least try. It's better than nothing.

I step outside and shiver when cold drops of water land on my skin. I'm wearing nothing but a flimsy black dress, and it's goddamn pouring out here.

"Half an hour? Cool. Bye." Those three sentences are all I catch of his conversation.

I walk to the front of the car, shaking rigorously from the sheer cold. I lift the hood and peer inside. Blowing away the smoke that is suffocating me, I check if everything's still in order. There's nothing leaking out, so that's a plus.

Oh, I have no idea what the hell I'm doing anyway.

"You a car mechanic now, too?"

I jolt up and the hood slams shut in front of me. Hunter's behind me, standing way too close for comfort.

"I just want to get this fixed as soon as possible," I say.

He chuckles. "Relax. They're coming. I got it covered. Get in the car before you're soaked to the bone."

Crossing my arms, I turn around and sigh. "I think I can make my own decisions."

He's right in front of me, literally in my face, his lips curved mischievously. "You don't just want to go home quickly. You want to get away from me. You're avoiding it," he chimes.

"That's right."

"You don't want to admit you don't like seeing me with other chicks. You want me for yourself." He leans in and places his big hands on the hood, trapping me between his arms. The air is suddenly thick, and it feels hard to breathe.

"You're an ass and you know it," I snap.

He laughs. "You're still under the impression that I was enjoying the party."

"You sure looked like you had fun with Scarlet!"

"Hmm … and that's where you're wrong."

He leans in so close, our foreheads almost touch. He's taunting me, gauging my reaction. I won't give in to his games. I won't lose. Not this time.

My teeth are chattering, but I won't stop looking him straight in the eye.

"She just wants to numb the pain. They all do. That's what I give them. I know what you're thinking, but it couldn't be further from the truth. My only role at that party was to hand out drugs. Period."

"It wouldn't surprise me if it was more than that," I retort. "You let them feel you up. Of course I'm thinking that's also one of the things you do."

He chuckles. "Thanks for the compliment. I feel flattered, but no, I'm not a gigolo," he muses. "God. You almost sound like a girlfriend."

My eyes widen and my entire body heats up from his comment. Only now do I notice his black t-shirt is completely soaked, and sticks to his delicious body. I can see every nook, each dent, all the hard lines and curves of his muscles. It's almost … bare. Just the mere thought of seeing him naked is turning my brains to mush.

"Oh, did I strike a nerve?"

"I don't know what you're talking about." My hands are shivering, so I clench the car behind me. It doesn't stop the trembling.

"You know, I quite like this quibbling. It got some fun back into my life," he says, chortling.

"You're just provoking me."

He frowns, but his lips still show his amusement. "I'm dead serious. It's funny seeing you get so worked up over nothing."

"It's *not* nothing!"

"Hmm … no, I know what you want. You want to be the first to tame me. And you want me to ravage you."

He squints, flashing a grin that's making me flush so badly.

My folds are getting wet, I can feel it. I can't help myself, even though I feel so fucking bad for feeling like this right now. He just does that to me.

But all he wants is to incite me to get angry.

"You're just making a joke out of this."

"Why would I?" His eyes are half-mast now.

"Because I told you I never really had a boyfriend before, and you think that's funny."

He closes his eyes, cocks his head and laughs loudly. I just stare at him, fazed.

"You really don't see it, do you?" he says after a while.

"What?"

"I've tried to keep you away from me. To show you that I'm a bastard. To make you see that I'm fucking messed up. And you still want me."

I suck in my lip as he says those last words.

"Who said I want you? You keep putting those words into my mouth. I never said anything like that."

He muffles a laugh, but it sounds more like a guttural groan instead. The sound turns on every part of my body. It's hard to ignore my pulsing nub, and the overwhelming need to let him be the first to take me.

My body is telling me to jump his bones, while my brain is telling me to run as fast as I can. I don't know what I really want anymore.

"And don't say those things about yourself."

He shakes his head. "But you can?"

"Yes, well—"

"Oh, just shut up already."

Suddenly he inches closer and presses his lips firmly down onto mine.

My eyes are wide open. Hunter's lips are crushing mine. He's kissing me.

Am I dreaming?

His hot mouth covers mine and ravishes me. Alternating soft kisses with harsh ones, he's driving me insane.

My eyes close as he keeps kissing me.

He's so fucking good at this, I swear I'm going to faint. I've never been kissed like this before. He's like a predator, a prowling animal, and I'm the feast he's indulging himself with.

His long, lavish licks turn me on so much that I moan in his mouth. He responds with a groan, sending shocks through my entire body.

We're kissing in the middle of nowhere, in the rain, both wet and wild, and it's amazing.

Soon his hands find their way to the small of my back where he digs his fingers into my skin. His kisses are sexy and sensual, and everything I imagined them being. Licking my lips in between his kisses, he forces my mouth to part and dips his tongue inside. He explores my mouth, and lets his hands reign freely over my back. Everywhere he goes, goose bumps pop up, and my body trembles from his touch.

Hunter steps closer and puts his hands on my waist. He lifts me up and sets me down on the hood of the car with no problem, continuing his wolfish raid on me. My thighs go watery as his legs part mine. He nudges me open, getting closer and closer as if he wants to claim my body right here, right now.

With his full, beautiful mouth on mine, I give up the fight. He's tempted me, chased me, persuaded me, and now I'm his.

His scorching kisses feel so hungry, so full of desire, I can't help but get completely wound up.

He moans one last time before retreating and gazing right at me. I don't want him to stop. The sensual look in his eyes seeps into every one of my pores, awakening my blooming sexuality.

"You're not fighting me anymore …" I don't know if that's a question or a statement. His husky voice turns me upside down and makes me feel so aroused.

"I told you I give girls what they want." The smug smile on his face is both annoyingly sexy as it is fucking vexing. "I knew I'd get you eventually."

Only after a few seconds does it register what he just said. Am I just a chase? He's been planning this?

He's still making a joke out of this, even after kissing me.

Then I realize I played right into his hands. He did that on purpose. I let him chase me and claim his prize.

He won.

I push him forward and wriggle my way under his arm to get away.

"Hey, where are you going?" he says, coming after me.

"I'm gonna sit in the car and wait this out."

"Why?" He catches up to me and grabs my wrist.

"Because you're still playing with me."

"What?" he says, his brows edging toward each other.

"Stop fucking playing around for once! What you just did was cruel. You can't just toy with my heart like that!"

He grabs both my arms and pins me to the car door, making it impossible for me to escape.

"I am *not* toying with you." I try to tackle him, but he traps my legs between his. "Unless that's what you want … I can play with you all night if you ask me to. And I *will* take that offer."

Oh. My. God.

There he goes again, making me all hot and bothered with his words. He knows it. That's why he's doing it. And it's fucking humiliating.

"What do you want from me?" I say with a desperate tone.

"I'm not playing with you. I just like to see you blush. Lucky me, I get to see it often."

"Why?"

He cocks his head and chortles. "Isn't it obvious? I want you."

I stare at him in amazement. Is this real?

He makes my stomach twist, and butterflies zing through my entire abdomen. It feels like my entire being has been waiting for this moment.

But I can't get it out of my mind that I saw Scarlet kissing him.

It's like she's sullied him. I know it's ridiculous, but that's how I feel. He was supposed to be … mine.

As if he ever was. He must've had plenty of girls before. I'm just another one to add to his list.

"What about Scarlet then? She kissed you."

"Who cares? I don't. She was just clinging to me. Doesn't mean it matters. At least, not to me."

"But—"

"I. Don't. Want. Her." He squeezes my arms, raising his eyebrows. "I want you," he says with a deep, husky voice.

He lowers his head, resting his forehead against mine. His piercing gray eyes are enigmatic and seductive. His lips are parted, but he remains still, as if he's waiting for me.

Then his tongue dips out and he licks his luscious lower

lip, sucking it in, biting a little.

Holy shit. I think I just died.

"Tell me what you want. What you really need. Do you want me to let you go? Do you want me to stop hunting for you?" he murmurs.

Taking in a sharp breath, I hesitate. I'm not sure what to say. It feels so unreal, and yet the look in his eyes tell me this is the truth. He looks so desperate, almost vulnerable, and it makes me believe him.

All this time he really wanted me.

"Kiss me," I say. "I want you to kiss me."

It doesn't take him a second to process my answer.

I feel his breath against my cheek, as he slowly inches closer to my lips. My brain is telling me not to do this. That he isn't good for me. That he's only in it for the fun and excitement. That I should pull back.

But I don't care anymore.

I've been dying to touch him and kiss him, and I'm not letting this moment slip by any longer.

As his mouth crashes into mine, shocks run through my entire body. He is quick and eager and ravishes me with his kisses. I can't resist. His hot mouth on mine is making me feel delirious. It's like a drug, so powerful.

Pinning my hands in a vice grip beside my head, he sucks on my lips. I moan out loud as he nibbles and then leaves short little kisses.

Every pore in my body screams out for him to touch me. Our mouths are a hot, wet mix. Anxious. Sultry. It makes me weak to the knees.

Desire swells as his kisses unleash a fever inside me. Lust is building, and I can no longer ignore it.

His hands slide down my arms to my waist as he dips his tongue in and out of my mouth, coaxing me. He groans, his lips dragging to my jaw, kissing me everywhere. I pant as he slips down my neck to the spot that makes me want to surrender completely.

My hands wrap around his muscular neck as he fervently kisses my jaw, dragging his tongue along the way. It's so freaking hot that I moan, and he chuckles in delight. When he nips my earlobe, I'm done for.

He retreats for a second, panting, visibly strained. His eyes are dark in a wicked way. "God, that dress," he murmurs. "Why'd you have to put that on?"

I giggle when he leaves another peck on my collarbone, almost too hungry to stop devouring me.

"Couldn't come to the party in a pair of sweatpants," I mutter.

"Hmmm …" The rumbling sound coming from his chest sounds like a growl and a groan at the same time. It's so fucking sexy.

"You look so damn hot … You don't wanna know what goes on in my mind when you're all dressed up like this. It's too dirty to handle," he whispers close to my ear.

I get goose bumps all over my body as his thirsty eyes sweep over my entire body from top to bottom.

"Although I wouldn't mind the sweatpants either," he says with a low voice. "Easier to take off."

Wow. It's still mind-blowing that he thinks about me like that. So sexual. So fucking arousing.

My mind is going blank. All I want is him. My blood is pumping into one direction, and I'm feeling more promiscuous by the second.

God, I want him to touch me.

He moves back to my lips and nips them, while his strong hands shift to my ass. As he squeezes it, I gasp, but he interrupts me with a feverish kiss on the mouth.

I wrap my arms around his muscular neck, dying with sensations. My fingers run through his spiky hair, gripping his head to keep him close. I want him so badly, a kiss isn't even enough.

His calloused fingers slide down to my legs. My nerve endings are on fire, as he slowly drags up my dress. Feeling the pads of his fingers brushing my bare skin is sending hot streaks through my body.

My nub is pulsing, and I want to press my body up against him. He responds by pushing himself against me, our clothes scraping, wrinkling up. I get all riled up by his sexy, insistent mouth, but when I feel his erection against my thigh I perish under his touch.

He's so fucking hot, and he wants me. He wants me.

That alone is already making me want to give it all up to him.

My hands slip down his neck to his pectorals, as I feel my way across his broad chest, wanting to explore every part of him. It's like a forbidden fruit has just been placed in front of me, and I'm finally allowed to take it. I don't want to stop feeling him, touching him, kissing him.

Suddenly, I want his tongue all over me. I want his hands to roam my body and expose all my secret titillating spots. I want him to take me.

But then he takes his mouth off me.

I'm fazed, feeling out of this world, and he gazes at me with wet lips that are just too good to leave alone.

As I lean in to press my lips back on his, he puts a finger between us. "Wait …" he mutters.

His eyes flick to the road beside us, while my mouth hangs open, hungry for more.

"Why are we stopping?" I say.

"They're here," he mutters.

"Who?" I stammer, still oblivious to the world around me.

He steps aside, and suddenly I'm feeling cold and wet.

We're both soaked, but only now do I realize we've been kissing in the rain without a care in the world.

A car drives up to us, and a man steps out. "You were the ones who called, right?"

Shit. I pull down my dress and straighten it, feeling like I've been caught doing something against the law.

"Yeah, thanks for coming," Hunter says, clearing his throat.

And there we have it. Our car will be towed away and the driver will take us back to the dorm. Hunter will have to explain to whomever he borrowed the car from that he won't get it back for a while.

To be honest, it's the least of my worries right now.

I'm so hot for Hunter, and now he's left me completely dry. A blazing fire left to sizzle out in the rain.

I don't think I've ever been more disappointed by someone showing up to rescue us.

CHAPTER 18
WHAT HAPPENS IN THE DARK, STAYS IN THE DARK

My clit has been thrumming the entire trip home. It's like my nerves have gone haywire. Every time I move even an inch, I feel my most sensitive parts scream out in agony. The desire to rub myself is so strong that I can barely stop myself, but I want him to be the one doing it.

Unfortunately, Hunter hasn't looked at me since. He hasn't even glanced at me. Not once.

Not after the kiss. *That kiss.* The one that made me red-hot with need.

My entire body is craving him, and he seems to be ignoring me completely. It's like he's doing it on purpose. Almost as if he doesn't want me anymore.

The look on his face shows agony, but at the same time he seems pissed and turned into himself. Like he's thinking about it too much.

I wonder what is going on inside his mind.

Swallowing away the lump in my throat, I clench my thighs together as my clit starts throbbing again. Each time I catch a glimpse of his luscious lips, all I can think of is having them all over me.

We walk up the stairs of our dorm, and when I spot the door to my room all I feel is misery. I don't want to go in there and be alone. That's torture.

He turns, opening the door to his room, and doesn't even look at me before stepping inside.

"Wait," I say.

With his back toward me he stops. He turns his head, but not enough to look me in the eye.

"Let's just go to bed. It's late."

What the hell?

"Don't you want to …"

Suddenly, he turns around and stares at me. The look in his eyes is deadly, but I'm not sure if it'll kill me or seduce me.

"I can't."

"Why not?" I say, frowning.

He sighs. "Let's just leave it at that kiss."

He wants to close the door, but I put a foot inside, preventing him from shutting me out.

"I want more," I say softly.

His half-mast eyes flick to the floor and then back up to my face, sweeping over my body again like he did before. He bites his lip and clenches the door firmly, as if he has to hold himself back.

"You say that now, but you have no idea what you really want."

"Don't decide that for me. I know what I want."

"We should stop this now, while we still can." He turns around, leaving the door open, and slumps toward his bed.

"What?" I say, angry. Tears well up in my eyes again. He can't be serious. This can't be happening again. He can't do that to me.

"I swear, if you just kissed me as a joke, I'll—"

"It wasn't. I kissed you because I couldn't hold back anymore."

"What?" I stammer as I step inside.

He drops down onto his bed, buries his head between his hands and sighs. It sounds more like a tormented grunt. Like he doesn't know how to deal with this.

"I don't get it. Why don't you want to kiss me again if you liked it?"

"I did, but we can't. I can't give you what you need."

I close the door behind me and walk forward, stopping in the middle of his room.

"You deserve a good guy. I'm not one of those. Nothing's going to change that."

"I don't want a good guy. I want you."

Lifting his head, he looks up at me with pure agony. I can see him trying so hard to repel me, and it's so goddamn hard to watch.

"Don't you see? I'm fucking bad for you. You don't know what the fuck you're getting yourself into."

"I do. Don't treat me like a helpless, pathetic kid. I can make my own decisions."

He immediately stands up, his fingers folded into a fist, and comes up to me. Shivers run down my spine as I'm reminded of his closeness, instantly awaking the desires stirring inside me. Hot memories of his kisses flash through my mind, and all I can think of is doing it again.

"I don't want to hurt you. I'm dangerous. Yet you stand here, wanting more," he says, towering over me.

"And I completely accept the consequences," I say.

"Are you fucking crazy? You have no idea what you're saying. There's a reason I ended it after a kiss. I won't be able to stop myself if we go any further."

"Then don't stop yourself," I say.

He chuckles, almost annoyed. "I'm Hunter. The guy who has sex like an animal. If you're with me, I'll fucking tear you to pieces."

"I can take it."

"You said you've never had a boyfriend. So you're a virgin, right?" He lifts his hand and caresses my cheek lightly. His rough finger is tingly on my skin, and I shudder.

"Do you even know what I do to virgins?"

I gasp. "No, but I'm curious to find out." I walk past him and sit down on his bed, reluctant to leave, even if he asks me to.

"Really? I think there's a lot more to it than that. You're still scared." He turns around and gazes at me with this predatory look in his eyes that intimidates me.

"What do you mean?"

"You think you have to give yourself to me in order to keep me all to yourself."

A flush spreads across my cheeks, and I start to feel lightheaded. At first I'm mad, but then the realization hits me that he might actually be right. Although I hate the way he says it, like he's all that, and I'm just a pining girl.

"I just don't want to … I want to …" I don't even know how to say this.

"I don't want anyone else. Anyone. Why do you keep thinking like this? You think I have sex with every girl out there?" he growls.

"Well I've never … and you're always …"

"What? Flirty? That doesn't mean I actually want something."

"Then why do you want something with me?" I say, gulping.

"Because you're different," he says. "But I can't. I can't do this to you. I can't turn you into something you're not. I already think I'm fucked up, but when I fuck you up too … God, no."

"You won't. I'll be okay. I can handle it."

"No, you can't," he growls, and takes a step closer. "You have to leave. Now."

"Why? Why do you keep pushing my buttons and then rejecting me?"

One of his eyebrows arches up. "Don't you see what you do to me? I need you to go so I can calm down. I get fucking hard just looking at you like that." He points at my dress, and suddenly I have the urge to cover myself up, feeling naked.

He shakes his head and sighs. "I mean, look at you. You're such a fucking good girl, with your books and your proper clothes. I'm like a fucking stain on your rep," he rants. "I could hold myself back, but now … after those kisses … God, now I can't stand it. I just want to rip your clothes off."

I think I'm not even listening to him anymore. After he mentioned getting hard because of me, everything feels like a huge blur. All I see is the huge bulge in his jeans, and now I'm desperate to find out what he looks like. What he feels like. What sex with him feels like. My first time.

"You have to leave. Right. Now," he snaps.

"No," I say.

"Listen to me for once," he says.

"No, you listen to me. I want you. I don't care about the rest. I want to … know what it feels like."

"Do you even hear what you're saying? I don't make love. I fuck your brains out."

"Then do it," I say. "You said you saw me looking. You knew I wanted you."

He chuckles, and the smirk on his face is so ridiculously sexy, I just want to plant my lips on his.

He comes closer, leans forward, and grabs me by the

shoulders. "Get. Out."

"No."

I don't want to leave. I want more from him. So much more. Now that I've seen and felt a glimpse, I don't want it to stop. I want to feel, touch, experience.

This isn't at all like me, but I don't want to be anywhere else. I don't even want to be me right now. All I want is him. No rules. No boundaries. Just finding out about sex.

I want to know what it's like. I'm turning off my restraints. I'll follow my heart tonight.

I've been waiting for the right person for so long, when all I was waiting for was someone like him. Someone who cares about me, someone who protects me. Someone handsome and sweet. So sexy, I could die.

I want him more than anything else right now.

"Get out now before it's too late to change your mind." He's right in front of my face now, so close I just want to pull him back onto the bed with me.

"No. I won't change my mind."

He squints, pursing his lips. "Say no one more time."

I scowl, confused. "Why? Do you get off on it?"

He grins, and it's a sultry, heavy grin that speaks volumes. "I told you, you don't know what you're getting yourself into. I like my girls feisty, and I like to claim them as my own. Especially when they're playing hard to get."

I gulp at those last words. My pussy is thumping like crazy, thinking of all the possibilities that encompass 'claiming.' Jesus. He really is an animal.

His head hovers close to my ears, and he whispers, "Just say it. Say the word, and I'll take you, right here, right now."

I gasp, my inhibitions shattering. "Please …"

He laughs, but it sounds more like a grunt, alerting all my senses. "You asked for it."

Not one moment does he waste. He grasps my arms, flings me down on the bed, and rips off my shoes like he's in some kind of frenzy, throwing them into a corner.

I crawl back on my elbows, peering at the predator in front of me.

"You want crazy? You'll get crazy," he says.

Hooking his fingers underneath his soaked black shirt, he pulls it over his head and throws it aside.

I'm baffled.

What appears is a sculpted body. Bulging biceps, broad shoulders, trained pectorals, washboard abs, and muscles everywhere. Oh my God.

My eyes are locked on his ripped body. I never imagined him being this fucking hot.

His abs contract when he stalks forward like the real Hunter that he is. He crawls onto the bed, looking up at me from above, his eyes aggressive, seductive. A boyish smile curves his lips, telling me how much he relishes this moment. Like he knows he's about to be the first to take me.

I love the way he looks at me.

Snatching one of my legs, he puts his lips on my foot, surprising me. He kisses all the way up to my ankle, and then drags his lips to my calves. From there his tongue comes out to play, sliding up to my thigh. It's the most exquisite thing I've ever felt.

"You sure about this, Leafy?" he says, kissing my thigh, setting me ablaze.

"Yes," I whimper.

He muffles a laugh, but it sounds more like a groan, making me all hot and bothered. "Here I come," he says with a husky voice.

He pushes himself up on his elbows and crawls right on top of me. I'm still completely dressed, but he feels amazing. I don't care about anything anymore.

Hunter has me by the shoulder and his other hand slides down my side to my ass, cupping it. He squeezes, hard, and crashes his lips into mine. I've been waiting for this since the moment he last took his lips off mine. God, it feels amazing.

My fingers drift through his hair, grasping him so he's closer. His hot mouth is so magnetizing. Our lips are raw, wet, and going numb from frenzied kisses, and I love it.

He's still wearing pants, and he rubs his leg against my thigh. He sucks on my bottom lip and nibbles on it as he undulates against me, making me feel his hard-on.

I struggle to get my glasses off and place them on the cabinet beside us. He's lying partially on top of me, his strong leg pushing up against my thigh. As it grazes my panties, I moan softly, and he bites his lip when he hears.

"You sound so fucking sexy when you do that," he whispers. "Makes me want to put my hands all over you." On his face is a cocky smile, like that of a boy who's proud he could make me squirm.

I love it.

His rabid kisses across my neck make me writhe. My hands drift over his rigid back, nails digging into his skin. He groans as I push my body up to meet his in a desperate attempt to be closer.

"I'm your first," he says in between his kisses.

I'm not sure whether it's a question or a statement, so I nod.

His fingers drift from my ass to my hips, and then slowly creep under my dress. I gasp, shocks coursing through my body as he crawls under my dress, nudging it up. The moment he reaches my panties, I hold my breath.

"You've never done this before, have you?" he whispers, nibbling my ear while frantically rubbing himself against me.

"No," I say in between breaths.

He chuckles, but it sounds more like a partial groan. "All the more fun for me."

His hot mouth crushes mine again, and it's so delicious I'm overcome with pure wantonness. I'm starting to feel possessed by him.

Moisture builds up between my folds as he pushes my wet dress over my panties and his hands make contact with my belly. It feels so good, and yet so dirty at the same time.

In a rush, he lifts my dress up and pulls it over my head, grunting.

A flush appears on my skin, and my hands immediately cover up my bra and panties. I still feel uncomfortable baring it all to him, to anyone for that matter. I'm so new to this, and yet I want it, too. Conflicting emotions take control of me.

"You're still scared," he says, throwing my dress across the room.

His eyes swipe over my body in one quick motion, and he bites his lip. "Why are you hiding? Are you ashamed of your body?"

"No. I'm just not used to this. I've never done this before."

"So no other guy has ever seen you like this?"

I shake my head, still clenching my own arms.

A devilish smile lightens his face. "Trust me, you look fucking hot."

I hide my smile by sucking on my lips, because I feel embarrassed by his compliment.

Suddenly, Hunter grabs my wrists. It takes him no effort at all to push them away from my chest and pin them above my head. "You wanted it. I'm doing what you asked," he says.

He kisses my sternum, his hands drifting down to my breasts. The moment he reaches them, I take in a sharp breath.

He waits, his eyes hungrily seeking my permission. I close my eyes and lick my lips, ready for more.

As he cups them, I moan with desire. He voraciously kneads them, taking pleasure in the fact that he's the first. I can see it in his eyes, that boyish, gratified look. All my sensitive spots are on fire.

He groans, nudging down my bra in an attempt to free my breasts from their cups. "I want to see you," he murmurs.

Kissing the nape of my neck, he pulls down my bra and exposes my nipples. I feel blatantly laid bare, but at the same time I want to give myself to him. To let him be the one to see and feel me this way. To experience this with him.

He moans inside his mouth as he works his way down my chest to my nipples. When his lips touch the peaks, I squirm and scrunch up the blanket with my fingers.

"Damn. Don't you ever cover up those perfect tits," he says, making me giggle.

He places his lips right on top of my pink tips and starts sucking. The explosion of desire is too much to take.

God, that feels good.

He muffles a laugh while suckling on my breast, his tongue sometimes flicking out to make me writhe. His free hand drifts down my waist again and inches up to my panties. I squeal when his fingers hook around the fabric. I'm drenched already, and he hasn't even touched me there yet.

"You want it so much, don't you?" he murmurs while sucking my other nipple. "Tell me how much you want it."

His hand slides down my panties, and I'm getting so fucking turned on I can't breathe.

"A lot," I manage to blurt out.

He chuckles and licks his lips when seeing me in agony. "Tell me you've touched yourself," he says.

My eyes jerk open, and I squint. "W-what?"

A sexy smile curves his lip. "Have you made yourself come before?"

I blush and suddenly feel very snuck up on.

"Never mind. You don't have to say it. Your blush says enough."

My eyes widen, and a sort of moan-laugh escapes his mouth. He loves this. It's obvious.

Of course I've done that. There's no girl that hasn't. But that was me, and my finger alone. Nothing else. Not him and his seductive, calloused fingers that would make any girl squeal.

"Next time you do it, you'll think of me," he murmurs.

Oh. My. God.

It's too much.

His lips drag up my neck again, all the way up my jawline, and then my mouth. I can't take my lips off him as his hand dives into my panties. The moment I feel him slipping down my wet folds, I gasp.

"Can I be the first guy to make you come?" he says.

I swear I just came, right there. Just from those words.

I'm too shy to answer.

I close my eyes and enjoy the feeling of having him explore the secret spots I deemed private all those years. His skilled fingers slip down my pussy, dragging up the moisture in between. He grunts in my ear, and pushes his legs up against me. His erection pokes my thigh, making me want to reach out and grab him.

Hunter pins me down with one hand, holding me hostage, which I'm enjoying. His other hand is roaming freely across my pussy, feeling his way down.

Powerful shocks run through my entire body, and blood pumps to that one spot between my legs. I struggle not to pant, feeling the pressure build as he works on me.

I can't believe this is happening, but at the same time I

want it so badly.

He licks my lips, kisses the edges of my mouth, and sucks on my skin as he flicks my nub. He knows exactly where to go and how to do it, just like I expected. He's a fucking sex god, and he knows it.

My body zings with sensations, and I feel like I'm about to fall apart beneath him. He's panting with me as I struggle not to give in to pleasure. I feel so dirty, and this feels so wrong and yet so good. His gray eyes stare right back into mine, full of longing, a craving, awaiting the inevitable climax.

And when it comes, it's massive.

It's a wave of emotions and shocks that run from my loins to my toes and up to the top of my head. It's amazing and freeing. I'm melting in his arms, heated up to the core. I feel drunk with lust. I've never felt anything like it before.

Hunter leaves little pecks on my cheek, and continues to rub me until I'm sated. As my panting subsides, he slips off me and lies down next to me. He gazes at me with a confident, satisfied smirk on his face.

"That was fan-fucking-tastic. Did it feel that way to you, too?" he says.

I let out a huge breath. "Definitely."

He chuckles, and it sounds cute. He leans forward and pecks me on my temple. He's being sweet, and I have no idea why. I just came, this isn't the time to be cute. This is the time for raw, hard sex.

"Why are you stopping?" I say, still catching my breath.

"Because this is as far as it goes tonight."

My jaw drops. "What about the sex?"

"What about it?"

"I thought …" I stammer.

"You came. You liked it. I loved it. That's all that matters."

I'm flabbergasted. Seriously, I have no idea what to say. I

feel cheated out of something I was promised, even though I wasn't.

"No, it's not all that matters," I say, and I pull up my bra, feeling very exposed all of a sudden.

"It's enough. For now."

"Why? You fuck all the other girls, too, don't you?" I say, feeling pissed.

"And you're not 'all the other girls.'"

I swallow. I don't know what to say. I can't believe he's doing this. After I've let him undress me, see my boobs, and touch me all over, this is what he gives me? He even made me come.

Fuck.

It was good, but now it's spoiled. This feels like another one of his teases, and I can't stand it.

Honestly, I feel humiliated. With me not being one of 'all the other girls' it's almost a direct insult. As if I'm not good enough to fuck.

And I just gave him my everything. He just took my innocence. He just saw me at my weakest, and he's taken advantage of it.

Snorting, I throw the blanket off me and get out of the bed.

"What are you doing?" he says.

I fetch my dress. "Going."

"Wait, what?" he says, and now he gets up from the bed, too.

"I don't want to be your plaything. I made a mistake coming here," I say, tears welling up in my eyes.

I should've known he'd do this to me.

He comes up behind me and grabs both my arms. "Don't go."

"Why should I stay?"

"Because I want you to. I need you."

"Stop playing around! You want me, but you don't want me? You just practically told me I'm not good enough to fuck," I say.

"No, you have it all wrong. When I said you're not one of those girls, I meant that you're special. Different."

I'm silently biting my lip, listening to him. I want to give him a chance, but the amount of times I'm still willing to do it are diminishing quickly.

"I want to take it slow. Not rush into things."

"Why?" I say.

"Because I like you too much. I don't want to spoil it."

He puts his arms around me completely, and kisses the back of my head. Resting his nose in my hair, he sniffs, taking in my scent. "I want this to be more than just sex."

"Why didn't you just say so?" I say, turning around in his arms.

He looks at me with hungry eyes. It looks as though he's still fighting the urge to jump my bones. Is he really holding himself back just so he can take his time with me?

"Because … You wanted me so badly … and I want you, too … But you're the first girl I want more with than just that. I don't want it to be all lust and fucking. I want you to like me for who I am, not for what I do in the bedroom. And maybe in the shower or the car …"

His bad grin makes me laugh. I feel better now, knowing he's doing it because he doesn't want me to be just a fuck. I'm not just a girl. I'm his Leafy.

"Is that why you call me Leafy?" I suddenly blurt out.

He muffles a laugh. "You want me to get into all the details?"

"If you want me to stay, spill it."

"All right. That first day I saw you with the leaf blower, I found your bracelet in the grass. I knew it was yours, and I wanted to bring it back, but I had no clue where to go. I didn't know your name, I didn't know where you were staying. Lucky for me, I found your bedroom quite close to mine," he says, chuckling, emphasizing the word bedroom. He's probably thinking of a whole lot of nasty things he could do to me there.

"Anyway, all I could remember was the girl with the leaves in her curly hair, so … Leafy it was."

"But I told you my name," I say.

"I know, but the Leafy thing just stuck with me. It has a nice ring to it. And it was fun, since you seemed to hate it. You blush every time I say it." He smirks, and I shove him forward.

I didn't expect him to fall back onto the bed, though.

"See? Training worked. You get stronger the moment you're angry."

"Oh ha-ha, very funny."

"So … will you stay?" he suddenly says.

I suck on my bottom lip and think about it for a second. Hunter looks like he really means it, and I want to believe it. I just hope what he says is true.

Part of me still believes this is a dream, and that I'll wake up somewhere in the middle of the night discovering it was all in my head. Then again, shouldn't I take this chance? He's made my life so much more fun and exciting, and he seems like he's really caring, even though he doesn't take care of himself that much.

Maybe that's why he needs me.

I step forward and he reaches out for me, grabbing my hand. He pulls me down to the bed with him, draping the covers over us.

"Let's just sleep, okay?" he says. He's taking off his pants underneath the blanket, and I can't help but gulp at the thought of him lying next to me in his boxer briefs.

"Hmm …" I groan.

We crawl farther onto the bed, pulling the sheets with us. I'm tired, and he's right, I do want to be with him. I can't say no anymore. Not to anything. Not because I can't, but because I don't want to anymore.

Somehow, I want this to work.

"Do you think you could stick with me a little longer? I don't want you to just be with me for the sex. I want you to stay for *me*," he says.

Damn, this is so unlike him. It's almost as if he's afraid to lose me.

However, it makes me smile. I feel like I'm suddenly someone's precious, like I'm special and needed.

"I'm not just in it for the sex," I say.

Hunter's arm is still around me, and he drags me to him so we're spooning. He nuzzles my hair and smells me. He feels warm and makes me feel safe in his arms.

"But you'd better not be abstinent until marriage."

He laughs and then pushes his hips against my ass, making me feel his erection.

"You can bet on it. I'm going to claim you soon," he says.

We cuddle some more, and then he yawns. We're both tired as hell. I doze away in his arms, happy, content.

I can wait. I can wait for him. I can wait for the answers to all my questions. I can wait to discover more about him. Hell, he's even waiting for me.

But I do know that I won't wait forever.

CHAPTER 19
THE MORNING AFTER

The next morning I'm still lying in his arms, confused as to why I'm here. I can smell his scent on the pillow we're sharing, and it's making me delirious again. When everything about last night seeps back into my mind, I feel crazily happy.

I'm really here, in his bed, sleeping with him.

His arms are still around me, and I can feel his chest going up and down against my back. Things can't get any crazier than this.

Well, maybe the sex could.

I giggle to myself and smile. Turning around in Hunter's warm embrace, I find him snoring loudly. He looks so goddamn cute right now. His face is the perfect thing to wake up to. Everything about him just makes me jittery.

Suddenly, the door slams open.

I'm startled. I jolt up from the bed, desperate to hold on to the blanket that's dropping off my scarcely covered body.

Jaret is standing in the doorway.

"Dude … Oh, shit," he says when he sees me.

Hunter groans as he looks up at Jaret with a drowsy look

on his face. "Huh? What's happening?"

"Sorry bro, I didn't know you brought her back here," Jaret says. His eyebrows rise playfully. "Hope you had fun last night."

I flush, and pull up the blanket even more, feeling very, very embarrassed.

"What are you doing here?" Hunter mutters with half a grunt.

"It's my room, too, remember? Glad I wasn't around to witness this last night. Had some fun myself, too! Crazy chick, though …" Jaret says, as he walks into the room like it's the most normal thing to do when you find two people in bed together.

"Dude, get out. Give us some privacy for fuck's sake," Hunter says with a croaky voice, scraping his throat.

"Sorry, bud, can't. It's important. I wouldn't have come otherwise, trust me," he says.

I reach for my dress lying on the floor and pick it up while holding the blanket firmly in place. It's not drenched anymore, but it smells bad. Although it stinks, I pull it over my head and drape it down until I'm no longer in my underwear. Better than having Jaret see me partially naked.

Hunter leans on his elbow, giving minimal attention to Jaret as he tries to wake up. "What?"

"I think I'm after the right guy. You know. The boss of Alpha Psi. I think I know who he is."

Opening his eyes wide, Hunter springs up. "What? Are you serious?"

"Alpha Psi? Is that a frat house?" I ask, but nobody answers.

"Yeah, that's why I need you to come with me right now. There's going to be another party tonight, and he'll be there. If you wanna catch him, now's the time. We have to prepare some kind of plan."

"Fuck," Hunter says, and he jumps out of bed wearing nothing but boxer briefs. I swear, if I wasn't on high alert right now, I'd be gaping at his package.

"What the hell are you guys talking about?" I say.

"You go get dressed first, I'll wait for you downstairs so we can get going. They're expecting us to do some work, too, today, so we really need the extra time."

"Work? You mean selling drugs and punching people in the face again?" I say, flabbergasted. "It's a freaking frat house behind all this?"

"All right, see you in a minute or so," Hunter says, and Jaret leaves the room again.

"Stop ignoring me!" I yell at him, and I come out of bed, too.

"I'm not, this is just way too important." He turns around toward me. "And yes, it's a frat house."

I step forward. "More important than telling me what the hell is going on?"

"You should go," he says.

"What? No! Not until you tell me," I say, frowning. "So you're in a frat house? God …" I slap my hand in front of my mouth in disbelief. Now I see why he's been selling drugs and punching people together with Jaret. Those are the people who put them up to it. I need to know more.

"Why do you want to go look for 'the boss'?"

Hunter shushes me. "Don't be so loud."

"Why? Does it matter?"

"Because … it's a freaking illegal frat house. We sell drugs, for crying out loud. Nobody can know about this. And yes, we're looking for the boss, but first we gotta find out who the courier is."

"The courier? What the hell is that?"

He sighs. "The one who brings the drugs from the boss to the top distributors. Those are the people I get my stash from." He runs his fingers through his hair. "I think I've answered enough questions now."

"Oh, c'mon, you've got to give me more than that."

"I can't. You don't know how dangerous that is."

"Why? Are you still too chicken to trust me?"

He gently cups my face between his index finger and thumb. "I care about you. I'm afraid you'll get hurt. That's why I don't tell you. It's better if you stay out of this."

I slap his hand away, and he turns around and walks out the door. I follow him as he goes into the guys' bathroom. I'm not letting him off the hook that easily. I take in a big breath before I walk in with him.

"I don't care if it's dangerous. I. Want. To. Know," I say.

He turns on the light, while I put my foot in front of the door, so he can't close it. Luckily there's no one else inside but us.

"You're not getting out of this, mister," I say, crossing my arms.

A smirk appears on his face. "I love it when you put your foot down like that." He quickly leans in and pecks me on the head, momentarily catching me off guard.

"But I'm going to take a shower now, and then I'm leaving," he says crudely.

"I'm going with you."

He laughs. "Fine. Suit yourself."

He lets go of the door handle and turns on the shower. The door is wide open, and now I'm staring at him, while he's taking off the only thing that was between me and his firm ass.

My eyes widen as he strips. He's completely naked, and I can see his bare ass tighten as he steps under the shower.

I gulp, seeing the rivulets of water stream down his

masculine body. The taut muscles grab my attention as he starts washing himself.

"You're a dirty girl, you know that? Peeping on naked guys," he says.

I gasp. "I am *not.* Trust me, I'm not standing here for that reason. I'm not even looking at you." I turn my head right away, feeling caught.

"I bet you were. And I also bet you liked what you saw."

God. Why does he have to be so fucking blunt all the time? It's turning me into a puddle of drool.

Closing my eyes, I sigh and lean sideways against the wall, waiting for him.

When he's done, he says, "You can open your eyes now. It's safe." The mischievous grin on his face is the first thing I see. I scowl at him as he chuckles a little. "You'll get to see me eventually. I can't wait to see the look on your face then."

"Whatever. I'm still not letting you out of my sight. I don't like what you're scheming one bit."

He's only wearing a towel around his waist, nothing else. He steps closer, and I have trouble not pulling off that towel that's between him and me, but I have to stand my ground.

"Oh, I didn't expect you to. Come to the party with me then," he says.

My jaw drops. "What? You want to take me with you?"

"Well, you just said I can't stop you, so I'd rather take you with me then. You're safer with me than anywhere else."

Somehow that doesn't make me feel comfortable at all.

"But if you don't want to, you can always just stay here, study a bit, you know, go about your normal life like you always do," he says, kissing me on the cheek.

"No, not a chance." I'd rather risk it than not know what he is doing for another day.

"All right. I'll pick you up tonight at your room at eight."

He walks past me, out into the hallway, and I follow him back to his room. There he grabs some briefs from his drawer, while I shut the door behind us. The towel drapes off his butt, and I gulp seeing the beautiful, perfect slabs of muscle that appear before me. He puts on his underwear, and then a pair of pants, covering up his body, making me pine.

"Fine, but if you don't, I swear to God I'll—"

"Yeah, I know, you'll kill me," he chortles. "Don't worry. I'll be there."

After he puts on a casual brown tee, he walks over to me and places his hand on my arm. I liquefy from his touch, even though I want to remain strong, to make a point. He just has this effect on me. I'm the melting candle and he's the burning flame.

"I'll see you tonight, okay?" he says, and he smiles sweetly.

He leans forward and looks at me for a second, waiting for my permission. I part my lips, pointing them up to meet his. Shivers run down my spine as his lips brush along my mouth. He leaves a short but scorching kiss, which makes the butterflies in my belly dance.

I don't want to stop kissing him, but he makes the choice for me.

♥♥♥

I study for the rest of the day, but I can't concentrate at all. I'm way too nervous. It's only ten minutes until Hunter's coming to pick me up, and I'm already sweating like crazy.

This party they're going to sounds scary. If it's going to be anything like last time, I'll need someone to back me up, in case Hunter's going to leave me alone. I'm sure he'll be too busy with whatever to entertain me.

Especially if he and Jaret are going after someone. I

wonder what they're up to.

I need someone else to come, someone I can really trust with all my heart.

I put my books aside and go to Scarlet's room. Before knocking on the door I clear my throat.

"Evie?"

"Not here." Well, it's her voice all right.

I roll my eyes. "Can we talk?"

"No."

"It'll be short, I promise. I'm not going to do anything stupid."

It's quiet for some time, but after a while she opens the door. "What do you want?"

"I j-just wanted to ask if you were okay," I say with a gulp.

"I'm managing."

I peek over her shoulders and see her side of the room is as messy as it was when she was still bunking with me. "Looks like you've settled in nicely."

"Yeah."

I don't really know what to say. She's really not talking a lot. "How's things with Scarlet? Can you hold out with her?" I say with a chuckle.

"Scarlet's quite nice, actually. Sounds weird, I know, but she's not as bad as we thought," she whispers.

"Oh, well that's good," I say.

Then it falls quiet again, and we're both staring at each other. She's tapping her foot, and I'm rummaging in my pocket. This is so awkward.

"Look, I still need my time alone. Could you tell me what you're here for?" Evie says.

"Oh … Well I wanted to invite you to a party tonight."

She frowns. "A party? Autumn Blakewood, going to parties? God, you've really changed."

"I'm not like Brody. This is different. I'm not turning into a douche bag."

"Okay …" she says hesitantly. "So you're going to that party?"

"Yeah, I got invited, but I don't want to go without my best friend. I'd love it if you could come, too." I smile at her, trying to make up for all the things I've done wrong in the past, but she barely shows any emotion at all.

"Please?" I add. "It would be really great if you were there."

She sighs. "I'll think about it."

"Okay."

She makes a face, and closes her door again.

"See ya," I say, but she's already closed the door.

Now I feel really bad.

I don't know what to do to fix this broken relationship. She's still not ready for us to start anew, and I'm feeling shitty because of it. I feel like I've lost my best friend, and all because of some stupid thing called love.

Dammit.

"Hey, you ready to go?"

I turn around and see Hunter standing in the hallway. He comes up to me, puts his arm around my waist, and pulls me in for a kiss on the temple.

"I just need to change into something else first," I answer.

He pats my back. "Okay, I can wait. It's early anyway."

I walk back to my room and go through my clothes, looking for something suitable to wear.

"Why don't you just put on that same dress you wore last night? It looked fucking amazing."

I flush, but laugh at the same time when I turn and see him standing in the doorway again. "No! I'm not wearing the same thing twice in a row without washing it first."

He chortles, the low, manly sound turning all my senses on hyperactive mode. "Too bad. I was looking forward to seeing you stretch that thing to its limit as you dance, and I'm there to watch." He wriggles his eyebrows, making me laugh.

"In your dreams," I say. I grab a pair of colorful skinny jeans and a white top. "Could you close the door?"

"Sure." He kicks the door shut, but stays put himself, crossing his arms.

I pull my shirt over my head, and look back as I see him gazing at my back. I'm still wearing my bra, but the look in his eyes tells me he's seeing me naked in front of him. He bites his lip, making me blush.

"Hey, I'm not giving a peep show!" I say, covering my chest area.

"I've already seen you. Nothing to be secretive about. Of course, I do love looking at you being naked."

I turn around and throw the shirt in his direction. "You're embarrassing me."

"I told you I love to see you blush."

"Turn around," I retort.

"Fine. If I have to," he says, and he closes his eyes indifferently.

I wait until he's fully turned around before stepping out of my jeans and putting on my new clothes. Before I'm done I check the mirror to see if everything's A-OK.

"You can open your eyes now," I say, as I put some earrings in my ears.

He grins, grunting a little. My nipples react to the sound by hardening, and my pussy clenches with need as he wraps his arms around me and kisses the nape of my neck. "You look sexy."

"Thanks," I say, licking my lips as he leaves small pecks on my shoulder. He's so skilled with his lips, he makes me shiver.

"I can barely wait to rip them off," he murmurs close to my ear.

That's it. I'm done for.

I close my eyes, turning into a meek lamb in his strong arms. "Let's not go to the party. Let's just stay here tonight," I whisper.

"Hmm …" he murmurs, the sound putting me on edge. My clit is thumping again, just from having his hands on my belly.

"I want to make love," I whisper.

He chuckles close to my ear, but it sounds more like a groan, too. It turns me on so much I feel the moisture between my legs building.

"As much as I'd like to take you up on that offer, there's something I need to do at that party."

I groan in annoyance.

"Don't worry," he says. "We'll get there eventually, and when we do … I'm going to make love to you so hard, you'll beg for mercy."

I chuckle, and he lets go of me after a short, hot kiss on the cheek.

"Let's go," he says, and he grabs my hand and pulls me to the door.

CHAPTER 20
COLLIDING FORCES

We drive to the party with Jaret's car. I'm texting Evie the address, in case she'd like to come. Hunter's been cracking his knuckles the entire time. I get scared just watching him do it. I wonder if he's going to beat someone up again tonight. I wish I could hold him back, but I know I probably won't be able to, even if I did show up in time.

Right before we enter the door to the house, which is a totally different location from last time, Hunter pulls me back and grabs me by the shoulder.

"One second," he says.

"Mind if I go on ahead?" Jaret says.

"No problem. You go watch them carefully," Hunter says, and they both nod as if they just made a pact or something.

"Pay attention," he says, turning his face toward me again.

I frown at the blatant command.

"You wanted to come, but I want you to promise me something."

"Okay," I stammer. "What?"

"Do *not* under any circumstance talk with the people I'm

involved with. Once I leave your side, don't come after me. No matter what."

"Are you kidding me?" I say with a scowl.

"I'm not. I don't want you to get involved in this."

I sigh, and he leans forward to look me in the eye. "I'll spend as much time with you as I can, but once Jaret calls me, I have to leave. Please promise me you'll just enjoy the party."

I make a fist with my hand, looking the other way.

"Please?" he pleads, squeezing my flesh. "Don't make me worry about you."

"Fine, whatever," I sigh. "Can we go in now?"

My heart is immediately weighed down by what I just said. I don't at all intend to just let him slip away. I came here to find out why Hunter's in this frat, and what he's up to with Jaret. I won't let him out of my sight.

"Oh, and one more thing," he says. "Don't take anything from anyone. Ever."

"Yeah, yeah, I get it. No drugs. No drinks from someone else."

"Right," he says, and he winks. "You're starting to get it."

"I'm not a little girl."

"No. You're my Leafy, and I want to see you safe."

Somehow the part where he says 'my' makes me gloat.

We go inside, and I'm almost blown away by the music drumming in my ears. It's loud and deafening music. They're playing Kanye West's song, 'Black Skinhead,' and I'm scowling just from hearing it. I hate these songs. I don't even want to call it music.

"Jesus," I say, covering my ears.

Hunter chuckles. "Probably *his* idea of partying."

With *his* I guess he means 'the boss,' whoever that is.

I'm glad when this song is over and the next one is Muse's 'Supermassive Black Hole,' which I think is a much better song.

It's also one of the few songs of theirs I've actually listened to.

Hunter greets some buddies of his with a fist bump, and I look around a little in the meantime. I catch a glimpse of Scarlet and Brody near a table. They both seem pissed, and from the looks of it it's a pretty heated conversation. They're arguing over something.

It shouldn't bother me so much, especially not after seeing Scarlet all over Hunter, but something about seeing them fight just makes my skin crawl.

Hunter grabs my hand and steps in front of me, blocking my sight. He pulls my hand up to his face with a seductive look in his eyes. "Wanna dance?"

"B-but what about—"

"It can wait," he says with a deep, rumbling voice that sends hot streaks to my core.

He brings my hand up to his mouth, keeping his predatory eyes on me like a hawk. When his lips press down on my skin, I shudder.

He pulls me back across the dance floor, licking the back of my hand. He makes me feel strange things in places I didn't even know existed. He's so fucking sexy, I can't resist.

Placing my hand on his shoulder, he drags me closer, pressing my chest up against him. This song is perfect to dance to, and my God … can he dance.

He twirls me around in his arms and puts his hands on my waist, swaying us both. Grinding his hips against my ass, we start to dance. It's extremely dirty, and I don't think I've ever danced like this before.

His hands are on my belly and waist, slipping and sliding up and down like he's feeling his way across my body. I can hear him breathing, he's so close to my ear. His scent is intoxicating, and I bite my lip in a frenzy.

He lowers his head, sinking his lips onto my neck. Leaving

long, luscious kisses, he moans softly against my skin, turning me on.

I'm getting wound up quickly. Especially after I feel his bulge poking in my ass.

He knows exactly what to do, pushing my buttons until I forget everything and everyone around me. All I can think about is feeling his body against mine, clothes grazing, hips colliding, clutching each other in a hot and sweaty dance.

God, this is the life.

I feel like a drooling teen around him.

"Hey," Hunter whispers close to my ear. "Isn't that your friend? Evie?"

I turn my head to where he's pointing, and I gasp when I see her dancing. She's here. She came.

With a girl.

My eyes widen as she glances at me and throws me a look.

I smile, and she smiles back.

Good. I'm glad she's happy. At least, a little. I want her to have a good time, even if it's without me.

"What's she doing here?" he asks.

"I invited her to come. I wanted her to have a good time. You know, relax a little. She really needed it."

"Are you sure? She looks upset," he says.

"That's because we're in a bit of a rough spot at the moment."

"How come?" Hunter kisses my temple.

I swallow away the lump in my throat. "I found out she's in love with me."

He chuckles proudly. "And you were already pining for someone else."

I flush. "Yeah, well, it's difficult," I say, still feeling a little insecure about the whole thing.

He grins, and a sound escapes his mouth that sounds like a

humming groan. "Too bad for her I got you first. Now you're mine."

Hunter presses a kiss on my cheek, and he drags it down to my neck, persuading me to close my eyes again. His tongue sometimes dips out, marking me as his. I am his.

I'm squirming against him as he feels me up and then some. It's hot in here, and I'm out of my mind, out of it because of him.

Suddenly I hear someone scream.

My eyes jerk open, zoning in on the exact spot the sound emanated from. We stop dancing, and Hunter releases me from his grip. There's a girl lying on the floor. Evie's standing right next to her, fuming. A guy stands across from her, laughing.

"You don't want a guy to join in on the fun? Pathetic," the guys says, and he flicks his wrists like he's all that.

My mouth drops open. Hunter's glaring at them, squinting more with each passing second, his jaw clenched tightly.

"Fucking dykes!" the guy screams.

"That's it," Hunter says, and he storms toward them.

"What the fuck did you just say?" Hunter says.

"They're a bunch of dirty fanny bashers. They're not allowed in here."

"You don't get to fucking decide that," Hunter growls.

"Who the fuck do you think you're talking to?" the guy says, and he spits on the floor. They're both bumping chests now. Hunter grabs the guy by the collar and lifts him up into the air like he weighs nothing.

"You're a fucking asshole, you know that?" he says.

"Dykes don't belong in an Alpha Psi party."

"I dare you to say that word again."

"D.Y.K.E. Dyke," the guy repeats in slow motion.

Oh dear.

With one quick punch, Hunter sends the guy flying into

the air. His knuckles aren't even bloodied, but the guy's nose is. He's on the floor, groaning, and when he sees Hunter towering over him, he crawls back on all fours.

"Get your fucking homophobic ass out of here!" Hunter yells.

The guy scrambles to his feet and back out the door, holding his hand to his broken nose.

"Dick," Hunter mutters, snorting.

"Are you okay?" I ask the girl who's lying on the floor. She nods. It's Evie's date, and Evie is squatting right next to her, making sure she's okay.

Hunter's face shifts instantly from completely pissed off to kind, and he holds out his hand to the girl. He helps her up, and she straightens her clothes while flushing quite badly.

"T-thanks," she says.

"Don't mention it," Hunter says.

"You girls all right?" I ask, and I look at Evie too.

She smiles, and her eyes flick from me to Hunter and back to me again. "Thanks. Both of you."

"Can we go home now?" The girl says, looking pretty anxiously at Evie.

"Yeah," Evie says, and she grabs the girl's hand. "We'll go home."

"I'm sorry," I say. I feel guilty for having invited her here. I should have known there would be dicks like that guy ruining everything.

"It's not your fault," Evie says, and she puts her other hand on my shoulder, smiling.

Somehow it makes me feel a little better about the situation and our friendship.

"See you later, okay?" she adds.

"Definitely," I say.

They both leave the house, and everything settles down

again. People start dancing, and it's back to partying like nothing ever happened.

Hunter is still cracking his knuckles.

"Are you hurt?" I say, grabbing his fingers.

"No," he says. "I'm fine. Pussies like him can't even graze me." He smirks at me.

Suddenly Jaret comes up from behind him, and I frown when I see him. Bad news always follows him.

"I found a distributor willing to talk."

"Awesome. It's time to go then," Hunter says.

"Wait, what? You're leaving?" I say.

"Not the party. We're gonna talk. See if we can find out who the courier is." Hunter kisses me on my forehead, and turns around.

"Okay …" I say, but the guys have already walked away. They've disappeared into the crowd.

Crap. What am I supposed to do now?

All this fighting and hip-grinding has gotten me thirsty, so I look around for a punch table. Instead, I find a bar in the corner with a few empty stools in front of it.

Brody is in the only occupied one.

I'm not really into talking with him right now, but it seems I have no other choice. Well, if he's in the same frat house, which he has to be, then maybe I can ask him some questions about them. Work out what the deal is.

Sighing, I make my way to the bar and sit down next to him.

"Hey, Brody," I say, swallowing away the lump in my throat.

"Hey," he says with a rather dull voice.

"Scarlet's not with you?" I say, curious and trying to stir up a conversation.

"Nah. Stupid fight." He picks up his drink and takes a huge

sip. "Anyway, what's up?"

"Nothing, just thought I'd get a drink," I say, and I order a lime coke, just to stay on the safe side this time.

He muffles a laugh. "It surprises me you're even here. I reckon it's Hunter's doing."

"Yeah, well, seeing as you guys are both in the same frat club, I don't think it's that weird."

"True."

There we have it. A confession. It's a small one, but it's a good step in the right direction.

He takes another sip, and his face contorts, probably from the high amount of alcohol that he's spiked his drink with.

"So, what do you do exactly?" I ask. "Just deal drugs or … something else?"

"Something else?" Brody laughs. "You mean the fighting?"

"Yeah."

"No, only the freshmen do that."

No wonder Hunter's always drummed up like a slave. I wonder why he lets them order him around like that.

"Okay … But what about you then?" I ask.

"I'm a distributor." Brody picks up his glass again and drinks up the rest in one go. He scowls, and then lets out a huge breath as he puts down his glass again.

"What is your boyfriend looking for exactly?"

I gulp when he says that. "Uh … What?"

"I heard some distributors talking about him, saying he wants information."

I don't know if I should tell Brody, or if I'm even allowed to, but at the same time I want him to tell me more. If I don't say it, he probably won't trust me with more. I should take the chance and hope for the best.

"He's trying to find out who the boss is."

"Why?" Brody's leaning on his hand, looking terribly

bored.

"I don't know," I say, taking a massive sip of my coke, almost choking on it. "Why are you so interested? I thought you guys didn't even know each other," I say.

"Who? Me and Hunter?" he says, swaying his glass back and forth.

I nod.

"I've been in Alpha Psi for two years. Hunter's a freshmen. Of course I hadn't met him before."

"Oh, well that explains it."

Brody puts down his glass and leans forward, gazing at me with an intent look on his face. "You know … I still wouldn't trust Hunter. He seems to be hiding an awful lot from you."

"What do you mean?" I say, my heart throbbing in my throat when he says that. How does Brody know that?

"Jessie, his brother, was a dealer for our frat house for years, too. Outside the grounds, of course. He wasn't in college."

I gape at him. "What? Are you serious?"

"Yep. Why do you think the guy's in jail now? Wasn't careful enough," Brody says. "There's a lot more Hunter probably isn't telling you."

"I can't believe this …" I mutter to myself, but it slips out of my mouth too, making Brody chuckle.

"And you know what else? If Hunter goes on the way he does, doing things out in the open, he'll surely end up there, too."

My lip starts to quiver.

No. It can't be.

Hunter can't end up in jail. He can't. Can he?

Just the thought of it makes my heart go wild. I don't want him to be put behind bars because of this. I don't care why he's doing it, I don't want to see him in there.

He said it himself, jail was a hellhole. No way would he be okay in there.

"I have to go," I stammer, and I get off my seat.

"See ya around, I guess," Brody yells after me, as I stumble through the crowd to the exit of the building.

Tears well up in my eyes. It's all becoming way too clear now. I've been swooning over a guy who's so freaking bad, he even told me he was, and I still didn't listen. If he ended up in jail, it would break my heart.

I don't want to see that happen. I can't handle it.

All I wanted was to get through college, and now life has become so much more difficult than that. And it's all because of Hunter.

CHAPTER 21
SECRETS AND DESIRES

I make my way to the exit of the building and go outside. I suddenly don't have enough air to breathe in. It feels like I'm suffocating in the realization that my life has been turned upside down by Hunter.

The door slams open behind me. I turn around. Hunter's barging toward me with a furious look on your face.

"Are you trying to get in trouble?" he yells. "Don't you know how fucking dangerous it is to go without me?"

"I don't care. I want to go home," I say.

He grabs me by the forearm, preventing me from going anywhere. "Why do you keep running away?"

"Fuck off!" I say, and I jerk my arm loose.

"What the fuck? Why are you so angry at me?" he says. "I didn't do anything."

"Brody told me all about you and Jessie."

His eyes widen when I say that.

"Your brother was dealing for the frat club, too. That's the reason he's in jail, isn't it?"

Hunter just stares at me, his jaws clenched tightly.

"You're always hiding things from me. Why can't you just tell me what you're doing? Why are you dealing drugs? Is it just for the money?" I yell.

"Partially … but it's not the biggest reason," he says.

"But you're broke all the time, just like me! What the fuck have you been doing with that money?"

"Saving it." The look on his face changes from angry to offended. "I told you I'm trying to get Jessie out of jail."

"By dealing? Doing the same thing that got him in there?" I say, pissed.

He steps closer, and his face is now hovering close to mine. "I'm doing what's right," he hisses.

"Right? Drugs?" I snort. "And here I thought you were a good thing in my life."

His eyes are growing dimmer by the minute. The flame behind them is dying out slowly, and it's my fault.

"Don't say that. You don't know what I've been through. You don't know how fucked up my life is. I told you it wasn't easy."

"My life isn't easy either, but now it's only getting harder with you doing things like this. I don't want to see you end up in jail. Your brother's in there because of what he did, and you're going straight after him."

"My brother is in jail because he tried to take care of me!" Hunter snaps. "We lived in the slums for years. He was the only one I had, the only one who cared for me. The only way he could earn enough to support us was by dealing. He doesn't deserve to be in jail for that. Not when the frat club practically used him as bait."

I'm shocked by his story, but I'm horrified as well.

"Then why in God's name are you in the club, too? They could do the same thing to you!"

"Because I owe it to my brother! I'd risk everything to get

him out of there. That's why I need the money; to bail him out." Hunter squeezes my arm. "Wouldn't you do the same if your family was in jail?"

"I guess …" I stammer.

"I want my brother back … It's because of him that I'm in college now. He saved up every freaking coin he could so he could get me some education, even with my learning problems."

My God. It's all starting to make sense now.

He's doing this all because of his brother. He loves him so much, he's even willing to risk jail time for it. And I've been so ignorant, so judgmental about it. I should've known better.

At the same time, I'm still scared Hunter will end up in prison. Why doesn't he just earn it in a legal way? I know it's less efficient, but at least there are no risks.

"B-but there are other ways to make money and to get someone out of jail," I stammer.

"Maybe, but there are other reasons why I chose to do it this way."

"Why? Does it have something to do with that guy you're looking for? The boss?"

"I can't tell you."

I sigh, rolling my eyes. "This again."

"Don't you see? I've tried to tell you, but you won't listen to me. I cannot tell you, because it would put you in harm's way. I don't want you to get hurt. I'll do anything to prevent that," he says.

Hunter wraps his arms around me and presses me firmly to his chest, almost smothering me. His heart is beating like crazy. He's shivering, too. I wonder why.

"I know I'm a screw-up, but I'm trying to get things together. You're the only good thing that's happened to me in my life," he murmurs.

Suddenly I feel all warm and fuzzy.

"College life has been hard on me, but I want to succeed so badly. I just don't know how. I thought that I could stand a chance with you. I thought, if that girl helps me out, teaching me how to learn quickly, maybe I can make it. Maybe I can make Jessie proud. Maybe the investment he made in me won't be in vain."

"It's not," I whisper. "I'll help you. I promise. I want you to be okay, too."

I look up at him, feeling glad he's finally given me at least a glimpse into his life. It's more than I ever thought was real. But now that I've seen how far he's gone for his brother, how much he cares about him, how much pressure he feels to save him because Jessie did the same for him, I have so much respect for him. I'm in awe at his kindness and pure will.

He smiles back at me, and I feel like I'm the luckiest girl in the world to be in his arms right now.

"I'm sorry for …" I mutter.

"Don't be. As long as you stay with me, I'm not mad. I should've told you sooner."

I nod, and the air feels cleared.

"Guess you wanna go back inside now," I say. "Look for that 'person.'"

"Nah. I think I'll leave it to Jaret for now."

"But it's important to you, right?"

"You're more important," he says, and he kisses my shoulder. "Let's go home."

"You sure?" I ask as I lean back.

He nods, his finger drifting up to my cheek, caressing it softly. He cups my jaw and leans in, looking into my eyes, asking for permission. I purse my parted lips and close my eyes as he presses his lips down on mine. It's soft and slow this time, unlike his voracious kisses from before. These are long and loving, and I'm shaken to the core by the intimacy of it. He's so gentle, and it feels like he wants to tell me I'm precious to him. I adore it. He's precious to me, too.

When Hunter takes his lips off me, he leans his head against my forehead and smiles at me. Seeing him in front of me like this calms me down.

He's beautiful, on the inside and out, even if he does what he does. His soul is good.

He's sweet, charming, sexy, handsome, helpful, protective, and he cares for people. He's everything I want in a guy.

"Wanna go?" he says.

He rummages in his pocket and takes out a key.

"How? We came with Jaret."

"I asked him to borrow his car. He said he didn't mind, as long as we didn't trash it. He's getting a ride from one of the other dealers."

Before I can say anything, he's already pulling me toward the car.

When we're on the road, I can't help but glance at Hunter. He drives like a real pro, his gray eyes sometimes flicking to me. My temperature soars each time his brooding eyes wash over me, and I can barely breathe.

His lips curve up into half a smile when he glances at me. When he licks and bites his lip, I gasp. He chuckles. I'm under his spell, and he knows it.

I can't help but let my eyes wander across his sleek body, and what I know is underneath those clothes. The way we danced really made me crazy for him; not even a fight can temper my feelings for him.

When we finally reach the dorm, I'm actually sad I have to get out of the car. It means I can't peek at him anymore, and I know we'll eventually part ways at our rooms.

I don't want to sleep alone tonight. I want to stay with him.

He looks at me, squinting his eyes, and then he leans

forward. At first I freeze, but then when he puts his lips on my cheek I relax. His lips slowly drag down to my neck, and he leaves sultry kisses everywhere. Blood rushes through my body as he groans against my skin.

"I just can't *not* kiss you," he murmurs.

His hands move from the steering wheel to my face, and he cups my jaw. Sucking my skin, he leaves red marks. Damn. I'm getting all hot and bothered again.

Then he takes his lips off my skin, and I suddenly feel cold.

"Why are you stopping?" I say, confused.

He chuckles. "We're still in Jaret's car. Better get to the dorm, don't you think?"

"Ah … Yeah. Right."

We step out of the car. My wobbly legs can barely hold me up, and I struggle to stay on two feet. Hunter comes to my side, and I clear my throat when he throws me a wicked smile. God, I hate him when he does that. It's like he's flaunting off his goods in front of my nose, but doesn't want to give them to me.

Hunter puts his hand on my back. As we walk into the dorm, his hand slips down to my ass. A blush spreads across my cheeks when he squeezes my flesh.

A soft humming sound comes from his mouth, like he's enjoying the fact that he can touch me like that without repercussions.

The moment I spot my door, I'm devastated. "Wait," I say, and I turn around toward him. I grab his hand and place it on my waist.

"What are you doing?" he says.

"I want a goodnight kiss," I say, pursing my lips.

A sexy smile appears on his face. I suck on the bottom part of my lip, and his eyes flick right down to see me do it. Biting his lip in return, he chuckles a little. "You're seducing me."

"I just want a kiss. Nothing wrong with that, is there?" I

say with one eyebrow raised.

"You've really changed," he says, leaning forward. "I like it."

His hot mouth crashes into mine, and he starts kissing me fervently. I wrap my arms around his neck as he puts both his hands on my ass. He's voracious, and pushes himself up against me. A loud thud is audible as we bump into the wall. We're in the middle of the hallway, making out like crazed teens, and I love it.

We drift to our rooms, stumbling over each other's feet. I can't take my mouth off his, he's that delicious.

But then he does.

My lips feel raw and swollen, and I need his kisses to soothe the pain, but he inches back.

"Don't stop," I say, but he grabs my wrists and drapes them off his shoulder.

"You're tired. I'm tired." He fakes a yawn.

"No I'm not. You're just making this up. You don't want to kiss me."

I cross my arms below my boobs, making sure they're nice and perky for him to see. Of course, when his eyes sink to my chest area, I muffle a laugh, feeling victorious.

"Hmm … You don't even know how much I want to kiss you. I want it so goddamn much, I dream about it. Ever since I met you I've been waking up with a huge hard-on."

I gulp at those words.

"I also know that when I do put my mouth on yours, I can't stop," he continues.

"Then don't," I say, hooking my fingers in his pants, urging him to come closer.

"No, I'm holding myself back already, don't make it so hard on me, please," he mutters.

"I don't want you to hold back anymore," I say.

"I told you before, I don't do sweet sex. You're a virgin. Sort of," he grins, probably thinking about our other night together. "I don't want to mess this up with you."

"Why are you so afraid?" I ask, leaning forward to kiss the corner of his lip.

I've never been so bold before, but I feel different today. Changed. He's turned me into a more confident girl. A girl who can handle herself. A girl who goes after what she wants. A woman. Fierce.

He gasps when I kiss his jawline. "God, you're making this really hard," he says.

He makes a deep, rumbling sound, alerting all my senses. My hand drifts up his shirt, and I feel my way across his amazingly tight abs that just scream to be touched.

"I don't think that's the only thing I'm getting hard," I whisper close to his ears.

He lets out an exasperated breath. "Fuck. Do you know how hot you sound when you say those dirty things?" he says, chuckling.

"I've always wanted you. I'm ready for you," I say.

My hand searches for the doorknob behind me, and when I find it, I open the door to my room.

Hunter's everything I dream about. He's the bad boy that keeps me alert. The guy who awakens my inner desires. The person who makes me overcome my fears and fight. We're complete opposites, and now I finally understand why they say opposites attract.

I'm not just attracted to him. It's so much more than that.

I want him to be the one.

"Please …" I murmur close to his ear. "Make me yours." And then I kiss him one last time on his neck.

"Fuck. That's it," Hunter growls. "You asked for it."

I'm taken by surprise as he grabs my arms and pushes me

through the door. He slams it shut behind him, and then smashes his lips onto mine. With his calloused fingers he grabs my face, and his tongue dips out during his fierce kisses. He's rough, and nibbles on my lip as I desperately try to get closer to him. I want to feel him, to have him, body to body.

He looks at me for just a few seconds with half-mast eyes. "I wasn't afraid. I didn't want to hurt your feelings. Nor your pussy." He licks his lips when he says those words, and I just want to put my tongue right there.

"I wanted to take it slow, give you time to adjust to me, but now you've done it," he says in between kisses. "I'm gonna take you, and I'm gonna fuck you until you scream my name."

Hunter turns me around, pushes me up against the door, and sinks his mouth to mine. He tastes so delicious, and all I can think of his having his lips all over me. I push my breasts up to his chest, my nipples aching, desperate for his touch, but he's completely fixated on my lips.

And oh God, the way he kisses me. It's as if he wants to show me what he can do. Like he's fucking my mouth.

Frenzied, my fingers latch around his body, trying to fuse with him. Each time Hunter breathes, his hungry eyes open to catch my gaze. My lips feel raw, and they're buzzing. I love it. He smiles when he sees me wired up because of his rabid kisses.

I reach for the bottom of his shirt and scrunch it up. He raises his arms, letting me jerk it over his head. I still marvel at the sight of his beautiful body, those taut muscles and square pectorals. I love that it's all mine.

"Am I the only one?" I ask, suddenly feeling a little insecure. I'm just a geek, and he's hot as fuck. It's hard for me to imagine him only being into me.

"Of course," he whispers. "You already had me the first time you said 'Yeah.'" The cute smile on his face makes me flush.

He puts his hands on the wall beside me, trapping me. I feel safe, though. With his predatory eyes on me, I don't even want to be anywhere else right now.

Then his mouth crashes into mine again, and I'm done for.

Trembling, I clutch his body and hold him close. Every few seconds our mouths disconnect to take a breath, and then we're right back at it. Our tongues are locked in a furious battle. His hips are grinding against mine, his erection poking my thigh. Groaning in my ear, he reaches for my hands and pins them against the wooden door.

This is so fucking hot.

"You want to be mine? I'll make you mine," he grunts.

His fingers curl around the fabric of my top, and in one go he jerks it over my head. My breasts don't even get the chance to bounce back into place before he's got his hands all over them again.

He kneads them softly, leaving kisses on my sternum, going lower with each kiss. My nipples harden, aching to be touched. I moan, and he chortles from the sounds I make. Then he flips my breasts out of their cups and squeezes them a little.

Within a second he yanks my bra loose, and it drops to the floor. I gasp, but then he puts his lips on the tips of my breasts and starts sucking, hard. He circles one nipple with his tongue, rubbing the other with his finger. A squeal leaves my mouth as he puckers my nipples to their limit, giving each one equal attention before returning to my lips. His mouth is hot with desire, and my stomach is fluttering. I'm overcome by need. The need to be even closer. To have him inside me.

Drifting down toward my jeans, he starts fiddling with the button to loosen it. All my sexual feelings focus on that one swollen spot his hand is drifting so close to.

I'm dying inside. Dying for him to release me.

"If this thing doesn't come off within the next six seconds,

I'm going to tear it off you." Sounds almost like a threat to my jeans, but I like it.

He jerks down everything but my panties, leaving me desperate and almost naked. Squatted on the floor, he gazes up at me with dirty eyes as he takes off my shoes one by one and then my pants, taking his time. He throws them aside, and starts kissing my leg.

I shiver from his hot mouth, the sultry lips that mark my skin. I feel abashed, but at the same time I want him to do it. I'm nervous as hell, but the sound of his chuckles puts me at ease.

"Too late to stop now, Leafy," he murmurs against my skin.

"I don't want to stop," I say.

My pussy clenches with need as his fingers caress my inner thigh, inching up toward my panties. When his lips reach the top of my thigh, he hooks his fingers under the fabric and rips it off.

I squeal and gasp, a stinging feeling grazing my skin. He just tore my panties to pieces!

"I told you I'm not nice," he says.

A hot streak spreads through my body when I realize he's staring straight at my pussy.

"Hmmm …" he murmurs, pressing soft kisses on my thigh. "I guess you never had this either."

I shake my head, feeling overcome with desire. When he puts his lips on my folds, I moan in agony.

He starts slow, but eventually increases his pace. He kisses me on my inner lips, sucks on my nub, and dips his tongue inside me. His licking is ravenous, and it feels as though he wants to eat me up and then some. I've never felt anything this good before.

"God, I love it that I'm the first. You're so fucking delicious," he says in between licks.

I crave more of his hot kisses, his hungry tongue, his skilled fingers. He answers my longing with more of everything. With his hands he nudges my legs apart, spreading them widely. I'm trembling from his eagerness, but he holds me still, lapping me up.

I gasp. The pressure of his tongue on my swollen, moistened clit is too much.

And then I come undone.

Sounds escape my mouth that I've never heard before, but I know it's because of the sweet, painful agony I feel, as waves of ecstasy flush through my body. I'm heated up to the core, and Hunter keeps up with my orgasm, even when it's already subsided.

As I pant, I fall apart against the door, my entire body shaking. This is bliss.

He muffles a laugh, but it sounds more like a groan. He comes to his feet again, and I squeal when he picks me up from the floor.

"No breaks. I want you. Now," he growls.

He twirls us around with his massive arms and throws me onto my bed with no problem. I love how cocky he is, how dominant, the sex oozing off him. I want it. I want it all.

Standing at the back of the bed, he peers at me with darkened eyes as he starts prying at his belt buckle. I watch him bite his lip, and it looks so fucking sexy. I swear, it's like he's trying to make me faint.

Especially when he jerks down his jeans and briefs in one go.

My eyes immediately widen, and I gulp. His sizeable cock is fully erect, bouncing up and down as his slacks drop to the floor. It's huge, big, and my God … so fucking hot. It's all I can look at.

But it scares me too, knowing he'll be inside me soon.

He smirks, seeing my anxious face. "Like what you see?"

I blush, crossing my legs because I suddenly feel very vulnerable. What if he doesn't fit?

He crawls onto the bed and over me with a wicked grin on his face. His hardness slides across my thighs as he inches up, and I swallow my next gasp for air.

Hunter leaves tiny kisses on my belly, dragging his lips up to my breasts. I squirm underneath him as he suckles on my hardened nipples again, the tips aching for his tongue. He squeezes my other breast, and my skin vibrates with his groans as he kneads.

All I feel is need. I need his body closer. It's never close enough.

My fingers coil around his back, desperately clawing him. He cups my face between his index finger and thumb and kisses my jawline voraciously. His tongue dips out and drags along my cheek as he reaches my lips and thirstily takes my mouth. He doesn't just latch onto my mouth. He claims me. Marks me as his.

"You have condoms?" he asks gruffly in between his ferocious kisses.

I nod, panting, and point to the left. "Drawer."

God I'm glad my mom added them to my suitcase before I left home.

Hunter pushes himself up on his elbows and leans on his knees as he reaches for the drawer of my nightstand. Taking out the condom, he doesn't take the time to rip it with his fingers. Instead, he brings the packet to his mouth and tears it to pieces, spitting out the condom. He snatches it from my belly, his fingers briefly grazing my skin, sending shocks through my body.

Arching his back, he rolls the condom over his length. I tilt my head to watch him do it, eagerly awaiting him.

When he comes back down like a tiger jumping on his prey, he grunts, and the deep roughness of his voice kindles a flame in my core. He looks so goddamn beautiful with his muscular shoulders supporting his weight, the unshaven jaw, his full lips, those dark, endless eyes I want to drown in.

I wrap my arms around him as he starts rubbing himself up against me, letting me feel what he can give me. His expression is dark, hungry, and lustful as the tip of his cock grazes my entrance. His muscles clench; I can feel his restraint. He's fighting the urge to plunge inside me. I want him to take me, and I even told him to do it, but still he's gentle with me.

"You ready for me, Leafy?" he murmurs.

"Yes. I was always ready for you."

I hold my breath when he slides into my folds. Digging my nails into his back, I close my eyes to enjoy the moment, to feel what it's like to physically connect with a man. It's so raw and powerful, and so full of desire.

"Here I come," he murmurs against my skin.

My legs part as he pushes his thighs into mine, slowly entering me. His eyebrows draw together as he locks his eyes with me, concentrating. He's tempering his wild side for me.

I reach for his face and cup it, forcing him to look at me as he presses deeper into me. "Make me yours," I repeat softly.

He licks his lips and then crashes his mouth into mine again.

His savageness is back, and in full glory. He sucks on my lips while pushing ever farther inside. He clutches my ass and holds me tight, breathing heavily against my cheek. I'm drunk with lust when he fills me. I feel so full and complete.

Our mouths collide in a hot, wet craze. Tongues slip in and out, sweat drips from our bodies, heat and wetness blend together, and I love every second of it.

He drives into me until every inch of him is inside.

Gasping, I push my hips up to meet his, clinging to the contact between us, wanting him further inside me. More. More. I'm delirious. Totally mad for him.

Hunter's pace increases, and he pumps inside me with long, deep strokes. My pussy responds to his cock, clenching with need. With my lips on his neck I beg him for more. His love is like a drug.

He whispers words in my ear, like *'you're so tight'* and *'do you like it?'*, and I can only respond with moaning, nodding, and gasping.

I think I even call out his name, just like he predicted.

Tension is building in his muscles, and I grasp him tight, holding him close to me. He fists my hair, clenching it tight as he arches his back. My blood is rushing to one spot, as wantonness grows inside my groin. The pressure between my folds is rising, and I feel myself growing increasingly elated. And then it happens.

A deep, drawn-out groan escapes his mouth. An expression of anguish combined with euphoria appears on his face. His jaw tightens, and his fingers clutch my waist. I moan loudly as I come apart underneath him. His member starts to pulsate, and warmth fills me up to the brim.

Still panting, he thrusts inside me, slowing down each time. When we're both sated, his trembling body drops down onto mine, and I wrap my arms tightly around him.

As his cock spills out of me, he takes off the condom, ties a knot in it, and hurls it to the bin. Then he falls to my side, exhausted.

Turning my head, I look at him. His head rests on my pillow, my hair tickling his nose. He smells me, and then he smiles. I smile back. He is beautiful.

No words can express what I just felt.

All I know is that it was wonderful, and that it was more

than I ever expected it to be.

I pull up the blanket, my body shivering from the coldness that suddenly washes over me. I'm naked in my own bed, and now that he's no longer ravaging me I need something else to warm me up.

"Did I hurt you?" he suddenly whispers.

It takes me a while to answer. Not because he hurt me, but because I have no idea how I'm supposed to feel after something like this. I feel full, swollen, raw. It's a little tingly, but that doesn't bother me. I'm just delighted. I'm happy. I'm happy because of him.

"No," I say, flashing a smile.

His lips curve up, too, and he presses his mouth against my temple, leaving a sweet, gentle kiss.

As he retreats, his hand snakes up my belly, curling around my waist and drawing me closer.

When I look at him, I feel so damn happy. There's nothing else in the world that has ever made me feel this way.

I think I'm in love.

"I … I …" I stammer. I want to say it, but I'm afraid. What will he say if I do? Will he reject me? I don't want this to end.

But I feel I need to say this. Hunter has given me the courage to follow my heart. My heart wants to speak up.

"I love you."

There. I said it. It's out now.

I couldn't hold it back any longer. It's the truth. He deserves to know. I want to let him feel it.

For a moment he just stares at me, his eyes half-mast, observing me. It's as if the words take time to register in his brain. I'm patiently awaiting his answer to my confession, wriggling my toes against his.

And then his fingers tighten around my waist.

"You're mine now," he whispers.

And with those words, he leans forward and presses his lips firmly on mine.

CHAPTER 22
LOVE IS A DIFFICULT THING

Rays of sunlight brighten the room. My eyes flutter open, sticky from the salt. I snatch my glasses off the nightstand so I can actually see something. When his beautiful face is the first thing I see, I'm filled with joy.

I'm also still a bit shaken by what happened last night. I can't believe I actually had sex. It was amazing, and everything went by in a rush. It's like I was on cloud nine or something.

And then it hits me: I'm no longer a virgin.

I wriggle my way under his arm, feeling suddenly very jittery. I don't feel different. Nothing's changed. The only thing that's different is my feelings for him. They're much more defined, clear as day. I love him, and I want to be with him for as long as I can.

He groans when I accidently wake him with my squirming. It's such a small bed, so it was bound to happen.

"Sorry," I whisper.

He slowly opens his eyes, which hide behind thick, dark lashes. He yawns, and my eyes follow the movement of his strong jaw. With his fingers he scrunches up the blanket, making grumbling noises. I smile at the sight of him. I can't stop looking at him.

I'm proud. Not because I have him, but because he is so much more than he tells himself he is. He cares so much for everyone around him, loves them with all his heart, so much that he'd go through hell for them. He calls himself bad for me, but he's made me feel stronger, vigilant, alive. I admire his devotion, adore his flaws, and the scars that mark his past and make him who he is. And I revel in his inner and outer beauty. The only thing he's been is good for me.

"Hey beautiful," he says softly, his voice still croaky.

I giggle and bump my thigh against his. "Wake up."

He grunts, and the sound stirs the butterflies in my belly. "Why?"

"Shower."

His hand slithers across my waist, and he pulls me closer to him, making humming noises. His groin presses against my side, and I can clearly feel his morning wood prodding my leg.

"Hmmm …" he groans.

I chuckle. "C'mon. I wanna shower. I feel dirty."

"I like that …" he says.

I laugh, and shove him away. One of his eyebrows arches, and he throws the blanket off him. "I'll take you up on that offer."

A manly, loud roar comes from his mouth as he raises his arms. His muscles tighten and look strained as he stretches them to their limit. I gulp just looking at his taut, ripped body. We're both still completely naked, and I don't feel insecure about my body anymore.

I get up from the bed and grab some fresh panties. Hunter growls.

I turn my head, and see him eyeing my bare butt. A flush spreads across my cheeks, and I hurry to grab my bathrobe.

"Aw …" he says as I close the robe and fetch a bottle of shower gel.

I roll my eyes at him. "Do you always blatantly stare at naked chicks?"

"No. Just you," he muses, and he jumps out of bed like a coiled spring. Damn, he has energy.

"And I'm not saying no to getting under the shower with you," he adds, wrapping a towel around his package.

I swallow away the lump in my throat. "When I said 'shower,' I didn't actually mean together."

Stepping forward, he gazes at me, and one eyebrow slowly creeps up on his face. A smile curves his lips. "But you do want to."

"What? I … uh."

He leans forward, his lips hovering close to mine. I can almost feel the sparks zing between us. "Don't deny it."

He grabs my hand, opens the door and pulls me through the hallway to the bathroom, locking us both inside.

It seems empty, but I look around just in case. We're in the girls' bathroom, and I don't want anyone to notice a guy is in here. Especially not *this* guy. Hunter Bane, the chick magnet of college.

Yes, I'm easily jealous. No, I don't want to share him.

He reaches for my glasses and carefully takes them off, placing them on the sink. "Too bad you can't shower with them. I love how you think you can hide your ogling behind them."

I flush, heat spreading across my cheeks.

Suddenly, he pulls my robe, forcing me to come closer. He rips it open, drapes it off my shoulders, and lets it drop to the floor. A sly grin appears on his face as he licks his lips, gleefully gazing at me as if he's wondering what I'm going to do about it.

Oh, I'm going to do something about it.

My hands reach for his towel, and with one jerk I tear it

away from his hips. He chuckles, and then twirls me around in his arms, pecking me on the shoulder. We walk forward, still in each other's clutches, and I turn on the shower as he pushes us inside.

The hot water streaming down my body opens up my pores. It also opens up my eyes. Rivulets of water stream down his pectorals, making me gulp.

He grabs my shower gel and squirts some on his hand. Then he starts lathering me with it. He runs his callused hands over my arms, along my waist, across my belly and up along my breasts. He cups the swell of my breasts and smears the soap all over me. I don't have to look down to know he's enjoying it; I can feel him prodding my thigh.

I have trouble not gaping down at his cock. I'm inching toward touching it. Some little devil on my shoulder is telling me to just go for it, but I'm embarrassed that I even have these thoughts.

I'd normally never be so lusty and horny, but Hunter has awakened a side of me I didn't realize was in me. It's kind of scary, but freeing at the same time.

He grins when he sees my blush, and I smile.

He's not skipping an inch of skin with the soap before washing his hands under the shower and then grabbing the head and spraying the bubbles off me. Not the hot water, but knowing he's caressing me softly is what makes me feel so warm. It's like he wants to take care of me.

Our connection has become infinitely more powerful after our intimate night. I still can't get it out of my head. What I said to him last night keeps replaying in my mind. I told him I loved him, and I meant it.

I want to do this every day. I want to shower with him, let him lather me up. I want to sleep in the same bed every night. I want to press my body to his, wrap my arms around him, and never let go.

I want to be with him forever.

I know it's too soon to know, I just feel like it. I'm not ashamed of admitting that to myself. I love the way he is. The beauty that lies in his imperfection. The way he makes me feel: warm and loved. That he's made me a different person.

We both need each other. I want him to tell me, though. I want him to make me think I'm way more than I thought I was. But I don't know why he would need me.

I want to feel special. I want to be the only one who can make him feel the way I do about him. The only one who can give him what he needs. I love him. I want him to love me, too.

I just didn't hear him say it. He only said I was his.

But does that mean the same?

I bite my lip, and Hunter's brow arches up. His lips curl up into a coy smile. "What are you thinking about?"

I stop biting and look at him, feeling caught in the act. "Nothing?"

He laughs. "I can tell when you're lying. You always blush."

Of course, I can't stop my cheeks from reddening now.

"C'mon, tell me," he says, placing his hands on my hips and pulling me closer.

"Do you …. Do you love me?" I say, hesitantly.

It's quiet after that. Hunter just stares at me. The silence is deafening.

It says enough.

Averting my eyes, my heart drops into my shoes.

"I …" he stammers.

"No. Don't," I say. "I don't want you to feel forced to say it. Then it's not real."

Hunter puts a finger on my lips. "I don't feel forced. I'm just baffled. But if I say it now, you'll think it is."

"Why are you baffled? It's not weird, is it?" I ask, swallowing away the lump in my throat. Oh God. Maybe I shouldn't have said anything. This is embarrassing.

"No, of course not." He pulls me closer and puts his lips on my forehead. "I just can't imagine someone could."

I frown, confused. "But you're Hunter Bane. Everybody …"

"Everybody what? Loves me? No. They only love my attitude, my looks, or what I offer. They don't know me. They don't like my personality, they don't want to know about my problems with school. And they definitely don't know anything about my family or my past."

"And I do?"

He gazes down into my eyes with a look that could stop hearts. "A bit. At least, I hope you do enjoy my company."

I chortle. "Of course I like you. I meant about the 'past' thing."

"Right, about that … I still need to tell you something …" he clears his throat, and I suddenly feel anxious. "Remember those guys at the restaurant?"

"I don't want to remember them, but I have no choice, really."

"It's been bugging me for some time now. I didn't want to tell you this, because I was afraid you'd hate me for it. I just can't live with it anymore."

"What?" I say, chewing on my lip.

"I was there for a reason."

I knew it couldn't have been a coincidence he was there to save me.

"I was supposed to do an exchange with them," he says with a sigh.

My eyes widen. "You what?"

"They're customers of Alpha Psi. I was waiting for them to

finish their meal, and I didn't notice them leaving until I heard your scream."

I'm shaking.

"Please don't be mad," he says, grabbing my arms. "I didn't know they were going to do that. I would never have let them leave the restaurant if I had. And I refused to have anything to do with them after it happened."

"I can't believe it …" I stammer.

"Yeah, me neither. They're probably pissed as hell after what happened. It wouldn't surprise me if they got their revenge sometime soon. Especially when the boss finds out what I did to them."

Hunter lifts his finger and brushes a strand of wet hair from my face, gently caressing my cheek.

"I will never let anyone hurt you," he says. "Even if it means getting my ass whooped."

I chuckle at his comment.

"So, you're not mad?" he says.

"Maybe a little …" I say with a devilish grin and a squint. "I mean, you should have told me sooner. But I'm glad you did the right thing."

Half a smile forms on his lips, and then he pulls me closer so he can kiss me on the forehead. "Good."

Suddenly a gut-wrenching scream fills the halls.

Hunter's eyes skid through the bathroom. I'm on high alert. We're both looking at the door. My eyes widen.

Oh God.

I recognize that scream.

Evie.

CHAPTER 23
UNFORESEEN CASUALTY

Every bone in my body screams. I need to get to her. Now.

I almost want to run out naked, but Hunter holds me steady. "Put something on first," he says.

"It's Evie!" I yell.

"I know. I heard it too." He turns off the shower, while I'm already grabbing the towels.

"I have to go to her!" I throw the towel to Hunter and start rubbing my own skin fairly hard, trying to get dry as fast as possible. "I've never heard her scream like that. Something's wrong."

I barely have my robe on before I run out the door looking for her. "Evie?" I shout her name, but she doesn't respond. I look around the hallway and the notice the faint sound of her whimpers. She's in the bathroom.

My breath hitches as I run down the hallway. Rushing to her, I pull open the door and call her name again. She stops crying for a second.

"Autumn?"

When I hear her voice, I let out a sigh of relief. At least I know she can still talk. "What happened?"

Squatting, I check each of the stalls until I find her feet, and then lean up against the door. She doesn't say anything. She's completely quiet, and it makes me scared.

"Evie? Open the door," I say.

It's silent for a few seconds, but then I hear her fiddle the door and I scramble back when she opens it. Tears are rolling down her cheeks. Toilet paper is crushed between her fingers, and her face is red all over. She looks miserable.

"What's wrong?" I say, coming closer.

She blows her nose and throws the paper in the toilet. Something really, really bad has happened.

She almost never cries.

"C'mon, you can tell me," I say softly.

Trembling, she lifts her head, her eyes watery and horrified. It looks like she's seen a ghost. Or something worse.

I'm not even sure I still want to know.

But I have to be there for her. She looks terrible, and I know there's something wrong. I have to brace myself for it.

I put my hands on her knees and caress the caps, trying to soothe her.

"I-It's S-Scarlet …" she says, catching her breath. She's having trouble breathing because of all the crying.

"S-she's …. Oh God." Her voice sounds croaky.

"What?" I say, grabbing her hands.

"I have to puke."

She turns around, pulls the seat up and throws up right away. I turn to grab a few pieces of toilet paper so she can wipe her face. She sighs, barely able to keep breathing. I seriously start to wonder what happened.

"Please tell me what's wrong, I'm worried about you," I say, patting her back to calm her down.

"S-Scarlet. H-her room. D-dead."

My heart stops. My breath is caught in my throat. All light disappears in front of my eyes. I can't speak.

I just stammer. "W-what? What are you saying? Dead?"

Her eyes scream out in agony as she sinks to the floor, bawling her eyes out above the toilet she just puked in.

"G-go look," she stutters.

I turn my head toward the door. Hunter's standing there in his sweatpants. His eyes are big and his face is darkened. He heard it too.

I swallow back the bile rising up in my throat. It can't be true.

No …

I run for the door, Hunter going in front of me. We both rush to Scarlet's room. As we step inside, my blood turns frigid.

Scarlet's lying in her bed. Her arms hang down over the bed. On the floor is a syringe. Empty. Below her face is a puddle of vomit mixed with foam still partially inside her mouth. Her eyes are dark, hollow. Life has left her long ago.

The true horror of what happened sinks in, and I collapse underneath my own weight. Sinking down to the floor, I hold onto the doorframe to feel grounded. It feels as though the world has been taken away from under my feet, and I'm falling into an endless pit.

"No …" Hunter mutters, walking closer.

He turns her body gently, inspecting her eyes, her face, her limbs. He's careful, but I still can't believe he actually has the courage to touch her.

Her. The body. The corpse.

She's no longer Scarlet.

It's just an empty shell. A nothingness.

I swallow away the rising bile, and try not to think about it, but seeing her body there, lifeless, is almost too much. It's shocking. I can't believe this is really happening. She's dead.

And oh God, Evie found her.

I crawl back up.

"Where are you going?" Hunter asks me, raising his eyebrow like he's still too busy with the examination.

"I need to be there for Evie," I say, and I rush out the door, not realizing she's already halfway across the hall. "What are you doing?" I say, confused, as I see her hold the wall as support while walking forward.

She doesn't answer, but falls into my arms instead. Crying, she breaks apart. I shush her and caress her back. "It's going to be okay."

"No," she whimpers.

She holds on so tight I can barely breathe. That, and I really feel like I need to throw up, too.

"Yes, it will. You have to keep it together."

"She's dead!" she screams. "I found her, dammit. I wasn't sleeping here last night … I only came back this morning. I didn't even know she was d …" Her breath gets caught in her throat. I pat her back to make her feel better, but of course I already know it won't do any good.

I guess I'll just ignore the fact that she just spilled that she slept at some other place last night. This is not the time and place to be asking about her relationships.

"I'm sorry …" I say, trying to concentrate on her sadness.

I don't know what else to tell her. There's nothing I can say that will make this all right. Scarlet's dead. She's never coming back.

I don't know how I feel about it. I don't feel like I need to cry. All I am is shocked and horrified. That's it.

But seeing Evie like this reminds me that she had a much stronger bond with Scarlet than I previously thought. It seems as though she really lost a friend. And I feel sorry for not knowing, for not being there in her place to find out about this so she wouldn't have had to witness it on her own.

God. How she must have felt seeing Scarlet in that state. By herself. With nobody to lean on.

"This isn't good …" Hunter mumbles, picking up the syringe from the floor carefully so as not to touch the needle.

I'm still calming Evie down, so it's hard to look at what he's doing.

"Fuck …" he says.

"What?" I say.

"Drugs." He holds up the syringe for me to see, but I'm too far away to see what it means. I don't have to; I believe him if he says it's so.

"She OD'ed?"

He lets out a huge breath. "Yes and no."

"Which is it? It can't be both," I say.

His jaw tightens, and he purses his lips. Hunter just stares at me, then flicks his eyes at Evie, and then back at me. He doesn't even need to speak to let me know what he's thinking. He wants to tell me something, but he doesn't want her to hear.

"Evie …" I mutter.

She looks up, her eyes swollen and red. I don't want to hurt her. She shouldn't have to watch this. She shouldn't have been here at all. It's all my fault. If I'd been a good friend, she would be sleeping in her own bed in our room, and she never would have witnessed this.

"You should go back to our room."

"B-but …"

I squeeze her shoulder. "It's better if you're somewhere you feel safe. Make yourself a cup of tea and crawl under the blanket."

She just gazes at me, her lips pouty. She sniffs.

I smile at her to make her feel at ease. "It's okay. Hunter and I will take care of it."

"W-we can't leave her like t-this," she stammers, and she briefly glances at Hunter.

"We've got it covered," I say.

"You should rest," Hunter says.

After a few seconds of staring her down, she gives in. Nodding, she turns around and walks to our room, still holding onto the wall. This has devastated her.

Dammit.

Hunter covers Scarlet's body with a blanket, careful not to leave any traces of him touching the evidence, except the syringe, which he places on the cabinet beside her bed.

I check to see if Evie's gone into the room before turning around. Holding my arms, I brace myself for the news he's about to share.

"That wasn't just an OD," he says.

I just wait for the next blow to come.

"She couldn't have gotten this drug from us. We never, *never*, sell this."

"What is it?"

"Heroin."

Holy shit. Heroin? That drug that turns people's lives completely upside down, scarring them for life?

"Maybe one of your guys made a mistake," I say.

"They're not my guys and they didn't make a mistake," he hisses.

"But she wouldn't do that, would she?"

"No. She only used the drugs as a means to escape. It was a one- or two-time thing. Nothing big. She wasn't an addict, and trust me, I know it when I see one; she wasn't one of them."

My breath is getting more ragged by the second. "Was she experimenting or something?"

"I don't know …" he says.

"Maybe it was an accident. Maybe she took too much," I

whisper.

"No, absolutely not. She'd never take too much. She told me she had too much to live for, I remember her telling me at the party when I asked her if everything was okay. I needed to check if she wasn't taking them to … you know …"

Suicide. He doesn't want to say the word, but I know exactly what he's thinking.

"She knew the risks perfectly well," he continues. "She wouldn't do that."

I sigh, leaning against the doorframe. I still can't believe she's really dead. It's so unreal.

"Something's wrong. This isn't even our product." He points at the syringe. "We only deal in powders and pills."

He checks her body, probably to see if he can find anything else, a mark of the needle or something, I don't know. I have no clue why he's doing it. As if it's going to change anything about the situation. Scarlet is dead. It was drugs. They're dealers.

The cops will inevitably get involved. And Hunter might go to jail.

No, not might. The question is when.

"She has bruises all over her body," he says, and I'm ripped away from my thoughts.

"I thought you said she OD'ed? Bruises don't come with that, do they?"

"They can, but this isn't drug related. Look at the marks," he says, pointing at her neck.

"No thanks, I'd rather stay here if you don't mind."

"Nobody would shoot heroin straight into their neck. Plus, these are really weird marks. They go all the way around her neck, centering on her esophagus. And they're on her wrists, too," he says, holding up her arm like a doll.

God, I feel sick to my stomach.

“Stop messing with her, please,” I say, holding my hand in front of my mouth. “You’re making me want to throw up.”

“Sorry,” he says. “But that’s the least of my worries right now. This should be a concern to everyone.”

“Why?”

“Because this wasn’t accidental. She was drugged with a dose far beyond normal.”

“Are you saying …” I can’t speak. My vocal cords are clamped shut.

“Someone forced his hand on her. It killed her.”

I shake my head. No. I can’t believe this. This can’t be true. Someone couldn’t have murdered her.

CHAPTER 24
WITH BAD COMES GOOD

I'm staring at the carpet, oblivious to the people passing me. My mind is astray, memories of that day repeating over and over in my head. Scarlet's contorted face. Her limp body. The puddle of goo drizzling from her mouth. The syringe. It's just too much to deal with.

And I feel bad for feeling only half as much as all the other people who are here. I don't even know what to feel.

Her friends are consoling each other, crying on each other's shoulders. One of them is staring at a photograph standing on a pretty decorated cabinet, uttering words I can't hear from so far away. I don't even want to hear them.

As if talking to her photograph is going to make her magically come alive. As if it makes up for what some bastard did to her.

Misery. That's all this room is.

I never imagined the dorm lounge could turn into the perfect room for a funeral reception.

It's morbid, really. Knowing what went on here. Parties, drugs, probably some fucking, too. This couch I'm sitting on disgusts me, but I have nowhere else to go. Evie's not here. She couldn't take it. She really got close to Scarlet, which I didn't see before. All those times they were studying must've opened her eyes.

And now it's too late.

Well, at least she liked the girl. I don't really know what to do, and every second I wonder what I'm doing here. I feel guilty for not crying, but I just can't. I don't feel anything. Just emptiness, hollowness.

Terror.

It sucks the life out of me like a light bulb blowing up, darkening the room. Too many horrific things are happening all at once, and they're all connected. It's terrifying the shit out of me.

Suddenly, I feel the need to run out and never look back. But it would be silly to do that. I have to be here. Somehow it feels like an obligation, my duty.

But spending one more minute on this couch will kill me.

Where else can I go? I don't want to stand alone, looking like a goofball. It's too crowded, and I feel uncomfortable just looking for an empty spot.

And I certainly don't want to stand next to Brody.

He's been here forever. Attended the funeral and everything. Most students weren't allowed on the premises, but he was her boyfriend, so they made an exception for him. I'm surprised they even knew.

Still, it irks me to look at him. The expression on his face has been completely blank the entire day. So bland, so emotionless. I haven't seen him cry. Not even once. He's just standing there in his corner, staring at the carpet just like me. It's like he doesn't feel anything.

Or he's just too shocked to register it all.

When he looks at me, I turn my head, hoping he won't

come my way. I don't want to talk to him right now. I'm still chicken-shit, sometimes. I wouldn't know what to say to him anyway. I don't want to be rude, but nothing I said would make her come back to life, so why bother? And it's not like I can help him with his grief. No one can.

I look around, desperate to get out of here, but knowing I can't. I could really use Hunter now to back me up and help me get through this day, but I haven't seen him since yesterday. Not since it happened.

He stormed out yesterday, cursing under his breath, and told me he had to talk to Jaret. I figured it had something to do with the suspicion of murder, but to me it just sounded so far-fetched. I'm not sure I can trust his crime-investigation skills. I think we should wait for the real police investigation to be over before drawing conclusions, but Hunter just went ahead and started a whole operation himself, I think. I have no idea what he's doing, but I know it's nothing good. The fact alone that he immediately ran away after finding her bothers me the most.

I mean, where the hell is he? What is he doing? Why hasn't he said anything? I'd expect at least a text message, but he couldn't even be bothered to let me know everything was all right.

I'm getting pissed just thinking about it. What the fuck could be so important that he couldn't wait one freaking day just to support his girlfriend during a freaking funeral reception?

I snort. Girlfriend. I let the word fly through my mind so often, and yet I've never even heard it come out of his mouth. Am I even his girlfriend? Everyone calls me that, except him, which is what matters the most.

God, what a time to think about these things.

I clear my throat and walk out of the room. I need to get out of here, fast.

♥♥♥

Stepping into my room, I notice Evie sitting there on her bed, staring at the wall. She looks up at me before sighing and flicking her eyes back so she can continue gazing at the spot on the wall.

I place my purse on the cabinet and walk over to her. Biting my lip, I sit down next to her and reach for her hand. When I grab it, she twitches, but doesn't pull back. She turns her head and looks at me with tears in her eyes. I smile, trying to console her.

She squeezes my hand. "Thanks."

"I'm here for you if you need me," I say.

"I'm okay," she nods, wiping away the single tear rolling down her cheek. "I feel horrible."

"Understandable, considering what happened."

"No, not about that. I couldn't go to the funeral. I just couldn't, and it makes me a horrible person."

"No, it doesn't." I put my other hand on top of hers too now. "Don't say that about yourself. You guys were friends. Everyone understands."

She snorts. "Yeah, well I sure as hell don't. I mean, I was finally feeling better, having another friend, feeling happy about who I am, finding another girl." She sniffs. "Not that the last part went anywhere."

"What do you mean?"

"Ah … you know, not really into each other. It was fun, but that was it."

"Oh …" I say. I don't really know what else to say.

"Well anyway, don't think you're horrible. If anyone's horrible around here, it's me."

She chuckles. "What did you do now?"

"Nothing! I just couldn't stay at that damn funeral

reception. All I could think of was what happened, Hunter and what he's doing now, and then I saw Brody and I freaked out. Like big time."

She laughs. "Nothing new to me. You're always out of it."

"Yeah, well, I'm glad I'm out of there. I'm really not good at those things."

"Who is?" she says, and then she sighs.

It's quiet for a few minutes, and we're both just sighing, trying to make sense of it all.

"Thank you for helping me," she says. "I really appreciate you sticking by me."

She leans her head on my shoulder and puffs. "And Hunter, of course."

I giggle. "Hunter?" I can't believe she even mentioned him and a 'thank you' in the same sentence.

"Yeah, he's a good guy."

"Oh, is he now?" I chuckle a little.

She pokes me in the side. "Don't laugh. I mean it. He isn't half as bad as I thought. Especially when he defended us back at the party."

"So are you telling me you actually like him now?"

"Maybe. I'm not saying 'like.' I mean, the whole drugs debacle is still irking me, but if you can deal with it, then I should be able to as well." She looks up at me and smiles.

I smile back. I'm happy she can accept him for who he is. Or at least accept the fact that I like him and that I want to be with him. I don't want to ruin the moment by telling her I haven't seen him all day, and that it's making me angry. I'd rather have this instead.

"I'm just glad he can make you happy," she says, and she laces her fingers through mine. "I'm happy for you two."

"Thank you," I say, putting my arm around her and hugging her. "It means a lot that you say that."

"I can't breathe," she whispers, while I squeeze her tight.

"Sorry," I say, laughing a bit and releasing her from my grip.

"It just makes me feel so much better knowing you're fine with Hunter and me being in a relationship."

"Hmm, so you're in a 'relationship' now?" She makes quotation marks with her fingers. At first my heart drops into my shoes. Her teasing makes me think she's still not okay with it.

But then she bumps her shoulder against mine and says, "Good on you, girl."

"I don't know, I don't even know what to call what we have. We just … After all those times we got together … it just happened."

"Oh. My. God." Her eyes grow big. "You had sex?"

I blush, feeling scrutinized. That, and I don't want her to feel bad. I know how she feels about me.

"This is for real? You? Autumn Blakewood? You had sex?" she squeals. "How was it?"

Wow. I did not expect her to react the way she did. Maybe she really is over it.

"It was … nice."

"Nice my ass. It must've been amazing!"

"I don't know. I never did it before, so I have nothing to compare it with. But it was … good." I turn red as a beet again, just thinking about what I did with Hunter. Or rather, what he did with me.

"God, I can't believe it," Evie says, slapping her own forehead. "I'm away for like one week, and you've already broken most of your nerd records."

I gasp. "What? You're making it sound like I'm some kind of virginal geeky holy Mary."

"You are."

She laughs and starts tickling me, making me squirm. She hasn't been this perky in ages, and I'll gladly let her make me beg for mercy while she tickles me to death. It takes us a few minutes to stop laughing and giggling.

"So … what do we do from here?" I say after a while.

"Well," she says, stretching her arms. "You seem to have a spare bed in your room, and I don't see anyone else's stuff lying around, so … mind if I bunk with you again?"

"Yes! Of course you can sleep here. Actually, no, I demand you bunk here."

She punches me in the shoulder, and I drop down onto the bed. She drops down with me, lying next to me, and puts her arm around me like she used to.

"I don't want anything to change, though," she says, and she lifts her head. "Is that okay? Can I still be the old me? Even after …"

"Shut up. You're Evie. You're always Evie. And you're always my best friend, no matter what."

She smiles, and I grab her hand to show her that I still care. I do. I don't care about what happened between us. I want things to be okay. I want my best friend back.

And now I have her back. On a day that was supposed to be miserable, gloomy, and sad, I somehow managed to get Evie back on my side. I should feel bad about being happy on a day like this, but I'm not. Good things can come on bad days, and I don't feel sorry for feeling happy.

I only wish things could stay like this forever. But I've learned from the past that bad things are always bound to happen, it's only a matter of time.

CHAPTER 25
INTO THE UNDERGROUND

Someone knocks on our door, and we both shoot up from the bed. Jaret steps in, his face dark and concerned. "Can I talk to you for a sec?" He signals me.

I look at Evie, and she nods.

"Uh … Sure," I say, and I get up from the bed. I glance at her one last time, feeling a bit anxious because Jaret looks like he has some bad news. Then I step outside with him.

"Hunter's having some … problems right now. I'm not sure if I should be the one to say this, but I don't want to lead you on either," he says.

"What happened to him?"

He comes closer. "Look, I can't really tell you, because my life is on the line."

"Okay …" I swallow. My throat suddenly feels raw and hot.

"I've been helping Hunter, but only because he asked me to. I didn't think it'd get this bad."

"What are you trying to tell me?"

"Look, they forced him to do something, because they

found out we're looking for the boss."

My eyes widen. Oh no. Oh God, no.

"What's going on? Where is he?" I say.

"Shhh!" he says, putting his finger on his lips. "Don't shout so much. Look, I really can't tell you a lot. I'm sorry. I don't want to get in trouble. If I'd known it'd get this tough, I would never have agreed," he sighs, rubbing his hands over his head like he's in some deep shit, just like Hunter.

Oh God. Where are they keeping him? What did they do to him?

"Is it bad?" I ask.

"No … Yes. No, he's done this before. It's what they always ask us newbies to do. It's just that it's never been this …" he swallows those last words.

"What am I supposed to do with this information if I don't know where he is? How can I find him?" I say.

Jaret rummages in his pocket and takes out two paper tickets. "Here. Take this. I got them from one of the distributors. Brody."

"Brody?" I scream. So Brody is a pawn in this as well?

Jaret puts his hand over my mouth.

"He probably got them from the courier. I had to give these to you, so my best guess is that he got the same order."

"You want to give these to me? What do I have to do with this?"

"I don't know, I'm just following orders, trying to get their trust back," Jaret says with his eyebrows raised.

I frown, while he presses the tickets firmly into my hand. "Don't look at them until you're in your room, and I'm gone."

He gazes at me one more time with a stern look on his face before turning around and walking away as if nothing ever happened.

Baffled, I go back inside and close the door behind me.

The scrunched-up tickets in my hand are the only thing I'm aware of right now.

I can't believe what just happened. Jaret basically told me Hunter's been doing what he's doing right now for a long time already, and it's all because of *them*. The frat club. Only this time … it's way, way worse. They even want me to see it.

Whatever it is, I need to find out and get him out of there.

Dammit, if only he hadn't gone after that boss, he'd be out of trouble now. Why in hell's name is he putting so much at risk?

"What you got?" Evie asks.

I'm startled, pulled out of my thoughts.

Unwrapping the paper, I walk toward her and sit down on the bed. We both stare at the tickets. They're entry passes into some sort of event tonight. Big fat letters exclaim the words 'Hunter,' 'V.S.,' and 'Killer.'

Chills run down my spine reading those last few letters.

It freaks me out to an impossible level.

"What the …"

"He's in trouble. Big time."

"Jaret gave these to you?"

"Yeah." There are two of them. "I guess he wants me to take you?"

"I guess …"

"Please, don't make me go alone." I put up my puppy-dog eyes.

She caves, laughing. "Oh, all right. How can I *not* go when you look at me like that?"

Her laugh doesn't make me feel any better. This whole thing is making me feel sick to my stomach.

I hope Hunter is all right.

♥♥♥

8 p.m.

We're walking through the city, our legs shaking from the cold. It's dark and scary outside. Lampposts barely light the streets, and it's grown increasingly deserted the last couple of streets. Cars don't come here. Nobody comes here. This is a place filled with abandoned warehouses.

And I have no idea what the fuck Evie and I are doing here.

I wish I'd never accepted those tickets.

Part of me wants to run back to campus and just wait it out, but my gut is telling me to get over my fear. I need to find Hunter and help him. I know he's in danger. I can feel it. If I run now, there's no way I can save him.

"I don't like this one bit …" Evie mutters.

Her teeth chatter, and she clamps onto her coat for warmth. I'm shivering, but I don't want to admit I'm scared to death. I don't want her to be afraid, and if I am, so will she be. I need to be the strong one now.

"Me neither, but we have to," I say.

"Remind me again why?"

"To find Hunter. For me. He's in danger."

"What?"

"Yeah, I just have this feeling in my gut that something is wrong."

"Oh … well, I hope he's okay, but I'm more worried about you."

"I've got you with me. I won't be in danger." I wink, and she smiles, trying to relax a little.

We cross the street, checking the signs for the way to go. It should be right around where we are now, although I still have no idea what I'm looking for.

"This is it," I say, as we walk into an alley.

"I don't see anything," she whispers, tugging my coat.

"There!" I point at the door, and drag her with me.

It says 'NO ENTRY,' but when I pull the door, it opens right away.

"You sure this is the place?" she asks, her voice trembling.

"Yes."

We both look at each other and gulp away our fears. Not that it helps one bit.

There's a staircase leading down into a basement. One light is dangling from the ceiling. Spider nests cover the walls. Scary shit.

"Ew … nasty," Evie says, as we walk through.

We go to the end where there's another door. I can hear loud noises coming from behind it. I wonder what the heck is going on down there.

"You ready?"

She nods, swallowing again.

When I open the door, I get the urge to close my eyes in case something comes flying my way, but there is only one person standing behind it. There's a man, at least six foot tall, with tattoos all over his arms and face, and he's right in front of me. His arms are folded, and he smells like hasn't bathed in years. On his shirt are the words 'Alpha Psi.'

"Tickets," he says gruffly.

Loud cheering and yelling comes from behind him. It sounds like there are at least a couple hundred people in this place. I peek over his shoulder, wondering what's up there. He blocks my view.

"Tickets," he snarls.

"Uh, yeah," I say, fishing them out of my pocket.

He snatches them from my hand, his fingernails scratching my skin. Dang, that hurts. He brings the tickets so close to his face, I swear I think he's sniffing them.

Inspecting them, his eyes sometimes flick to me, then to Evie, and then back to the papers in his hands. He squints, grumbling.

Shit.

Unexpectedly, he gives them back. "You can pass."

For a moment I just stand there, baffled, while he moves to the side.

"Well?" he says, his voice growing impatient.

"Thanks!" I grab Evie by the coat and drag her with me.

We enter what looks like a giant warehouse, but there are rows and rows of bleachers forming a circle around the center. In the middle of it all is a cage.

We're on a lowered part of the warehouse, so I can only see the top of the bars. It echoes with screams and shouts, people who are cheering for something. Or someone.

It gives me the chills just listening to their chants.

Killer, Killer
Make him be the spiller
The floor will flood
With all of his blood
Killer, Killer

I swallow. The horror that fills my heart unsettles me. Everything about this screams danger. Still, I press on.

Evie and I hold hands as we walk to one of the bleachers. Angry men with tattoos and piercings glare us down. Evie squeezes my hand. We slip past them, up the bleachers. There are a couple of spots left in the middle, so I set my gaze on those and make my way toward them, ignoring everything and everyone around me.

Groans and thuds are coming from the center of the room,

the cage, and I recognize the sounds to be human. The audience cries out in enthusiasm.

Shivers run down my spine hearing them roar at the sound of someone's bones cracking.

I close my eyes as we sit down. Sweat drops roll down my shirt. My fingers are tingly, and I'm not sure if it's because Evie's squeezing the life out of them, or if it's because I'm going to faint.

"Can you look?" I ask.

"Why? You have eyes," she scoffs.

Neither of us are remotely interested in watching, but I want to know what's going on.

"Please? I'm scared."

She sighs. "Fine."

It's quiet for too long, so I ask, "What do you see?"

"Oh. My. God."

"What?" I say.

"You have to see this for yourself." She lets go of my clammy hand.

I feel left in the dark. I know I have to open my eyes eventually, but I'm scared of what I'll see.

Breathing out slowly, I gather the courage to look.

And what I see shocks me so much, I think my heart temporarily stops beating.

The guy in the cage getting beaten to a pulp is none other than Hunter Bane.

CHAPTER 26
BRAWL OR DIE

I stare in complete and utter abhorrence at the cage in the center of the warehouse. Hunter is going all out in a fight with a guy twice his size.

They're punching, jabbing, thrusting their whole bodies at each other as much as possible. Every second a quick jab is thrown out. I can't even follow their movements, they're so fast. They're like two raging bulls storming at each other, continuously beating each other up.

So this is what Hunter has been doing all this time. Each time he came to my room all busted up, he'd been in a fight just like this. In a cage, beating up his opponents until they passed out.

I'm trembling in my seat, trying to make sense of it all.

Evie's equally as terrified as I am; she hasn't spoken since we both saw Hunter fighting.

Is this what they make him do? Fight people for money?

And how long has he been doing this? Hours? Days? Has he been locked up in here ever since he left after Scarlet's death?

I can't believe he would let them do this to him. That he'd

agree to something this horrible.

It's hard to watch.

Hunter's nose is bleeding, his jaw is purple, and his eye is swollen. It looks like he's already taken quite a beating.

He wipes his nose with the back of his hand, which from a distance looks covered in bruises. The look in his eyes is bloodthirsty, murderous. Clenching his jaw, he runs toward his opponent and rams him down with brute force.

The guy flops down on the hard concrete ground, and I think I hear something crack. The audience goes 'ooh,' and I wince when the guy places his hands on his ribs, his face contorting with pain.

Hunter prowls toward him with a smug smile on his face. Grabbing the hem of the guy's shirt, he lifts part of his torso up into the air, and raises his fist. He mouths something, but nobody can hear it. Then he punches the guy straight in the face.

Multiple times.

My eyes widen. I'm shocked.

Hunter beats the guy's face to a pulp and doesn't let go until he's fainted, his body limp in Hunter's hands.

I'm disgusted.

The crowd bursts out into cheers, while I want to throw up in a bucket. I can barely hold down my dinner.

"It's a win for the Hunter!" A big tattooed guy dangles a key between his fingers and opens a barred door right behind the fainted guy. Hunter backs away, spitting out some blood, and goes back to his side of the cage. Clinging onto the bars, he gazes at the crowd, peering at each and every one of them.

When his tongue dips out of his mouth, and he licks his lips, I can't help but feel hot.

And then he roars. The crowd goes mad.

"Who's the motherfucking Hunter?" he yells.

"You are!" the crowd chants.

Apparently they've found a new favorite.

I can't blame them. He's my favorite too.

Although I don't want to admit it, because this is so fucking bad I can't even describe it, he looks goddamn sexy as hell in that cage. His red sweatpants hang low on his hips, his V-line clearly showing. He's half-naked. His abs are bulging as he flexes his taut shoulders, and drops of sweat roll down his chest.

A smug smile appears on his face as one of his fans, a girl with a pink blouse and boobs the size of melons, hands him a bottle of water. She squeals when he snatches it from her hand and throws the contents over his head and body.

I could enjoy seeing that, if I were to forget for even one second that he's actually fighting people for money. Damn.

The big guy whistles, alerting two other guys to come pick up the body and drag him out, while the guy with the keys stares Hunter down. He blocks the exit, his hands hovering over his hips. In his pocket there's a glinting object. A knife.

I gasp.

And then Hunter looks my way.

I freeze, my breath faltering. His eyes narrow as he looks at my face, and then they widen as he realizes it's me.

I bite my lip; his jaw drops.

No. I don't want him to know that I'm here. That I'm watching him do this fucked-up shit.

But now it's too late.

Another guy enters the cage, this one much bulkier than the previous. He bellows, slapping his own chest like a gorilla. The guy with the keys locks the door again, trapping Hunter inside.

Hunter barely takes his eyes off me.

But I can't take my eyes off the guy who just came into the cage.

My heart is beating in my throat. I don't think I'm

breathing.

It's the same guy that once tried to rape me on the street.

Those tattoos, I'd recognize them anywhere. It's him. It's really him.

Now I understand what he meant when he said that he'd meet Hunter in the arena. This is the arena. This is his rematch. A fight for revenge.

Fuck.

The guy approaches Hunter from behind, and I watch in horror as he drags a distracted Hunter away from the bars and pounds him right in the back. Hunter arches his back, the blow too much for him to take, and blood shoots from his mouth.

Hunter immediately hits the guy in the balls with a backward kick, and releases himself from his grip. He pants, turning to his opponent, and barely manages to stand up straight. He winces, the pain clearly showing on his face.

"I'm going to kill you!" the guy yells in his face.

Cracking his knuckles, Hunter waits until the guy comes at him, while I bite my nails in frustration and fear. Suddenly I notice the guy has a knife in his back pocket.

I panic.

"Hunter!" I scream. "Knife!"

Hunter turns his head toward me, his eyes filled with primal despair as he responds to my cry. Temporarily distracted, he doesn't see the jab coming straight for his face. It's my fault.

His body can't absorb the blow, and he's hit so hard that he flies across the cage. I hold my breath as I see him crash into the bars of the cage. His eyes show an expression of pure agony.

Tears well up in my eyes. I can't watch this. I can't be here. I'm only hurting him. I can't watch him do this to himself. To be the victim of someone else's frenzy.

I stand up and run all the way to the end of the bleachers.

"Hey!" Evie screams, coming after me. "Wait up!"

I run through the crowd toward the door as Evie catches up to me.

"Where are you going?" she says.

"This is horrible, I can't watch him getting beaten to a pulp."

She grabs my hand before I walk away. "I'm going with you."

We pass the guard near the door, who flashes us a look, and then we go out through the door. The noises behind us are still too much to take, so we go all the way up the stairs until we're outside on the streets again. I can finally breathe again.

"Damn, that was scary," Evie says. "What the fuck is going on? Why did you get tickets for this? Is Hunter in some kind of underground fight club or something? Those guys all wore the same shirt, something with Alpha Psi on it. What the fuck does it mean?"

I stare at her, panting. She squints.

"You've not been telling me the entire story, have you?"

"I didn't know it was this bad," I say. "Yes, he's in a frat club. An illegal one. And they deal drugs and fight with people."

"What?" she snaps. "Deal drugs? Are you fucking kidding me?"

"I wish I was, but it's the truth. Hunter's involved in something way beyond normal."

"No shit. And you knew about this?"

"Partially …" I say.

She taps her foot on the floor. "Well, I don't expect you to share everything, but the least you could've told me was that your boyfriend is a freaking criminal!"

"He's not. He's doing this for his brother, Jessie."

"His brother? What does that have to do with any of this?"

I sigh. "It's hard to explain right now. There's a lot more to it. Can you just trust me? I promise I'll tell you when this is all over."

She sighs, frowning. "Fine. As long as we go home right now."

I bite my lip. There's nothing more that I want right now than to go home and forget all about this, but something inside me wants to go back to Hunter, too. I want to talk to him. No, I need to. I need to know why he's doing this, and why he never told me about the arena. This is about more than just the money, it has to be. There's no way he'd be looking for the boss of Alpha Psi, putting his own life at risk, just for money. There must be something I'm missing.

"I want to talk to him," I say.

"Oh fuck no, you're not being serious, are you?" Evie says.

"I am. Look, you just go on ahead."

"What? I can't let you go in there by yourself. Nu uh, no way."

"Please. I need to talk to him. I don't want to drag you any more into this than I already have."

"It's dangerous down there."

"That's why I'm saying you have to go. Go to the dorm. Let me handle this."

"No."

"Evie! Please," I beg.

She rubs her face with her hand, groaning. "Are you sure about this?"

"Yes, I need to do this."

It's quiet for a few seconds before she says, "Okay. But you have to promise me you'll come back."

"I will."

"No, you'll be in perfect health, no scratch on you. I don't want to see you get hurt."

"I promise, Evie, I'll look out for myself," I smile.

She hesitantly smiles back. "Okay. See you back at

campus."

She turns around, still looking back at me over her shoulder, while I open the door and go back inside. Back down the stairs of hell.

CHAPTER 27
TRUTH UNFOLDS

I take one huge breath before I storm into the building again. I hold up my ticket for the guard to see, in case he doesn't remember me storming out two minutes ago. He doesn't even groan this time, and I pass him without an effort. I guess they're used to fiery types here.

I walk through the crowd again, but instead of going toward the bleachers, I go straight for the cage.

I easily reach the center, and cling onto the bars as I peer inside. No one stops me. Apparently, nobody cares.

I look inside and see the man who tried to rape me lying lifelessly on the floor, his body limp. I swallow away the fear I had of Hunter going down this time. I look up and see him standing there, buckled over, holding his own head. Blood drips from his mouth. He's still breathing, but barely.

"Hunter," I yell.

In an instant he turns around and gazes at me with furor. Fear settles in his eyes the moment he realizes it's me.

He immediately steps toward me and grabs my hand. "Fuck," is the first thing he says. "I can't believe you came here."

"I can't either. What the hell are you doing? Is this just for the money?"

I jerk my hand loose.

"No, wait, let me explain," he says. He reaches for my hand, but I step back. I can't handle his touch right now.

"Why are you doing this? How could you …" I say.

"They found out Jaret and I were looking for the boss. They put me in here as a punishment, so I could regain his trust."

"Why would you agree to that?" I yell, tears welling up in my eyes. "You just beat people up in here, and you think that's okay?"

"I need to do this. There's no other way. Besides, I can't get out, they locked me in here."

"Why in the hell would you let them do this to you?"

His face grows dark, full of regret, but also like he just made a pledge or something.

"There's no other way to save my brother. I need their trust, so I can finish this." He leans forward, putting his head through the bars. "Listen to me. I never wanted you to see this, but you have to go, right now."

"Why?"

"Because it's fucking dangerous in here. And now I finally understand why they got you in here. They're testing me by using you."

I gasp.

"Where did you get the tickets?" he asks.

I frown. "What does that have to do with any of this?"

"It's important. I wouldn't ask if it wasn't. C'mon!"

"Jaret gave them to me. He said he got them from Brody."

"Fuck!" Hunter slams his hand against the bars. "This is really bad."

"Brody just helped me understand what the hell it is you're doing here."

"No! Don't you see? He gave you those tickets so he could use you against me."

"What? But he—"

"He's not who you think he is!" Hunter yells. "He wants to have power over me, and he's using you to do it. You have to get away from here as fast as you can. You're in danger. I'm the one they're after. I don't want you to get hurt."

"What are you talking about?"

"Jaret and I found out who the courier was."

Sighing, I close my eyes and cross my arms. All I want is to leave here as fast as I can. I wanted to give him a chance to explain himself, but all he's done is made it worse. He's still talking about 'finding the boss.'

"Listen!" he yells, because I've turned my head away from him. "The courier was Scarlet."

My jaw drops. "What? Are you sure?"

"Yes, I'm sure. She was diverting our attention every time. Her buying drugs from us was just a diversion to make us think nobody knew who the courier was."

"But she's dead!" I scream, unable to hold back the tears now.

"Time for the next round, bud. Stop chatting up your girlfriend," the guy with the keys says, chewing some gum.

It's all just a fucking show to them. Hunter is bleeding so they can have some fun. All for the money.

This is sick.

"Yes, she's dead. That's exactly why I'm telling you you're in danger. You have to go. Now," Hunter whispers, his eyes flicking back and forth between me and the guy with the keys.

"Time's up," the guy says, and he opens the cage doors and lets another fighter in.

I gulp.

"Go. Home. Now!" Hunter says, clinging to the bars for as long as he can before he's dragged back into a fight.

Shaking my head, I back away from the cage slowly. I can't believe this. This isn't happening. Scarlet was the courier? She was the one delivering the drugs to the distributors? She was the one in direct contact with the boss?

She died.

"And whatever you do, do not go to Brody. Do you hear me? Don't go to him!" Hunter yells. "Promise me! Do *not* go to him. I don't want you to get hurt. I can't get out of here. Please, don't put yourself in danger."

I'm not listening anymore. My brain feels like it's going to explode.

Brody. He was a distributor. He said he was. Jaret said Brody gave him the tickets.

No, this can't be.

Maybe Brody knew she was going to die. Maybe Brody is something more than he claims to be.

He *will* explain this.

♥♥♥

I bolt through the dorm, racing up the flight of stairs until I reach Brody's room. I don't even bother to knock on his door.

"Brody, we need to talk."

He's sitting at his desk, and the moment I storm inside, he casually turns around. On his face is a relaxed smile, and he sways a pen back and forth between his fingers like everything's normal. Well, this is anything but normal.

"Well, hi to you too. Did you enjoy the show?"

"What the hell is wrong with you?"

He chuckles. "Wow, you seem happy."

"Time to talk," I snap.

"About what?"

I slam the door shut behind me. "I know you're in the frat house. You told me you're a distributor."

"So? That's nothing new."

"You knew Scarlet took an overdose. She was the courier."

His eyes narrow. "How do you know about this?"

"It doesn't matter." I pace up and down his room. "The point is, I need to know what the deal is with you and this entire Alpha Psi club. You guys are bad. You forced Hunter to fight."

"And your point is?"

"What the fuck is wrong with you for thinking this is okay?"

He stands up from his chair, his demeanor suddenly changing into something much, much darker. Something creepily scary.

"He had to be punished," he says with a strong voice.

"Just like Scarlet? Did she have to be punished, too?"

He prowls forward, the pen dropping to the floor.

I inch back, swallowing. "She was poisoned. Murdered. And you know it."

Brody stops in his tracks, carefully assessing me from a distance. "Yes."

I find it hard not to breathe. I was right all along.

He was the one behind it all.

"She was a threat. She wanted to expose me for who I am. Of course I don't want that to happen. There's a lot at stake here." He leans forward and picks up the pen. "Do you know what I've been through? Do you know how much I've sacrificed to get this business off the ground? How much I've suffered to finally be able to afford things?"

"Was it worth it?" I snap.

Brody squints and sighs. "Damn right it was. After our

fight, Scarlet probably realized how advanced this whole operation was. She wanted out. I didn't let her, yada, yada, I killed her. You know the drill." He flicks his fingers like he just told a simple story.

I'm frozen in place, mortified.

"You killed her … You … You're the—"

"The boss. Yes." He balls his fists. "Unfortunately, your fucking boyfriend had to go ruin it all by pursuing me. I still have no idea how he managed to find out she was the courier, but it doesn't matter. He's locked up now, and he'll be dead before the end of the night."

"No …" I gasp.

"Yes," he says, chuckling. "I was hoping he'd keep you out of this, but now he's left me with no choice but to do the same to you."

He clenches the pen in his fist, pointing it toward me. "You see, I'd do anything to keep my business going. It's my life. There is nothing more important."

Oh no. Oh God no.

This can't be happening.

I don't want to die.

I step back as far as I can, but Brody's right in front of me, blocking the only exit out of this goddamn room. My fingers curl around the edge of a cabinet, trying to get as far away from him as possible.

I should've known. Dammit, I should've seen this coming!

Hunter was right. He was always right.

"Don't do this, Brody," I stammer.

"What? Kill you? Autumn, you've left me no choice. You should've just stayed out of this. Now it's too late."

He lurches forward.

I scream. My body twists in a way I didn't expect to be possible. The pen barely shoots past my waist. Brody has me by the shoulder, his fingernails digging into my skin. I can feel the blood flowing.

I scream as loud as I can, grabbing a hold of his arm to keep him from stabbing me. It's my strength against his. His deadly eyes are gazing into mine, almost searing their way into my soul.

He moves his hand toward my neck and starts squeezing, hard.

I'm coughing, choking on my own breath. Burning pain follows. My esophagus is being crushed by his hands. I fight to untangle his fingers from my throat, but he keeps strangling me. I'm trying to gasp for air, but nothing comes in. Life is slipping away from me. I can't breathe, I can't breathe. I don't want to die.

The door slams open.

Brody shifts his hand, holding the pen like a knife. He tries to strike me with it, but I avoid it by arching my back. My eyes can only focus on avoiding the pen. I don't know what's happening.

Someone comes in and grabs Brody by the shoulders, dragging him away.

Panting, I buckle over and suck in the air that was pulled from my lungs. I'm gasping for air, trying to get as much in as possible.

And then I see who it is that saved me.

"Don't you fucking lay a hand on her, you motherfucker!" Hunter yells.

He grabs Brody by the shirt and wraps his other hand around Brody's wrist. He turns Brody's arm until he squeals, forcing him to drop the pen he tried to stab Hunter with, too.

"I fucking knew it," Hunter says. "You were behind it all along."

"Damn right I was." Brody spits in his face.

Hunter balls his fist, pulls it back, and then punches Brody in the face so hard he flies through the room. Landing on the floor, he groans, spitting up blood and a couple of teeth.

Hunter picks him up and puts him on his chair.

"Hand me those ties," he growls, glancing at me.

I clamber up to the bed, open the cabinet, and grasp a few ties. I struggle to get to Hunter.

"Tie them together," he says, still holding down Brody so he doesn't move from the chair.

My breath is still faltering, but I somehow manage to tie some knots, and hand the long line over to Hunter. He starts wrapping it around Brody, strapping him to the chair.

When the final knot is tightened, Brody is incapable of moving.

"Are you okay?" Hunter asks me, briefly placing his hand on my upper arm.

I sigh. "Yeah." And then I smile. He visibly relaxes.

My gaze drifts back to the murderous old friend sitting on the chair. "Why …" I stammer, still catching my breath.

Brody only groans.

"Why did you do all of this?" I say, looking up at him.

He chuckles, coughing up blood. "Growing up in poverty isn't easy. You should know that. I grabbed a chance at fortune."

"Money? Is that it?"

Brody shrugs, averting his eyes.

I can't believe it's true. Did he do all of this just for the money? Start up a drug gang, a frat club, just for the money? He killed Scarlet just so he could keep his money?

This is so messed up, I can't even begin to describe it.

Suddenly I hear loud sirens screeching outside.

I look up at Hunter, who immediately walks toward the window and peers outside. "Finally."

"What? Are those the cops?" I say, rubbing my neck because it still feels sore.

He nods, then turns around and leans against the window. His wounds from the arena are still fresh, and he looks like a complete mess. Blood is all over his face, both his eyes are black, and he has bruises all over his ripped muscles.

"Fuck," he mutters. "I'm glad I came here in time. Lucky I could get ahold of those damned keys to open the cage myself and slip out."

I gulp. Hunter went through all that trouble to free himself. He came to my rescue. I put myself in danger, knowing what he said about avoiding Brody, and still I came here. Words can't describe how grateful and lucky I feel to be saved by Hunter.

"Thank you," I say softly.

"Don't thank me yet."

"What do you mean?"

He looks up at me, and then his eyes flick to the door.

A couple of cops storm into the room, and their gazes flick from Hunter, to me, to Brody.

"Agent Williams." The chief cop holds up his badge. "Is this him?" he asks.

"Yep," Hunter says. "Like I promised."

"Where are the goods? I need proof," Agent Williams says, and he starts untying Brody.

"I'd be careful with that motherfucker if I were you. He just tried to stab us with a pen," Hunter says.

"Thanks, my partners here will make sure he doesn't move," Agent William says, as he cuffs Brody.

"You have nothing on me," Brody says.

"Oh no?" Hunter lifts an eyebrow, and then directs his attention toward Agent Williams. "Check the bottom of the drawer. Especially the screws."

Hunter steps forward as I gape in confusion. "How did the cops get here so fast?" I ask.

"I already alerted them back at the arena, once I got hold of a cell phone."

"You were right," Agent Williams says, holding up a piece of wood. "There's a double bottom." Then he carefully takes out packets of powder, pills, and needles.

Agent Williams instructs the other cops to take Brody away, while another one starts plowing through the room. Williams himself walks up to Hunter. "Well, since you upheld your agreement, I'll make sure we do the same."

Hunter's lips curve up into a smile. Agent Williams holds out his hand. Hunter shakes it. "Thanks."

"What agreement?" I say.

"The one where they reduce Jessie's sentence to a week."

"What?" I say, gaping at him.

"I'll fill in the paperwork tomorrow. You can come pick him up then," Agent Williams says. "Now, we have to clear the room, so please, if you will." He points at the door, and Hunter escorts me out.

When the door closes behind us, I feel like I just closed off a part of my life I can never, ever return to.

CHAPTER 28
EXPLANATIONS

"It's true," Hunter says. We walk to his room in complete silence. My throat feels thick, and I can barely swallow. So much information is being processed in my brain right now.

While I sit down on his bed, Hunter closes the door behind us, and he grabs a water bottle to hold against his face. The bleeding has stopped, and he's wiped away most of it.

"My brother got himself involved in this crappy frat house so he could pay my college funds," he says.

"Yeah," I say, acknowledging I already knew that.

"Well, the Feds wanted to catch the damn bastard behind it all. I made a deal with them. I'd lead them to the boss of the entire operation, if they'd reduce Jessie's sentence so I could bail him out and take him home."

My jaw drops, and I can only stare at Hunter. I'm completely baffled.

Hunter places the bottle on his desk, and then takes a step forward. I freeze.

"This is the reason I couldn't tell you anything. I was afraid it would blow the entire operation."

"So you were basically … undercover?" I mutter.

"No … not really. Sort of, maybe," he chuckles. "I'm not a cop, if that's what you're thinking."

"Oh …" I don't really know what to say. I'm flabbergasted.

"I'm just a poor student, enrolled thanks to his big brother. I was just there at the right moment at the right time. They needed to roll up the gang, I had an easy way in. One plus one equals two."

"So they got you to do their dirty job?"

"Yeah, well, it was that or let my brother rot in jail. And that wasn't really an option."

He sits down beside me and gently curls his arm around my waist.

"So you were only in the frat house to get your brother out?" I say.

"That's what I told you, isn't it?"

"And the drugs, the dealing, the fighting, it was all for this?"

"I needed to gain their trust to climb up higher in the ranks. It was the only way I could find out who was running the entire thing."

"Wow …" I let out a huge sigh, trying to process it all.

Biting his lip, he looks up at me from under his dark lashes. For the first time I see those gray eyes from a whole different perspective.

"Please don't be mad at me for not telling you sooner." He squeezes my waist and places his hand on top of mine. "I don't want to lose you."

"I'm not mad," I say after a while. "I just can't believe that's what was really happening."

"I couldn't tell you, because I knew it would jeopardize your safety. I could never risk that."

"You didn't jeopardize my safety; I did," I say, chuckling. "Going to Brody was the stupidest thing I've ever done."

"Yeah, that was pretty stupid," he says.

I gasp and pound him against the shoulder. He winces, laughing, but is barely moved by my pitiful strength. "Good punch."

"Nah. Not as good as yours."

"I can teach you. Just like old times." He wriggles his eyebrows. "I can take you anytime."

I chortle. "God, you and your sexual innuendos."

"I just got a thing for you, can't help it." He inches closer and plants a kiss on my cheek. "Tell me you'll forgive me. I need you."

A flush spreads across my cheeks. After everything that's happened, he still wants me.

"I just need to know one thing," I say. "Was I part of your little operation?"

He frowns, confused. "No, of course not."

"Seeing as I was Brody's friend."

"No. That wasn't why I wanted to spend time with you."

I lift my head, my eyes meeting his. "Then why?"

Hunter raises his hand and caresses my jaw. The pad of his thumb skidding over my skin creates goose bumps all over my body.

"I'm such a screw-up. I've always been a screw-up," he says. "I wanted to free Jessie and sold my soul to the devil to do it. And then I met you. You're like an angel, the complete opposite of me. You caught my attention the moment you walked into our campus, with your untamed hair, and pretty little eyes you hide behind those cute glasses."

He licks his lips, his eyes flicking down toward our entwined hands, and then back up to my eyes. "Remember when I asked you if you thought I was trying to change you?"

Swallowing, I try to suppress the nerves, but lightning shoots through my veins.

I nod.

"I wanted you to change *me*," he says. "To help me keep my promise to my brother. To keep me from failing at school. To keep me on the right track. To make me a better person. Because you can do all those things, and you did."

He squeezes my hand, and I lace my fingers through his. Happiness buzzes through me, forcing a smile onto my face.

"I think you're the only one who sees me for who I really am. Who knows what it's like to be the underdog. You're the only good thing that has ever happened to me. And I was so, so goddamn afraid I was gonna lose you over all this shit." He lets out a big breath.

The moment of silence between us feels nice, and it's the first time I've actually enjoyed not knowing what to say. I want this moment to last forever.

"And when you told me you loved me … I … I just …" He sighs. "I thought I didn't deserve it. Something this good doesn't happen for fuck-ups like me. I was always afraid of getting too involved with girls, so I kept them at arm's length. I didn't want to feel the responsibility that came with a relationship. It meant having even more to take care of. But then I never really had a girl like you before."

He smiles. "You're different."

"Different how?" I say, muffling a laugh.

"Good," he says with a wink. "Very good." He comes closer, gently leaning his forehead against mine. His hot breath is on my skin, and it calms me down so much I barely remember what went down before. Being in his presence is soothing, and I don't want this to end.

"And you know what? I think I love you," he says.

A smile quirks up his lips, and I can't hold back my laugh.

"What's so funny?" he says. "You think it's funny?"

I can't stop laughing.

Hunter grabs me by the arms and pushes me down on the bed, while I'm laughing like crazy.

"Am I funny, huh?" he says, looking me straight in the eye.

"I'm sorry," I say, still laughing. "I can't help it."

"Is me loving you funny?" Hunter's fingers move to my belly, and then he starts tickling me ferociously. His skilled fingers make me squirm underneath him.

"No, no, it's not funny at all," I squeal, laughing hysterically. "Stop!"

"Beg me," he says.

"Please!" I stammer.

He grins. His hands move up, gripping me tightly, and his fingers curl around my shoulders.

"I like it when you say please," he says, licking his lips. I give him a playful slap. "See, you can't resist my charm, Autumn."

I frown, still chuckling. "What? You've never called me by my name."

"Guess there's a first time for everything. I still prefer Leafy, though." He brushes a strand of hair from my face, his index finger briefly grazing my cheek.

'Me too," I say.

Hunter cups my chin between his index finger and thumb and then presses his lips down onto mine. It's a soft and tender kiss, full of love. One I've been wishing for ever since I met him. His kisses swiftly turn into the more rabid, ravenous sucks and licks, as he starts pecking me all over my face and neck. I squirm underneath him.

"You're my Leafy now, and I'm never letting you go. Ever."

He places his hand on top of mine, pinning it above my

head. I gasp for air as he takes my breath away, never taking his mouth off mine. Our lips are locked in a hot, sexy battle, our tongues dipping out to meet each other. He groans, heightening all my senses. I moan in anticipation of what's coming, knowing what his love can do to me.

I'm delirious, and I love it.

I love everything about him. Who he is. What he's made me be. We're both strong, no matter the cost. Fierce.

And I'm his Leafy. Forever.

ABOUT THE AUTHOR

Clarissa Wild is an avid reader and writer of sexy stories about hot men and feisty women. Her other loves include her furry cat friend and learning about different cultures. In her free time she enjoys watching all sorts of movies, reading tons of books and cooking her favorite meals.

Want to be informed of new releases and special offers? Sign up for Clarissa Wild's newsletter on her website clarissawild.blogspot.com.

Visit Clarissa Wild on Amazon for current titles.

Thank you for reading FIERCE!

Enjoyed this book? You could really help out by leaving a review on Amazon and Goodreads. Thank you!